ALSO by JUDITH A. BARRETT

DONUT LADY COZY MYSTERY SERIES

MAGGIE SLOAN THRILLER SERIES

RILEY MALLOY THRILLER SERIES

GRID DOWN SURVIVAL SERIES

SWEET DEAL REVEALED

Donut Lady Cozy Mystery

Book 3

Judith A. Barrett

SWEET DEAL REVEALED

DONUT LADY COZY MYSTERY, BOOK 3

Published in the United States of America by Wobbly Creek, LLC

2019 Florida

wobblycreek.com

Edited by Judith Euen Davis

Cover by Wobbly Creek, LLC

ISBN 978-1-7331241-1-9

DEDICATION

SWEET DEAL REVEALED is dedicated to good friends, imaginary sprinkles, and the color pink.

CHAPTER ONE

A clap of thunder startled me awake. I threw back my bed covers and squinted at the clock. *Five o'clock. How could I have overslept? I should have been at the donut shop a half hour ago.* "Colonel," I called out. "Why didn't you wake me up?"

I leaped out of bed, and my German shepherd lumbered into the bedroom. As I hurried to my closet, Colonel flopped down in front of the door. I sidestepped to dodge him and tripped over the trash basket. I grabbed at the wall and hit my face on the door jamb in perfect timing with a flash of lightning and an instant crack of thunder.

"I need to slow down." I groaned and pulled myself up. As I collected the scattered papers, Mia waltzed into the bedroom and meowed. She jumped onto my bed and kneaded my pillow.

"What's wrong with you two?" I crossed my arms. "Wait. It's Sunday, isn't it?" I shook my head and stumbled to the kitchen to start a pot of coffee.

The whoosh of the wind and the rhythmic beating of rain against the windows resounded through my cozy two-bedroom bungalow. The window-shaking booms of thunder added emphasis to Mother Nature's early morning performance, and I shuddered. Mia curled up next to me on the sofa, and Colonel laid his chin on my knee. His soulful eyes comforted me. The two of them stayed close until the fast-moving storm was gone.

"Storms still bother me, but I have another feeling I can't shake."

While I dressed, the shadows gathered at my bedroom door. "You feel it too? Maybe we can walk it off. Who wants to go along?"

The shadows disappeared when I picked up Colonel's leash, and Mia scampered to the pantry.

I carried the folded leash while Colonel dashed ahead and splashed in the puddles on our stroll to downtown. The fragrance of flowers and damp grass and the cheery bird songs brightened my morning mood.

"Let's be adventuresome and go to Ida's Diner for breakfast. We never have time during the week."

Colonel quickened his pace to a trot. He stopped at the end of the block and waited. When I caught up with him, he loped to the end of the next block.

"Is this our version of leapfrog?" I asked.

When we reached Ida's, Colonel flopped on the sidewalk under the awning where it was dry. I opened the door and inhaled the comforting diner aroma of old grease mixed with frying bacon and baking yeast bread. The heady fragrance of warm sugar and cinnamon beckoned me inside.

"Where's Colonel? What happened to you?" Mary Rose asked. Her long dark hair was piled on top of her head with a hair clip. Tendrils escaped at her neck and around her face.

"Greeting customers out front. I tripped and hit the corner of my closet door." I touched my cheek gingerly with my fingertips. "Does it look bad?"

"You've got a red mark on your cheek. Don't think it will bruise. Hey, Sully," Mary Rose called to the kitchen. "Colonel's playing maître d' out front."

"On it," a low male voice said.

"Sit wherever you like, Ms. Donut Lady. You want coffee?"

I slid into a red vinyl booth midway back and faced the door. I had a view of the parking lot and Colonel.

"Whatcha want?" Mary Rose asked as she poured a fresh cup of coffee.

I stared at the menu. "Everything. Recommend something."

"You want eggs. Sully brings fresh eggs from his farm. If you don't mind waiting a few minutes, he'll be pulling out the cinnamon rolls. Bacon or sausage? Grits or home fries? How you want your eggs?"

"Eggs over easy, bacon, grits, and a cinnamon roll."

"Hungry Donut Lady special," Mary Rose called to the kitchen.

"On it."

I raised my eyebrows. Mary Rose snickered and strutted to the kitchen waving my ticket.

"Y'all have an unfair advantage," I said. "You've been awake longer than I have." I wrapped my hands around the hot cup and inhaled the steamy elixir.

Two white pickup trucks pulled into the diner's parking lot. Four men who wore jeans, chambray shirts with a construction logo, and muddy work boots stopped and greeted Colonel. They stomped their feet on the porch and then came inside. The four of them headed to the big booth at the opposite side of the diner. Mary Rose was a whirlwind as she refilled coffee, delivered menus, and took orders. She glided out of the kitchen with a steak on a plate and took it out to Colonel. When she scurried inside, I raised my eyebrows and she laughed. "Maître d' special."

A middle-aged man and a young woman came in. The man was over six feet tall. His curly, dark brown hair was clipped short. His face was ruddy, and he had a full beard that matched his hair except for gray streaks along his jawline. His beard skimmed his shirt at the neckline. He wore khaki slacks and a white dress shirt that stretched across his abdomen.

The young woman was slim and just over five feet tall. She had straight, long black hair and dark skin and wore jeans and a tight black T-shirt. When they passed me, he clenched and unclenched his fists.

"No need to be a prima donna. Hurry up," he growled.

They continued to the last booth. My back was to them, but I had the hearing of a teacher. I snickered when I glanced at the window and saw their reflection. *And eyes in the back of my head.* The young woman faced the door.

"Whatcha drinking?" Mary Rose asked.

"Coffee," the man said. "And bring the check."

The woman scowled. "Water for me. And a cinnamon roll to go."

Mary Rose delivered the coffee, water, and a white paper sack. On her next pass through, she dropped off the check and refilled the man's coffee.

The woman stared at the man and held out her hand with her palm up. She wiggled her fingers and raised her eyebrows. He slammed a fat manila envelope on the table.

She peeked inside. "Is it all here?" Her eyes narrowed. "Good stuff?"

"Of course," he said.

"I hope so for your sake." She slid an overstuffed white envelope across the table.

Mary Rose brought me my breakfast. "Enjoy."

"Maître d' special?" I asked.

"Sully and Colonel go way back. Remind me to tell you the story sometime."

I spooned my grits out of the bowl and onto my plate next to my eggs. I stabbed the yolks, and the thick egg creaminess oozed into the grits. I scooped up a bite with my fork. *Mmm. Heaven.*

Mary Rose refilled my coffee. "Ever have farm eggs before?"

"If I have, it was long ago. These are delicious. Absolutely defy description. Thanks for the recommendation. And I haven't had grits in years. These are perfect."

The bacon was salty and crisp, and the cinnamon roll was gooey sweetness. I licked the velvety icing off my upper lip. *Good thing I can't come here every morning for breakfast. I could put on ten pounds in a month, no problem.*

The young woman rose to leave the diner, and the man followed her. When they reached the parking lot, he grabbed her arm, snatched a handful of hair, and jerked back her head. He leaned down for an open-mouth kiss. Colonel rose to his feet. His hackles were up, and his low growl grew in intensity. One of the men in the booth narrowed his eyes and frowned at the parking lot. After Colonel growled, he rose and headed to the door.

The man outside jerked his head toward Colonel, and the young woman grabbed his hand, bent his small finger backward, and slammed his sternum with her elbow with the force of a woman who takes care of herself. "Forget it, bud. Not in the deal."

He yowled as he released her and stumbled back. Colonel's growl intensified. She sprinted across the parking lot and out of sight. The man clutched his hand to his chest and glanced at the diner. The customer returned to his friends, shadows drifted in front of my window, and I focused on my plate.

"That was interesting. Undercover, do you think?" I shook my head. *Talking to shadows?*

Mary Rose waved the coffee pot, and I nodded. *I won't sleep for three days.*

"There was a man in here earlier," I said while Mary Rose poured. "He sat in the back booth. I'm pretty sure I went to high school with him, but I couldn't remember his name. You ever have that problem? He's a big guy and has a big beard."

"Omigosh. All the time! That's Mr. Wallace. I ran into my best friend from fourth grade at the grocery store and couldn't remember her name. I kept calling her *Hon*." She giggled.

"I'll have to remember that." I grinned and sipped my coffee. "Does Sully make cinnamon rolls every morning?"

"Nope. Just Sundays." She lowered her voice. "He says he can't compete with the Donut Lady."

"He did not." I laughed.

"Maybe not, but it's true," she grinned.

* * *

The next morning, Tiffany, my talented baker, punched down a batch of dough. She brushed the flour off her dark brown hands. "Remember you told me the sheriff asked for his favorite donut—something like pomegranate, pineapple, and coconut mai tai? A little bird named Emma told me his birthday is tomorrow. Don't you think we owe our sheriff a nice surprise? I can't figure out what to call them, though."

"What about over the hill mai tai?"

"Love it." Tiffany covered her last batch of dough to rise. "I'll get cocktail umbrellas we can stick into the donuts."

"I've got another one. Older than dirt donut. Use chocolate cookie crumbles for dirt."

"You are on a roll, Miss Lady. What about scones?"

"I'll need to think about that. You have any ideas?" I sipped my coffee.

"Remember the sheriff suggested jailbird donuts?" Tiffany asked. "What about jailbird scones?"

I choked and spewed my coffee. I grabbed a cloth and cleaned up the counter. "Remind me not to drink coffee while we're brainstorming. I assume cranberry-orange scones with orange drizzle?"

"Wait before you pick up your cup, Miss Lady. I was thinking maybe an orange frosting smear with orange zest and black bars on top. I can pipe the black stripes with dark chocolate."

"Perfect. And I love the taste of orange with bitter dark chocolate."

We high-fived, and the bell jingled.

"A high five in the Donut Hole?" the sheriff asked. He narrowed his eyes. "You two are up to no good, right?"

"You're certainly suspicious this morning, Sheriff." Tiffany flipped her dishtowel over her shoulder and served his coffee and donuts.

"Better watch that, Sheriff," I added. "We'll start thinking you're a lawman and clam up."

The sheriff shook his head. "Of all the donut joints in this town, I have to come here."

"Casablanca," I said.

The sheriff raised his eyebrows. "Not everybody knows that."

"What are you two talking about?" Tiffany asked. "Are we changing the name of the Donut Hole?"

Sheriff and I laughed. When the bell jingled, Shirley bustled in, and the sheriff picked up his hat and ambled to the door. When he glanced back, I mouthed, "Coward."

He saluted with two fingers. "Here's looking at you, kid."

"Yep," Tiffany mumbled, "older than dirt."

Shirley perched on a stool at the counter and pushed her short, curly blond hair behind her ear. "The sheriff's always in a hurry. He must have staff meetings every morning. Karen, since you wouldn't let us have a housewarming party after you moved back to your remodeled house, Woody and I came up with another idea. Actually, Woody did. He said he got the idea from the animal rescue adoption day. You know, when we got our cat, Chase. I won't tell you because it's his idea. We'd like to come by after school this afternoon so he can tell you. We already cleared it with Monica at the library, but zip." Shirley pinched her thumb and index finger together and motioned across her pursed lips. "I won't say. It's a great idea. You'll like it because you're a teacher. Are you glad your cast is off? That was a silly question. Of course, you are. But I noticed your pink long-sleeved shirt, and it reminded me of your cast. Thanks for the coffee and my sack, Tiffany. I have to run. I have a meeting, but it's not at the sheriff's office." Shirley giggled as she dashed out the door.

"Books," Tiffany said. "If Ms. Monica cleared the idea, it's books. Or magic." She dropped donut holes into the fryer.

I stared at Tiffany. "You know about Monica and magic?"

"Sure. Ms. Monica's hobby. She does a magic show for the little kids." She dumped the donut holes on the wire screen to drain.

Nice cover for a magical librarian.

"Write Now authors meet at nine today, Miss Lady. I was thinking blueberry scones. They liked them the first time they were here. I've got maple and strawberry glaze for donuts."

"Finish up your donuts, and I'll get the scones going," I said. "Do you think they might like school glue scones?"

"I'll whip up some vanilla crème. Why school glue scones for the writers?"

"I don't know. Just a feeling."

"Fine. Don't tell me. And I suppose I need to make blood scones too?" Tiffany crossed her arms and scowled.

I studied the ceiling. "Yes. I guess you do."

Tiffany squinted at the ceiling, and I carried napkins into the meeting room to hide my smirk. *Made you look, Tiff.*

The mayor hustled into the shop at eight thirty. "I should have called first, but my calendar cleared. Any meetings this morning? Can I help?"

"Writers group, Mayor. Of course, you can help. You're our official greeter."

"Thank you, Donut Lady. I love this job." He hustled to the storeroom for his apron. I followed him. "The leader for Write Now called me last night. The group has had an angels versus vampires controversy going for a couple of weeks. She wanted to know if we could help her defuse the argument. We have school glue scones and blood scones for them, but we aren't going to tell them. It's going to be messy when they bite into the scones. Tiffany doesn't know yet. Sure you want to prank Tiffany and a writers group? There's the risk that both of us will be fired."

"I love my job." The mayor chuckled and turned around. I tied his apron, and he hurried to the pink room.

The Write Now members sauntered in. The leader stopped by the counter and paid me. "We all set?" she asked in a soft whisper.

"You've got angels and vampires scones. The angels have vanilla crème inside, and the vampires have dark raspberry blood. Both of them will provide a lovely trajectory of white or red sticky goo. The mayor is your greeter, and he is all in."

When the mayor took in the platter of scones, I explained angels and vampires to Tiffany.

"I've been stressing about this all morning. Why couldn't you just tell me? As soon as you make me boss, I'm firing you. Not funny." She stomped into the storeroom and slammed the door.

"You snickered," I said.

Tiffany opened the door and slammed it again.

Screams and laughter came from the pink meeting room.

The major opened the door. "We got a hit, Donut Lady, but we need more napkins. A lot more napkins."

Tiffany tiptoed out of the storeroom and peeked into the pink room. The mayor grabbed her hand and pulled her in. "Ladies and Gentlemen, may I introduce your baker and perpetrator. Remember Tiffany in your next book." The room exploded with the sounds of laughter, applause, and whistles.

After the group left, Tiffany and the mayor scrubbed the sticky table, chairs, and floor.

"Best job ever," the mayor said as he took off his apron. "I'll take my apron home and wash it."

"That was wild, Miss Lady. After they realized the scones oozed, they tried to squirt each other." Tiffany chuckled and handed me a folded napkin with *Donut Lady* hand-printed on it. "I found this on the buffet behind the clean cups. Guess it's for you."

I stuffed the napkin into my pocket.

Tiffany cleaned the equipment, and I swept the shop. I sat at the counter, unfolded the napkin, and read a scrawled note: "Be careful. He's a snake."

I shuddered. "Tiffany, you have any idea who wrote the note?"

"Don't know. Why? What does the note say?"

"Nothing really."

"There was a new person, youngish, at the meeting. Never saw her before. She was quiet and kept her head down. Long dark hair. Strange, now that I think about it. She had this air of—I don't know—authority?" Tiffany read over my shoulder. "That's not nothing. Who is 'he'?"

I shrugged. "I think it's a prank."

"No, you don't. Who?"

"I saw a short, young, dark-haired woman with Mr. Wallace at Ida's Diner yesterday morning."

"If it's the Mr. Wallace I know, he is a snake. You don't have anything to do with him, do you?" Tiffany frowned.

"No. What do you know about him?"

"He's involved in something illegal, maybe drugs. Whatever it is, he's in deep. Not a nice person. I heard he left the area and went to Atlanta. Wonder what he's doing in town?"

* * *

After we closed the shop for the day, I headed to the soup kitchen on impulse. "Not sure if Melinda Wallace will be there, but I have a feeling she might need a friend, Colonel."

The soup kitchen's heavy metal doors with the wired windows were unlocked. When I pulled a door open and entered the foyer, the silence was eerie.

"Hello. Anybody here?"

Colonel and I walked through the dining area and past the door to the commercial kitchen to the hallway where shadows gathered and swirled. When we reached the hall, Colonel whined and raced down the darkened corridor to a closed door and barked. I hurried to join him, and he scratched on the door.

A feeble voice said, "In here."

I opened the door a few inches, but it was blocked. I pushed against the door and opened it enough to see inside. I gasped. Blood spatters were on the wall, and pools of blood dotted the floor. The storeroom was in shambles with shattered jars, cans, food boxes, and flour strewn on the floor. I pushed against the door, and it opened enough for me to see what blocked it.

Melinda lay on her side with her back against the door. Her pale green shirt and jeans were spattered with blood.

"Oh my." I grabbed the door handle to steady myself.

"Melinda?" I pushed again and scooted her enough for me to squeeze into the room. I stooped next to her and brushed her brown, gray-streaked hair away from her battered face and touched her shoulder gently.

She opened her swollen eyes. "You're here. I'm okay," she said in a weak voice.

I pulled out my phone and called nine-one-one. "Tess—no, I'm fine. But I'm at the soup kitchen. In the storeroom. Melinda needs an ambulance. She's been beaten. Yes. Badly."

"Cold," Melinda said.

I spotted a pack of commercial tablecloths. I struggled to my feet and ripped open the package.

"Ambulance is on its way. Where does it hurt?"

"Hurts."

I spread a tablecloth over Melinda and scooted glass and debris away from her. "I'm going to open the door a little wider. Let me know if it hurts."

When I pulled the door open a little wider, it slid Melinda toward me. When she winced, I stopped.

"Can you breathe okay?" I crouched close to her.

"Been better."

"Who attacked you?"

"He hurt me."

"There's a lot of blood. Is it all yours?"

"Dropped jar. On his head."

"Good girl."

Melinda closed her eyes. "Yes."

I scanned the floor. Pickles, pickle juice, and blood surrounded the shards of a broken gallon jar near the ladder. Colonel howled. I didn't hear any sirens, but he must have.

"Donut Lady?" A familiar male voice called from the kitchen.

"Down the hall in the storeroom." I shouted. Colonel barked.

Roger stuck his head into the room. "Wow."

"Melinda's against the door. Maybe if the rescue crew can put her on a backboard, it will be easier to move her."

"Any of this blood yours?" Roger waved his pen. "Did she say who attacked her?"

I glanced down. My jeans and hands were covered with blood. "None's mine. Melinda didn't say who, but she did say she dropped a jar on his head. I think it was that gallon pickle jar."

Roger bit his lip and scribbled in his notebook. "Y'all are going to get me fired yet. Sheriff's not going to believe this."

Colonel howled.

"Ambulance is here. I need to check the building. You be okay?"

"Yes."

Melinda mumbled. I leaned closer. "Knew you'd come."

* * *

The lead paramedic, Carol, came in first. She raised her eyebrows and scanned the room while her team logrolled Melinda onto a backboard. "You injured?"

"No."

She followed her team out, and they were gone. I surveyed the room more closely and noticed the man's bloody footprints that led to the closet.

"Come on, Colonel. The sheriff's waiting in the hall for us." I struggled to my feet and closed the storeroom door. I leaned against the wall while my heart pounded, and I hyperventilated.

Roger appeared at the end of the hallway. His eyes widened. I put my finger to my lips and tiptoed to him.

I whispered. "Roger, I saw bloody footprints. I think the man is in the storeroom closet."

Roger called for backup and edged his way to the storeroom with his gun drawn. I followed him for a few feet until he turned and glared. I eased back. Colonel waited at the storeroom door.

Roger opened the door and went inside. Colonel followed him. I fumed. *How is that fair?* Deputy Jeff came up behind me.

"Roger and Colonel went in the storeroom," I whispered. Jeff slipped down the hallway and assumed his backup position at the door. The crackle of the radios startled me. Jeff ran past me to the outside door.

I headed to the end of the hallway, and Colonel caught up with me. Melinda's office was on my left. Colonel faced the office and whined. The turn to the hallway leading to the dining area was on my right. I turned to the left. When I touched the doorknob, the door to the office swung open. "You're my witness, Colonel. I didn't force my way in at all."

Papers were scattered on the floor, and the desk and file cabinet drawers were open. "Déjà vu, Colonel?" I tiptoed to look behind the desk. *Nothing.* I exhaled in relief. When I turned to leave, shadows billowed between me and the door and slid to the ceiling and then to the corner of the room.

I jumped. A stocky young man stood in the corner. He wore an oversized black Bulldogs T-shirt stuffed into jeans pulled high on his waist. His brown hair was slicked down except for the cowlick at his crown. His pale hands shook, and his cheeks were streaked with tears.

"Andrew, I didn't hear you. You were so quiet. Are you okay?"

Andrew stared at the shadows as they shrunk under his feet and disappeared. He sniffed back tears and swiped at his face and nose with his shirtsleeve. "There was yelling and noise. I got scared. Lot of noise. I hid." Andrew covered his ears.

Colonel pushed the door wide to enter and approached Andrew. "Can I pet him?" Andrew asked.

"He'd love it."

Andrew stroked Colonel's back. "I don't like noise. Can we go find Deputy Roger?"

"That's a good idea."

On our way to the kitchen, Andrew asked, "Is Ms. Melinda okay? I peeked when the ambulance came. She looked hurt bad. I didn't help her."

He stopped and stared at the floor. "Is she going to be mad at me?"

"A bad man hurt her. She'll be happy you were quiet and stayed in her office."

Andrew nodded and headed to the dining room. "I saw the bad man."

My eyes widened. *Didn't expect that.* "I think Deputy Jeff is outside. Can you tell him about the bad man?"

"Deputy Jeff is nice."

"He is. Let's see if we can find him."

Jeff approached us when we stepped outside.

"Deputy, Andrew was in Melinda's office. Hiding, right, Andrew?"

"I saw the bad man, Deputy Jeff."

Jeff blinked. "Let's find a place to sit and talk, Andrew. How about in the soup kitchen dining room?"

"Yes, sir." Andrew followed Jeff inside.

"Let's go home, Colonel."

After we had gone half a block, the sheriff's car pulled to the curb. "Would y'all like a ride home?"

Sheriff Grady stepped out of his car, circled around to the passenger's side, and opened the back door. Colonel leaped inside and laid his chin on the back of the front seat. The sheriff opened the passenger's door. "So why did you go to the soup kitchen in the first place?"

I slid in. "I had a feeling."

"Of course, you did." He shook his head and slammed the door.

CHAPTER TWO

After the sheriff gave me a lecture on staying out of trouble and dropped us off, I took a quick shower and changed my clothes. I put my soiled clothes in the washer and changed the dial to cold to rinse out the blood. I poured a glass of sweet tea, and Colonel and I went to the backyard. I sat on the steps and sipped my tea while Colonel checked his property and marked the perimeter.

Tires screeched in front of my house. When the knocking on the door turned to banging, I ambled inside. When I swung open the front door, Jack, my tall handyman and self-proclaimed protector, lost his balance. He snatched at the outside door handle, jerked the door against his shoulder, and stumbled backward.

"Are you okay?" he asked.

I raised my eyebrows and bit my lip. "You want to start over?"

His neck and face turned crimson. "Good idea. Hello, Donut Lady. How ya doing? Are all the neighbors watching? I'm afraid to look." He brushed his jeans and glanced over his shoulder.

I laughed. "Come on in, you goof."

He sat at the dining table, and I poured him a glass of tea.

"It's tough for an engineer with no social skills to be a knight in a red flannel plaid shirt." He took a big gulp of tea. "I was at the gas station and heard you found Melinda hurt at the soup kitchen. There may have been some embellishments of the story. Did you know your fan club meets at the gas station?"

"I can't wait to hear Tiffany's version of the story in the morning. Hers is always the best."

"So, what happened, really?"

"I'd really like to visit Melinda at the hospital. Want to go along?"

"Only if I drive. I need to redeem my self-worth."

On the way to the hospital, I described finding Melinda and Andrew. "Pretty short story. Not very exciting," I left out the part about the shadows.

After Jack parked at the hospital, he said, "Did you know Andrew is one of Alfred's helpers for the anger management program? Andrew helps work with the boys who have issues."

"I didn't know that. But Andrew takes longer than most folks to process his thoughts. How does he help?"

"Alfred assigns a project to a team made up of an adult, Andrew, and one of the boys. I've worked on several. Andrew stays focused on the project. We're challenged to emulate him. It's life-changing."

Jack offered his arm, and I slipped my arm through his and rested my hand on his forearm as we walked across the grass to the sidewalk. When we reached the hospital doors, I dropped my hand. "Thanks. My vision these days, especially on uneven ground, isn't the greatest."

"Glad I could help," Jack said.

When I stepped up to the information desk, he mumbled, "Wish you'd let me help more."

I chose to ignore him. "Melinda Wallace?" I asked.

The clerk popped her gum and checked her computer. "She's still being evaluated. Are you family?"

"No. Close friend. She doesn't have any family in town."

"Good enough. Call tomorrow to see if she's up to having visitors. Here's the number to call." She scribbled on a notepad and tore off the sheet.

"I'll get the truck and pick you up." Jack strode away to the parking lot.

"Your husband is very thoughtful," the clerk said.

"You're right, he is. But he's a close friend."

"Friends are nice to have," she said as she answered the phone.

On our way back to my house, Jack said, "Where would you like to go out to dinner? You have to eat. No reason to eat alone."

"I'm not up to—" *Friends are nice to have.* "I love to cook, but cooking for one isn't fun. How about if we stop at the grocery store, and I'll make you a homecooked chicken dinner?"

Jack frowned. "Is that your polite way of telling me you won't go out to dinner with me?"

I raised my chin. "Yes."

Jack guffawed. "You win, Donut Lady. Let's go grocery shopping. I'll buy. You cook."

After I selected potatoes and salad ingredients, Jack met me at the poultry case and put a half-gallon of ice cream and a bottle of wine into the cart.

While the chicken baked and the potatoes boiled, we sipped hot tea.

"Why did you buy the donut shop?" Jack tilted his head and peered at me.

"I wanted to be my own boss and stay busy. I just had a feeling it was the business for me."

Jack finished his tea. "Are your feelings always right?"

I set my cup down. "Interesting question. I never ignore them. Not sure that answers your question."

"Maybe it does. Can I help with dinner? I'm good at salads."

"That's great. I'll get the gravy going, and we can eat in ten minutes."

Jack showed off his knife skills as he chopped and sliced, and I stirred my roux for the gravy. "It's nice having help while I cook."

"I like feeling useful." Jack set our salad bowls on the table. He peeked over my shoulder at the skillet as I added and stirred chicken broth into my roux. "Wow. That's gravy magic."

Jack scooted back his empty plate after we finished eating. "Oven-fried chicken, mashed potatoes and gravy. You're a great cook, Karen. Thanks for turning me down."

"Any time, Jack." I laughed.

"I set myself up on that one, didn't I?" Jack smiled.

I dished up the mint chocolate chip ice cream, and Jack opened the wine.

"Shirley told me that white wine counts as champagne when it's served with ice cream," I said.

"I never knew Shirley was a philosopher." He carried our empty bowls to the sink. "Refill on your wine?"

"No, thank you."

Jack headed to the door, and I followed him.

"I'm going to let Colonel out the back. Are you going to drive around to the alley to guard us?"

"I could just stand here. Save the gas." He crossed his arms.

"Fine. You do that. Want to go out, Colonel?"

Colonel and I walked to the back door. When Colonel returned, I double-locked the door.

"Thanks again. Dinner was wonderful."

"Thanks for the company."

Jack stood at the door and stared at me. He sighed and left. After I locked the door and clicked the deadbolt, he stepped off the porch and started his truck.

The shadows filled the hallway.

"Time for bed, everybody."

* * *

The next morning, I opened my eyes at three. *No way can I sleep.* When Colonel and I stepped outside at three thirty to walk to the Donut Hole, I was glad I wore my sweatshirt for the chilly morning air.

"This is going to be a great morning, Colonel. Today is the sheriff's birthday."

When we neared the Donut Hole, the lights from the shop cut through the darkness like a beacon. Shadows danced in the street.

"Guess we're not the only ones excited about today." I unlocked the door, and the bell jingled.

Tiffany stopped the mixer and grinned. "I had a feeling you'd be here early. We got a regular conspiracy going. Tess will occupy the sheriff with paperwork until seven. Ms. Emma, the mayor, half the town, and most of the school will be here by seven."

I grabbed my apron. "I'll get busy on our jailbird scones. What do you think about setting up self-serve coffee?"

Tiffany shook her head. "The mayor's heart will be broken."

"You're right. He might think he's been fired."

"Woody and Ms. Shirley will be here at six to decorate. Aunt Gee's raffling one of your *Got Sprinkles* caps. She'll use the proceeds to buy supplies and sports equipment for Mr. Gibson's program. Ms. Emma said that's one of the sheriff's favorites."

"You organize all this?" I stared at Tiffany.

"Me and Ms. Emma. You were too busy fighting trolls and dragons yesterday. I can't wait to tell you what really happened, but when did you start carrying a saber? I'm planning on six batches. Do you think that will be enough?"

"Maybe seven. And I'll do a triple batch of scones."

The door jingled a little before six. Shirley held the door open, and Woody carried in a ladder. The two of them hurried out and returned with each one of them carrying a large box.

"You need any help?" I asked.

"We got this," Shirley said as she opened up the ladder near the reading table. "Right, Woody?"

"Yes, ma'am."

Tiffany and I pretended to work on donuts while we watched Woody hang a banner with Shirley's help. After they finished, the four of us stood at the front door and admired the handiwork. The lower part of the pennant was four feet from the floor.

"What do you think? We got a flat sheet from Gee's shop. I cut it in half lengthwise, and Woody decorated it," Shirley said.

"*Happy Birthday to the oldest sheriff in Asbury.* That's brilliant."

"It was Ms. Emma's idea. She said the sheriff would be surprised," Woody said.

"We have permanent markers so everyone who comes in can sign the banner," Shirley said. "Woody added the pink-sprinkled donuts across the top because they are the sheriff's favorite."

"We've got balloons too," Woody said. "Pink and black. Pink for the donuts."

"And black for the old sheriff," Shirley added. "We'll be in the meeting room."

The bell jingled, and Isaiah came into the shop. "I had nothing to do with this. Make sure the sheriff knows that." He carried a three-foot ceramic cookie jar shaped like a stack of donuts—chocolate dipped, sprinkled, strawberry dipped, and blue dipped. "I have no idea where Mama finds this stuff either." He placed the crock on the reading table and went into the meeting room. "You got the sign for the donation jar, Woody?"

Gee carried in a fishbowl and set it on the counter near the cash register. "For the tickets for the drawing. Where's my hat that I'm raffling?"

Tiffany wrote the day's specials on the board while I handed Gee her hat. *Over the Hill Mai Tai and Older than Dirt Donuts. Jailbird Scones.*

Gee leaned against the counter and laughed. "Y'all have certainly outdone yourselves. This raffle money might be diverted to bail money. Nope. Can't do that. I'm no jailbird." She laughed even harder, and Tiffany and I joined in.

I fanned my face with a napkin and caught my breath. "Gee, I'm not sure if we're laughing at you or with you, but you are hilarious this morning."

Gee straightened her back. "I'm hilarious every morning."

The bell jingled, and the mayor and Emma hurried in. "Did we miss something?" Emma asked.

The mayor's eyes widened as he surveyed the shop. "Genius. Of course, I expected nothing less." He hurried to the storeroom. "I've been thinking," the mayor tied his apron. "What do you think about setting up a self-serve coffee station in addition to our regular coffee machines? I have a feeling we're going to get swamped. And I've got six gallons of orange juice in my car. What do you think about free orange juice for the kids?"

"I think you're awesome," I said. "Maybe we can set up a juice station too."

Tiffany set up the large coffee maker on the buffet in the meeting room while the mayor scurried to create a coffee station.

"Do you have donuts for those of us who aren't over the hill, older than dirt, or jailbirds?" Amber stood at the doorway with her hands on her hips.

"We've got special donut holes—maple loopholes for the lawyer," Tiffany said. "We didn't want you to sue us."

Emma high-fived Tiffany. "You're quick, Tiffany," Emma said.

The principal, two teachers, and thirty children crowded into the shop. "We thought we'd just blend in," the principal said. "Pretend you can't see us. We'll bring the children in shifts."

Alfred, Andrew, and two teenage boys came inside. Andrew wore hearing protection and a big grin. Alfred touched my elbow. "Okay if we stand by the back door and crack it open a bit?"

"Fine by me. Thank you for bringing Andrew."

Roger opened the shop door. "Sheriff's driving up. Might want to keep the noise down for a minute or two." He stepped inside and joined Tiffany near the fryer.

Colonel padded to the back door and leaned against Andrew. Everyone shushed each other and stared at the front door.

The bell jingled, and the sheriff walked in. His eyes widened as he surveyed the room. He gazed at the specials board. The children giggled. Emma held up her hand and signaled with her fingers, "One. Two. Three."

"Surprise!" everyone shouted, and the children jumped up and down and danced.

The sheriff shook his head and chuckled. He held up his hand, and the shop became quiet.

"Deputy Roger," he said, "Round up the usual suspects." He glanced at me and winked.

The principal led the children in a birthday song. Everyone applauded, and the sheriff bowed before he pulled out his usual stool. I set the sheriff's coffee on the counter along with two specials and a scone. Emma sat next to the sheriff, and I poured her a cup too.

Gee pointed at a folding table, and Isaiah hurried to set it up out front. Woody, Gee, and Amber carried out boxes with donut holes, napkins, and cups. The mayor and Isaiah set the orange juice on the table. Balloons on strings trailed behind Shirley when she headed outside. She tied them on the shop corner posts and on the table. Shirley handed out permanent markers and encouraged everyone to sign the banner. The principal led the children to Isaiah's table where they lined up for donut holes and orange juice before they left for school. Shirley and Woody left when the children did.

Adults crowded the register for donuts and scones. Tiffany and Amber served pastries and collected money. Gee sold raffle tickets, and the mayor and Alfred staffed the donation jar and reminded everyone to sign the birthday banner.

"What's your favorite, Grady?" Emma asked. "Are you over the hill, older than dirt, or fond of jailbirds?"

"That's an easy choice. I've developed a soft spot for jailbirds. What about you?"

"I think I'm over the hill. These are really good," Emma said. "May I have another one to make it official, Ms. Donut Lady?"

The mayor put his hand on the sheriff's shoulder. "Happy birthday, and thank you for your service to this town, Sheriff." The two men shook hands.

Jack slipped onto the stool next to Emma. "I'm older than dirt. Donut Lady, and you are amazing. Look at this town coming together."

He inclined his head in the direction of the mayor and Alfred who stood together at the donut jar.

"I can't take the credit." I poured a cup of coffee for Jack and set a chocolate covered donut in front of him. "Tiffany and Emma coordinated everything."

Tiffany set three boxes of donuts and scones on the counter. "Tess called in an order, Sheriff. You want to deliver it?"

"I sure would. You want to go along, Emma?"

"Lights and sirens?" Her face lit up.

"You are a person of interest. But, no," the sheriff laughed.

We had a steady stream of customers all morning. At eleven o'clock, Gee announced, "Time for our raffle drawing. Come pull a ticket, Donut Lady."

Gee stuck her hand into the fishbowl and stirred the coupons. I closed my eyes, turned my head, pulled out a ticket, and handed it to Gee.

"Andrew!" she squealed.

"Seriously?" Alfred asked. "Andrew? He bought a ticket?"

"Sure did," Gee said. "I sold it to him myself."

"Is it okay if I take his cap to him?" Alfred asked.

"Can I go along?" Isaiah asked.

"Of course. You can present it to him."

"Wait a second," Gee said. "I have a gift bag to put it in." Gee returned from her car with a red Bulldogs sack, and she dropped the cap inside.

"Thanks, Ms. Giselle. He'll love it," Alfred said.

I narrowed my eyes at Gee, and she shrugged.

"Time for me to head back to my store," Gee said.

When the shop cleared, the mayor said, "I'll take care of the meeting room. I told Alfred I'd bring the donations by the bank this afternoon. We'll get an official count of the proceeds and let everyone know."

After the mayor left, I said, "I'm officially tired. What's our inventory?"

"We sold out before eleven. All except for the one scone you asked me to save."

* * *

After lunch, I drove to the hospital and went straight to room 215. The door was partially open. I tapped on the door jamb.

"Melinda?"

"Come on in, Donut Lady," she mumbled.

Melinda's face was dark with bruises, her left cheek was puffy and bruised, and her left eye was black. Her lip was split and swollen. She had a patch of hair above her left ear that had been shaved and bandaged. Her forearms were wrapped with gauze, and her hands and knuckles had abrasions. The head of her bed was raised to a sitting position.

"Tell me I'm not a mess," she said. I smiled back at her crooked smile and twinkling eyes.

"You're not a mess. You look awesome. Like a fierce warrior."

"Good. That was the look I was going for. Pull up a chair. You look tired."

I scooted the visitor's chair closer to her bed. "We had a surprise birthday party for the sheriff at the shop this morning. It was wildly successful."

"Sorry I missed that. Did you bring me a donut?"

"We sold out. However, I do happen to have a jailbird scone. Want a taste?"

I handed Melinda the scone on a napkin.

"This is brilliant. Orange behind bars, right?"

"Exactly. Tiffany's idea, and I agree it's brilliant."

She pinched a small piece of scone but was careful to include the orange frosting. "Mmm. The scone just melted in my mouth. My jaw's a little sore, so chewing isn't my best skill." Melinda pinched off another small piece. "I'm starving. This is wonderful."

"Can I ask who attacked you?"

She pinched off another bite. "It was a man I didn't know. Large and beefy. Gray hair. Bushy eyebrows. Has a huge cut on the top of his head and scratches on his face."

I snickered. "You told me you dropped a jar on his head. Do you remember? I found a gallon pickle jar broken on the floor. You're awesome."

"When he tried to pull me off the ladder, I had just rolled the pickle jar down my arms to my chest. He grabbed my arm, and when I felt the jar slipping, I'm not sure what I had in mind, but I remember thinking, *oh, what the heck*. I turned toward him and raised my elbows and dropped it on his head with all the force I could. Isn't that bizarre?" She put her fingers up to her lips and snickered. "I can't laugh. My mouth and jaw are too sore."

"Your warrior instincts kicked in," I said.

"He knocked the ladder off balance. I think he had trouble seeing with the blood running down his face. I fell, and he tripped over me. When I got up, that's when he hit me in the face. I'm not sure what all happened next until you were there. I knew you'd come."

"That's what you said. How'd you know?"

She raised her eyebrows. "Because it's what you do."

"Did you know Andrew was at the soup kitchen?"

"Oh no. Was he hurt?" She straightened her back and leaned forward. "Unh. Bad move." She exhaled and eased back against the pillow on the bed.

"No. Andrew heard the noise, and it scared him. He hid in your office."

"That's a relief. He helps me put inventory away. He's helped in the storeroom since he was ten. He is very sensitive to loud noise. I'm sure the crashing and yelling terrified him."

"Your office looked like it had been ransacked." I offered her the ice water with a straw.

"Thanks." She sipped on the straw. "That's good. The attacker kept asking, 'Where is it?' I didn't know what he was talking about."

"I just can't imagine how awful it was for you."

"The good news is the doctor says I can go home tomorrow if my sister can stay with me a few days. She's asked for a few days off."

"What can I do?"

"It's okay to say no, but there is one thing. My dog. One of the soup kitchen volunteers picked her up and took her to the kennel. She loves the kennel, but I always pick her up before the end of the day. Her name is Pepper. She' a Yorkie mix and loves other dogs and people."

"How is she with big dogs? What about cats?"

"She's only been around cats at the kennel in crates. She loves big dogs. The kennel uses Pepper to socialize dogs that are unsure or nervous."

"Really? A lot of smaller dogs are threatened by big dogs."

Melinda's crooked smile reappeared. "Pepper thinks the sole purpose of people and dogs is to play with her."

"Colonel and I could go meet her. If she and Colonel get along, she could go home with us. Mia will either hide or teach Pepper about cats."

"That would be great. The kennel has Pepper's favorite food and sleeping pad. I'll call and let them know you and Colonel are coming by for a get-acquainted visit, and she might go home with y'all." Melinda's face and shoulders relaxed. "Thank you, Donut Lady. I've been worried about her."

When I got home, I took Colonel out back for a break. "Let's go visit a kennel."

I carried Colonel's leash into the kennel office. Colonel stayed close to me. A slender clerk in her early twenties came out from behind the desk and stooped to greet Colonel. Her shoulder-length sandy-brown hair slid over her face. When she stood, she flipped her hair back, and her blue eyes twinkled. "Ms. Donut Lady, I'm Tammy. I'll whistle for Pepper. Cover your ears. I'm loud." Tammy put two fingers to her mouth and whistled. "She has free run of the place. She thinks she's the owner. She'll be happy to show Colonel where the play yard is."

Pepper was a blur of black and tan as she dashed down the hall. She slid to a stop in front of Tammy who gave Pepper and Colonel a treat.

"I love the touches of gold in her silky coat," I said. "She's a pretty girl."

"She is, isn't she?" Tammy beamed. "Play yard, Pepper."

Pepper pranced down the hall, and Colonel trotted along behind her.

As we followed the dogs, Tammy said, "We pick up donuts for the staff every Friday. We love surprises. How do you come up with all those different ideas and flavors? Is there a donut blog you subscribe to for ideas? Our headquarters in Albany is jealous of us. We don't really rub it in or anything, but we write up the details for the Friday donuts as part of our weekly report. I wouldn't be a bit surprised if they move their monthly meeting to Asbury on Fridays. The Donut Hole is famous in two counties."

We walked outside to the grassy play yard. When Tammy opened the gate, Pepper raced inside and around the perimeter. Colonel sat and watched her. He strolled to the middle of the yard and flopped down on the grass. Pepper ran her circle two more times and then flopped next to Colonel. Colonel returned to the gate, and Pepper danced alongside him.

"They're fine. Ms. Melinda said you had Pepper's food and favorite dog pad?"

"We've got them all packed up for you. We knew Colonel would be fine, and all the dogs here love Pepper. Even the grouchy ones."

Tammy picked up Pepper's things and walked out with us to my car. Pepper jumped into the back with Colonel. He stretched out across the back seat, and Pepper scrunched into the small amount of space at his feet. On the way home, I glanced in the back. Colonel had curled up and given Pepper more space.

When we went inside the house, Mia padded out of her pantry and stalked Pepper. Pepper flopped down next to Colonel and ignored Mia. When Colonel ambled to the back door, Pepper trotted next to him, and the three of us went to the back yard. Pepper darted around the perimeter while Colonel sniffed the corners.

I put Pepper's dog bed next to Colonel's in the living room. She dragged her pad to the kitchen near the pantry door.

"I guess Pepper wants to make friends, Mia." Mia flicked her tail and circled Pepper's pad.

CHAPTER THREE

The next morning when my alarm woke me, Colonel was on the small rug next to my bed. I tiptoed to the kitchen. Pepper and Mia were curled up on Pepper's pad. Pepper woke when Colonel and I reached the back door and trotted outside with Colonel. Pepper dashed around, and Colonel sniffed the grass. I left them to do their business while I dressed.

I fed Mia and opened the back door. The two dogs raced inside, and I fed them. When I was ready to leave for work, I stopped. "I didn't think this through, Colonel. Do you suppose Pepper can be a shop dog?"

I clipped the leash onto her collar, and the three of us went to the shop. When we went inside, Tiffany's eyes widened. "New dog?"

"Pepper is Ms. Melinda's dog. Colonel and I picked her up at the kennel. We have her until Ms. Melinda gets out of the hospital today. I just hope Pepper doesn't scare our customers or run away."

I unclipped the leash, and Pepper trotted to Tiffany. Tiffany put her hand down for Pepper to smell, and Pepper gave her a kiss. "I think she'll be fine with our customers."

"What's our plan for today?" I tied on my apron.

"We have only one meeting; the Historical Society meets at eight thirty. I thought strawberry glazed and maple. I think my brain is getting fried. I couldn't come up with anything for scones."

"What about amaretto scones? We could use almond extract. Maybe don't call them amaretto scones. Amandine scones? What do you think?"

"Sounds fancy. Let's do it. I'll bet Mr. Otto has a recipe." Tiffany scooted to the storeroom to check the secret recipe book. She came out of the storeroom waving the booklet. "Got it. And it's easy."

"I'll work on scones, and you can get back to your donuts," I said. I scanned through the recipe. "Why did we never do this before, Tiffany? This is easy."

"Told you."

After we had all the donuts except the last batch done, the bell jingled, and the sheriff strolled in. Pepper dashed to the door to greet the sheriff.

"What? Did you trade Colonel in for a compact?" the sheriff asked.

Colonel snuffled in his sleep.

I snorted. "This is Melinda's dog, Pepper. And I think Colonel just grumbled at you. So, did you get sufficiently harassed about your birthday yesterday?" I put his coffee and donuts at his spot at the counter.

"Yes. Quite sufficiently, thanks to you two and my wife, but it was all for a good cause. Not to mention Alfred and the mayor working together after all these years of not speaking. I never expected to see them work together. Awesome."

"It was." I poured a cup for myself and sat next to the sheriff. "Can you tell me anything about the bloody footprints I saw at the soup kitchen storeroom?"

He chuckled. "I know it isn't funny, but it appears the attacker opened the wrong door in his hurry to escape and was stuck in the dark until he found the light switch. There was blood smeared all over the walls. There was blood on the window and the window sill where he climbed out. His blood trail led to the parking lot in the back."

Pepper danced around the sheriff's feet until he reached down and scratched her ears. "Is Melinda getting out of the hospital soon?"

"Maybe today."

The sheriff drained his cup and finished off his donuts. I refilled his cup.

"What's an amandine, Tiffany?" he asked.

"It's a fancy word for almond. We're upscale today," Tiffany grinned.

"Y'all are just full of surprises." He chuckled and gulped down the rest of his coffee. "Gotta run."

Shirley dashed in, and Pepper raced ahead of her to the display case. "Who's this? You got a new puppy? Is that okay with Colonel? What about Mia? Are you going to sell the donut shop and start a dog rescue?

No, you'd never do that. Donuts are in your veins. Aren't they? You'd never walk away from the donut shop. Would you?"

"This is Pepper. She's Melinda Wallace's dog. We're dog sitting today."

"Of course, you are. I should have known. I'm relieved. I don't know what I'd do without your coffee and donuts. Maybe Tiffany will buy your shop. Then you can have your dog rescue business. Is that what you're planning?"

"Shirley. Stop." I put my hands on my hips. "Pepper's just visiting. Who's the Donut Lady?"

"You are." She tilted her head and sighed. "I dropped into my old habit. Sorry. Thanks for the coffee and donuts. Here's my money. I don't want you to go broke and have to take in more dogs. See you later."

I stared at the wad of money in my hand, and Tiffany laughed.

I handed the cash to Tiffany. "Here, pay Shirley's bill, and the rest is for you."

When the Historical Society was leaving, one of the members approached the counter. "Tiffany, we appreciated that you used the correct spelling for Amandine. Very refreshing. We took up a collection for your college fund." She handed Tiffany an envelope. "This is from all of us."

"Th-thank you, ma'am," Tiffany stuttered. Tiffany went to the storeroom and closed the door.

When she came out, her eyes were red. I turned away. She deserved some privacy, and I was a little weepy too.

"Remember when I got out of prison, and you told me it would be better in a week?" Tiffany asked. "You forgot to tell me that it gets better every week."

"Pretty cool, isn't it?"

"Yes." Tiffany busied herself with the meeting room, and I sprayed and wiped down the counter. Pepper dashed to Tiffany and back to me.

"She's doing great, Pepper," I whispered.

My phone rang. "That's great news, Melinda. Colonel and I will bring Pepper by in a bit."

I called to Tiffany, "Melinda's out of the hospital."

Tiffany pushed the utility cart out of the meeting room. "That's excellent news. When are you taking Pepper home?"

"After we close up, we'll get her things from my house and take her home."

At the end of the morning, I hung up my apron. "I have a question. Why do we never check the calendar the day before?"

Tiffany frowned. "We enjoy the thrill of being surprised? Are you going to check now?"

"Nope. I think we enjoy the neatness of wrapping up today and being done."

Tiffany brushed her hands together. "Done. You know tomorrow's Thursday, right?"

I laughed. "No, I actually forgot. I guess our surprise is if we have a second meeting in addition to our regular Thursday book club."

Colonel, Pepper, and I stopped by my house and picked up Pepper's bed and food. When I parked at Melinda's house, Pepper barked and scratched to get out of the car. When I opened the car door, she dashed to the house and yipped while I gathered her things. Colonel lumbered to the porch and sat in the shade.

"You're right, boy. We aren't staying."

Melinda opened the door, and Pepper yipped and ran tight circles around Melinda. Melinda reached down, and Pepper jumped into her arms.

"I missed you too, Pepper, girl." Melinda stroked Pepper's head and cooed.

I carried in Pepper's food and pad. "Are you okay if Colonel and I head out? Do you need anything?"

"I'm just sore. The doctor said I was lucky because I didn't have any internal injuries or broken bones. My sister is hoping to be here later, and Pepper and I can take a nap in my chair. Thank you for everything."

I stood on her porch to listen for the deadbolt. *Learned that from Jack.* I chuckled.

* * *

I woke with a start. Colonel was on the sofa next to me, and my book was on my lap. My neck ached from sleeping in a cramped position. "Let's go to bed, Colonel."

I checked the doors and trudged to my bedroom. I checked the clock. "It's only nine thirty. Guess I had a sleep deficit."

I snuggled down and relaxed to the soft, rhythmic sound of Colonel's snores.

A thud and a scream woke me. I sat up. I was on the ground in a forest with the shadows all around me. Colonel nudged my arm, and I picked up Mia and Pepper. A tall pine tree ten feet away swayed and crashed next to us. The ground around a large oak tree swelled as the tree rocked. The oak screamed and teetered toward us, and we ran. When the tree cracked and fell, the ground trembled, and the top branches raked my back. The din of toppling trees surrounded us. We ran faster until a tree crashed in front of us. It was so big that I couldn't see beyond it. We turned away and ran to a creek. I stepped into the icy cold water. Colonel stayed on the bank and barked.

"Come on, boy. Come on." I cried. "We have to stay together." The water rose to my chin, and Pepper whined. Mia scratched me and tried to get away. I slogged through the water clutching the wet shivering animals and climbed onto the bank next to Colonel. The forest caught fire, and Colonel barked. And barked.

Colonel is barking. I shivered from the cold and opened my eyes. All the covers were on the floor, and Colonel barked. I wrapped myself in a blanket.

"Colonel. What is it?"

Colonel dashed to the bedroom door, faced the hallway, and growled. The shadows scattered, and he whined.

I tiptoed down the hallway to the living room with Colonel by my side. I glanced at the shadows behind me. "You have my back or you planning an ambush?" I mumbled.

Colonel hurried to the back door, and I peeked out the kitchen window. A raccoon had knocked over the neighbor's trash can and was waddling to the neighbor's front yard. When I opened the back door, Colonel dashed to the back fence.

When Colonel and I came back into the house, I heated the kettle for tea and glanced at the clock. *Three thirty. Might as well feed Colonel and Mia and get ready for work.*

"Let's take the car today, Colonel. Want to go, Mia?" Mia sauntered into her carrier, and the three of us went to the shop where the lights were on.

The bell jingled when I unlocked the door.

"Just the book club today," Tiffany said. "I'm working on the Thursday pink sprinkles and maple donuts. What scones for today?"

"How about mixed berry scones? Cranberries and blueberries?"

Tiffany disappeared into the storeroom and returned with Mr. Otto's secret recipe book. "What made you come up with that? Mr. Otto has a cranberry and blueberry scone with sour cream. Doesn't that sound good? Maybe drizzled with classic vanilla glaze?"

"Sounds great. I'll get busy on the scones." I hurried to the storeroom for my apron.

Tiffany dropped the last of her first batch in the fryer. "I'm planning on four batches. I thought regular pink sprinkled donut holes today."

"Do we have sour cream? I can't remember. I guess I could look." I opened the refrigerator. "No sour cream. The supercenter opens early. Should I run get us some, or do we adjust our recipe?"

"It would be easy to adjust, and nobody would know." Tiffany peered over my shoulder at the recipe. "But I think I can keep up with the donuts and start on the scone recipe if you want to run to the store."

"It's our Thursday surprise. I'll be back in a half hour."

I grabbed my purse and keys and scurried to the car. After I parked, I realized I still had on my cap and apron. I shrugged and dashed inside to the dairy section. *Thirty-two-ounce containers. Perfect.* I checked the expiration dates and put four in my basket. No one was in line at the self-checkout. I bit my lip and crossed my fingers. *Too easy.*

I parked at the shop and unlocked the door. I headed to the refrigerator, and Tiffany glanced up. Her eyes were red.

"What's wrong'" I reached for the counter to steady myself. *Who's hurt?*

"I burned a batch of donut holes," Tiffany sobbed. "I've never burned any donuts. Ever. I'm a terrible baker." She ran into the bathroom and slammed the door.

I put the sour cream in the refrigerator and tapped on the bathroom door. "You done?"

"Yes, ma'am."

"I need to know where to pick up with the scone recipe."

She came out of the bathroom. "With the sour cream. Thanks."

"For what?" I asked while I measured the sour cream.

"For not embarrassing me."

"You're welcome. What's going on? Really."

Tiffany dipped donuts into the maple icing. "Nothing. Except I haven't heard from Roger in two days. We had kind of a fight, and I told him I never wanted to see him again."

I divided my dough, patted my first batch into a circle, and cut the scone triangles. I put the triangles on a baking sheet, popped it into the oven, and set the timer.

I lifted out my second batch of dough and patted it into a circle.

"That was stupid, wasn't it?" Tiffany asked.

I met her gaze. "You'll have to ask someone else. I have to work with you every day." I held my breath.

Tiffany burst out laughing. "You win. You know you say the most outrageous things sometimes, Miss Lady. Do you think he's just stubborn?"

I cut the triangles and put them on a baking sheet.

"Aren't you even going to talk to me? What kind of friend are you?"

"An old one." I put the sheet into the oven.

"Well, I told him I never wanted to see him or hear from him ever again, but I didn't mean it. I was mad. He said he wasn't going to apply for a job in Savannah that would be a promotion because he didn't want to leave Asbury. Because of me. I told him that was no reason. He couldn't blame me because he didn't want to better himself."

The timer dinged, and I pulled out the first batch of scones and put in the second. "Sorry. I missed that. Why doesn't he want to leave Asbury?"

"He said because of me."

"Oh."

"You think I misunderstood what he was saying, don't you? I need to apologize for blowing up so I can ask him what he meant, don't I?"

"Do you have the donuts done? Can you make the drizzle for the scones?"

"Donuts are done. I'll make the drizzle. You finish the scones." Tiffany measured the powdered sugar. "Thanks for the talk. You have a way of putting things into perspective."

The bell jingled. The sheriff strolled into the shop and stood at the counter. "Can I have my coffee and donuts to go? I've got an incident I need to cover."

I handed him his coffee and a sack with two pink-sprinkled donuts and a plain scone. After he left, I said, "He's never done that before. Must be something big."

Tiffany paled. "I need to text Roger and tell him I'm sorry."

Shirley scurried into the shop. "Did you hear the news? Melinda Wallace's husband dropped dead on their porch this morning. I heard she was arrested, but that can't be true. Everybody knows he's running around except her. She talks about how busy he is and how much he has to travel with his job. I think she should give him the boot, but I guess she can't now. It must have been a heart attack. He was overweight, and all that extracurricular stuff couldn't have been good for his heart. He should have joined a gym. Maybe I should join a gym. Do you work out, Karen? You could join a gym with me. Neither one of us is getting any younger."

"Here's your coffee and your sack."

"Thanks. I have a meeting. I'll find a gym for us."

"I'm not interested in—"

She was gone, and I was talking to the door. "—a gym."

My phone rang. "This is Melinda Wallace. Remember what Mr. Otto said? It's more than the biddies, life is getting me down. Would you mind having lunch with me?"

"I'd love it. I'm sorry about your husband."

"Thank you. I need fresh air. I think it will be good for me. Do you mind eating in the park? I can bring sandwiches. Would you bring me a donut? Or a scone? Meet at Sycamore Park at noon?"

"Will do. See you then." I grabbed the tongs and put two doughnuts and two scones in a sack. Mia rubbed across my legs.

"It's an emergency meeting. We need reinforcements."

Mia flicked her tail and marched to the storeroom.

After the last customer bought our remaining four donuts, Tiffany got a text. "Miss Lady, do you mind if I leave now? Everything's clean."

"Go ahead. I'm ready to leave too." After Mia pranced into her carrier, the three of us went home.

A little before noon, Colonel and I left for the park.

I parked at the curb, and Colonel bounded off after a squirrel. When I was in the fourth grade, my class planted tiny bare-root trees in the new Sycamore Park. I stared in awe at the size of the tall, spreading pecan trees.

Melinda sat at the picnic table in the middle of the park and waved when she spotted us. She was a shock of color with her button-up pink blouse, bright red capris, and deep purple sweater that was wrapped around her shoulders. Colonel ran toward her, and I followed him until he diverted to chase another squirrel.

I set my sack of donuts and scones on the table. Her black bruises had perimeters of dark blue.

"How do you like my widow's weeds?" She shook her head. "I'm reaching the point of hysteria. I needed to talk to a fellow outcast before I totally lose it. I even had a craving for unsweet iced tea. I am a total outcast."

I snickered. "You definitely are a splash of color. Or should I say a clash of color? I need to know, where did you even find unsweet tea? When I first moved to town, I'd order unsweet tea, but most of the time it was sweet. I finally caved. I'm back in Georgia. I drink sweet tea."

"I was teasing about the unsweet. You're right. It would have to be imported or something. We have sweet tea. Let's eat. Then we'll talk." She waved at the picnic bench.

After Melinda finished her soup, she pinched a bite of scone. "Edward was a cheatin' jerk. He thought I believed his phony story about going out of town every week, but he was actually spending his money on two-bit—"

Melinda picked up a napkin and fanned herself. "I got carried away. I heard a while ago he lived with a woman and her two small children in the next county when he's not home. He is—was—using the name Sam Clinton. I suspect the children are Edward's. Another complication. I filed for divorce, and it was supposed to be final next month. Leave it to

Edward to check out while we are still married and stick me with all his mess. I don't even know what to do about a funeral for him. It's going to take forever to find all the money he's squirreled away. And for some reason, I'm worried about those small children. The older one is six, and the little one is three. Is that crazy?" She tilted her head and gazed at me.

I met her gaze. "No. I understand being concerned about the children. As far as money is concerned, while I was on trial for Terry's death, the only thing that kept me going was the satisfaction of rooting out all the money he hid from me. I'll give you a list of my searches. What else can I help you with?"

"The list will be a big help." Her shoulders relaxed. "You've saved my sanity, thanks. I'm not sure what my next step will be. But—" She stared at the ground.

"What are you thinking?"

"When I tried to talk to him about his business, he'd get angry. Now I think he was hiding something. I'm going to go through our tax records." She rose from the bench. "Thanks for meeting me. I think I wore myself out." She shuffled to her car.

Colonel sprinted across the park to chase a long-gone squirrel. A white pickup truck pulled into the parking lot, and Roxie pranced to join Colonel.

Jack strolled to the picnic table and sat on the bench across from me. "I didn't want to interrupt. Are you looking into who killed Melinda's husband?"

I glowered. "Of course not. His death was obviously from natural causes. What gave you that idea?"

He scratched his chin. "I know my regulars."

I snorted. "So, what do you hear?"

"This is gas station information, so you know it's true, right? Clarissa was pumping gas and screaming on the phone at Edward two weeks ago. Something about his kids in Conway. And she mentioned Sam Clinton. No details on who Sam Clinton is."

"Wow. So, the whole town, except for me, knew about his family in Conway. Melinda knew too, right?"

"Seems to be the general consensus. Basis for her divorce proceedings. So, Ms. Not-Investigating-Anything, feel like a little trip to Conway?"

"Oh yes. County courthouse? I need to take Colonel home. It's too hot for him to wait in a vehicle."

"I'll drop off Roxie and pick you up in twenty minutes or so at your house."

"That works."

On our way to Conway, I pulled out my phone and spent several minutes searching the internet.

"I found an address for Sam Clinton in Conway. Want to drive past the house?"

"Sounds like a plan. Can you search marriage licenses on your phone?"

After a few minutes, I said, "Ugh. It's too hard. I keep running into popup ads and sketchy links."

"We can wait until we get to the courthouse. Want to split up? Check marriage licenses and property records?"

I nodded and leaned back to enjoy the passing countryside. "Still some cotton out there. Isn't it getting late for harvesting? I missed the cotton fields and didn't know it."

"I don't keep up, but cotton prices might be too low to make harvesting the lower yield fields profitable."

"Farmers have to be masters of agriculture, business, and economics too? I never thought about how complex farming is."

Jack slowed when we passed the address I had for Sam Clinton. Azalea bushes brightened up the neatly trimmed front yard, but the paint on the soffits was peeling on the small gray house. A bicycle with training wheels leaned against the side of the house, and a tricycle was on its side near the front steps.

Jack parked at the courthouse.

"I'll go to the Probate Court and ask about marriage licenses. I'll bet they're online, but I'll learn what I can," I said.

"Tax office is across the street. I'll start there for property records. If I finish before you do, I'll come looking for you at the courthouse."

After an hour, Jack sat next to me at the computer table where I scrolled through the past ten years of marriage licenses. I rolled my shoulders. "Nothing," I said. "Nothing for Edward Wallace or Samuel Clinton."

"I was more successful. The house was purchased by Edward Wallace ten years ago and deeded to Samantha Clinton a little over two years ago."

"Dang. I wonder if I was the only one who assumed 'Sam' was Samuel?"

"Would you have noticed Samantha Clinton in your marriage license search?"

"I'd like to say yes, but my mind's fried. I think since I didn't find anything for Edward Wallace, we don't care, but now I know how to get to the online records if we change our minds."

On our way to the truck, I said, "It's somehow comforting to know the house belongs to Samantha."

"I understand," he said. "Have you heard of the Pie House here in Conway? Supposed to be the best in the state. How about some pie and coffee?"

"Sounds like fun."

I read the paper menu and sipped my coffee. "How'd you know about the Pie House? The tart cherry pie sounds great to me."

"Us bachelors share information about the best places for home-style cooking. I've wanted to try the Pie House for ages. I think I need chocolate pie."

When the server came to our table, she said, "The cherry pie's been out of the oven for only ten minutes. Okay if we add a little homemade ice cream to your pie to cool it down, ma'am?"

"Oh my, that would be great."

"I have to change my order," Jack said. "I need warm pie with ice cream too."

After our server left, Jack leaned across the table and whispered. "I think if you say à la mode in here, you get tossed out. Not sure why. We'll need to research. Ask the competition or something."

I chuckled, and Jack beamed.

When the server brought the check, I snatched it off the table. "My turn to buy."

"Okay, Donut Lady. Next time is my turn."

I smiled. *Hope that was a joke.*

On our way to Asbury, I leaned my head back. "Even if we hadn't found anything, the pie and ice cream made the trip worthwhile."

"It did, didn't it? I'll have to take you to some of the other secret bachelor-recommended restaurants."

I turned to examine the countryside. *Not sure how I feel about making this a regular thing.* I glanced at Jack. *I'm probably making too much of a casual conversation.*

"I never would have thought Conway was the place for pie," I said. "Thank you."

CHAPTER FOUR

The next morning, Colonel and I hurried into the shop. "It's Friday, Tiffany. What's our special today?"

"Reading. Special request."

"Sounds great. Who requested it?" I put on my apron.

"The high school principal, Woody, and Shirley, but you don't know. It's your surprise housewarming, but it's going to be at the school right before lunch, not here."

"So, what do you have in mind?"

"Bookworms. That was easy," Tiffany said. "We'll just do our older than dirt donuts and add gummy worms. I'll show you."

"What about dragon donuts? For fantasy," I said. "Let's put a little cayenne in the flour for heat, and we can make different colors of glazes—pink, orange, blue, green."

"And blood scones for mysteries?" She frowned and bit her lip. "We just did blood scones. What about—" Tiffany dashed to the storeroom and returned carrying a small box.

"I spotted this pushed all the way back on the top shelf a few weeks ago and meant to mention it." She set the box on the counter, brushed the dust off the lid, and pulled out two spice jars.

"Spices? What spice?" I asked.

"It's jars of sparkly sugar. Gold sparkly sugar." She handed me a jar.

"Well, then. Let's make cranberry-orange scones and sprinkle golden sparkles on them. They'll be—" I stared at the ceiling. "UFOs. For sci-fi." I wiggled my eyebrows.

Tiffany's eyes widened. "Genius. Some people read tea leaves. You read ceilings. Let's get busy."

"How many dozen donuts do we take to school?" I asked while I mixed the dough for the scones.

"The principal said 'gross.' I never knew Mr. Castillo had a sense of humor."

I chuckled. "What do we want to do for the donut holes? Oh, I've got it. Dragon eggs."

"I'm on it," Tiffany said. "I got the gummy worms yesterday. I wish I could claim I had a feeling, but the principal called yesterday while you were on your phone."

When the sheriff sauntered in later, he frowned at the specials board. "Bookworms and dragons? And I think I'll need a UFO. I see the bookworm in my donut. But a blue donut? That's a dragon? Not sure I get it." He bit into the donut. "Umm. Good. Oh, it's spicy." He took a sip of coffee. "Kind of grows on you."

"Not too spicy?" Tiffany asked.

"No, it's good. Love how it sneaks up on you." The sheriff took another bite. "Need the UFO," he said with his mouth full.

Tiffany whistled between her teeth while she carried the plate with the UFO high over her head and hovered it into place in front of the sheriff.

"It sparkles," he said with his eyes wide. "Where do you two come up with this stuff?"

"According to Tiffany, all answers are on the ceiling." Tiffany and I posed and stared at the ceiling.

"Not looking up," the sheriff mumbled with his head down. He turned his head to the side and peeked at the ceiling.

"Made you look," Tiffany danced around the room.

"I hate this place. Give me a UFO for the road," the sheriff grumbled. "But first, I've got a couple of calls to make." He winked. "Tess, we've got a report of a UFO at the Donut Hole. Yep. Spelled U. F. O. Might need reinforcements. Good plan, Tess." He chuckled and hung up. "How about a refill on my coffee? I need to sit here and plan my day."

It wasn't long until Roger burst into the shop. "I brought the UFO spray, Sheriff. Tess said you'd need it." Roger dropped to a defensive crouch and pointed an aerosol can around the room.

"Hold your fire, Roger," the sheriff said. "They might be friendly."

I stared at Roger's can of plastic string. "You two just disarmed the UFO with your fast-thinking."

"We won?" the sheriff asked. "We won, Roger!"

"It isn't a competition," Tiffany said. She flipped a dishtowel over her shoulder and stomped to the meeting room. She glared at Roger and slammed the door.

"You got the glare that you wanted," I said.

"Yes, ma'am." Roger bounded to the meeting room.

"Get out," Tiffany yelled, and Roger went inside and closed the door.

"They'll be fine, right?" the sheriff asked.

"They will." I refilled our coffee. "This was fun."

"Roger's been moping all week. I needed the two of them to make up. What was that about a glare?"

"Roger said when Tiffany glared at him like she glared at me, he'd know."

"Know what? Something on the ceiling?" the sheriff looked up.

"No," I chuckled. "He'd know she trusted him. She could be mad at him, and he'd still be there for her."

"Thanks for the interpretation. Hopefully, I've had my full dose of drama for the day."

The bell jingled when the sheriff left, and Roger bounded out of the meeting room. "Oh no, he left. Am I in trouble?"

"Probably." I carried dishes to the sink.

Tiffany followed Roger to the door. "Miss Lady's just trying to break the tension. I'll see you later."

I turned in time to see Tiffany kiss Roger on the cheek. Roger winked at me, and I covered my mouth to keep from giggling.

After Roger left, Tiffany said, "It's not easy to trust, is it?"

"No, it isn't. Congratulations. Roger's a wonderful man."

"I think so too." She sniffed and brushed her cheek with her shirt sleeve. "I'm a little emotional today."

"Let's get one last batch going. Donuts and scones. I have a feeling."

Tiffany hurried to the storeroom and returned with more flour. "I love it when you get a feeling."

Shirley scooted into the shop a little before nine.

"Do you have a nine o'clock appointment?" I asked while I added her sugar and cream. "Here's your coffee and your donuts and scone."

"I'm running late. I've got a meeting at eleven at school about Woody. Can you go with me? I might need moral support. We can take the principal's donuts to him. Maybe Tiffany can come too. I'm worried about Woody." She bit her lip and stared at the floor. Tiffany rolled her eyes.

"I'll be happy to go with you. Do you want me to meet you there?"

"That's a great idea. Yes. Wait for me out front. Eleven. Don't go inside the school. Did you hear about Melinda's husband? He didn't die of natural causes. At least that's what everybody's saying. Do you think Melinda poisoned him? He was running around on her. I already told you that, right? I can't stand around all morning. I've got to go." She placed a few folded bills on the counter.

After she left, Tiffany put the change into the "Shirley jar" under the counter. The phone rang, and Tiffany picked up.

"That was Tammy at the kennel," she said after she hung up. "Her company is having its district meeting this morning at the Asbury facility. She wants to surprise them with donuts and scones. She'll be here in ten minutes. Good call, Miss Lady."

Tammy hurried into the shop and stopped to read the specials board. "Bookworms, dragons, and UFOs? Y'all are awesome!" She paid for her pastries. "Do I have any donut holes?"

"Sorry, no," Tiffany said. "Only dragon eggs."

Tammy squealed. "I love this place! I'll bet I get a raise."

"Much deserved," I said.

After Tammy left, I beamed and held my hand up. Tiffany smacked a high-five. "Best day ever," I said. "I just remembered. Colonel and I walked this morning. Do you think Gee would like to help deliver donuts and go to a meeting?"

"I suspect she's in on it. I'll text her."

Tiffany's eyes widened. "I didn't expect that. Aunt Gee says she's not sure she can get away, so Mr. Jack will pick us up."

"Dang it. That was slick. We may have to brainstorm our retaliation later."

* * *

At ten thirty, Jack came into the shop. "Gee said you asked for a ride to the school. Do you have the donuts packed up?"

"Almost, Mr. Jack," Tiffany said.

"We'll need to clean up the shop after the school meeting," I said. "Tiffany, Colonel, and I can walk back. The day's nice. I do appreciate the ride. Don't think we could have walked the four blocks carrying a dozen boxes of donuts."

"I'll be glad to hang around and give you a ride back to the shop. Want to get some lunch afterward?"

"Maybe not today. Too much going on."

The bell jingled, and Josh from the gas station sauntered in. "I heard you had dragon eggs, Ms. Donut Lady. Can I have a box of dragon eggs and a dozen bookworms for me and the mechanics? My boss sent me."

Tiffany boxed up his order, and I took his money.

"Josh, I threw in four UFOs for you," Tiffany said.

"You're the best," Josh beamed. "You too, Ms. Donut Lady."

After Josh left, Jack said, "Y'all have a fan there."

Amber came in; she wore her gray suit with her turquoise silk blouse. "I don't know which fan Jack's talking about, but I'm another one." She stared at the board. "One of each. And then I'll sign up for the half marathon in Conway."

When I stepped to the coffee pot, she said, "To go, please. I've got a pre-court meeting."

After Amber left, Jack loaded the truck with the donuts.

"Are you sure you don't want me to stay here and keep the shop open?" Tiffany asked.

"I do hate to close down without any notice to our customers," I said. "We should make Gee mind the store for us." I chuckled. "No. That's letting her off too easy."

"I'll stay. It's decided," Tiffany said.

"What's decided?" Jack asked.

"Tiffany and Colonel are going to stay and keep the shop open. I'm ready."

When Jack and I arrived at the school, Shirley and Woody stood near the flagpole. Shirley waved, and Woody rolled a wagon to the truck.

"I got a wagon from the library to haul the donuts inside. Twelve dozen is too many to carry."

Woody led the way inside. When we entered the school cafeteria, the students and teachers cheered and applauded. A homemade banner across the wall proclaimed *Reading Challenge!*

Woody rolled the wagon to a table, and four teachers unloaded the pastries. Monica from the library stood behind another table piled with books. She grinned and waved her silver pen across the books on the table. I blinked as the books sparkled.

Shirley stood next to Jack and me near the door. The principal spoke into a microphone. "Ms. Donut Lady, in honor of your dedication to reading, we're dedicating this year's reading challenge to you."

The principal handed the microphone to Woody. "Miss Lady, our reading motto this year is *Reading is a Treat.*"

Shirley beamed and applauded. "I'm so proud of him," she shouted over the applause.

After the applause and cheers died down, the principal said, "We're kicking our challenge off with donuts before lunch. Why? Because—"

The children shouted, "Reading is a treat!"

The children lined up for donuts, and I beamed. Shirley hurried to Woody's table to join him.

Ginny's class was next to where Jack and I stood. After they returned to their table with donuts, she stepped close to me. "All of the children, including several who aren't our usual readers, signed up for the challenge. You've made a huge difference in their lives through your dedication to teach Woody to read." She hugged me, and my eyes welled up.

When the last table of children went through the line, I turned to Jack. "I'd like to leave now. Do you mind?"

"Not at all. I'm glad I was here."

On our way to the shop, Jack asked, "Want to reconsider lunch?"

"Can I have a raincheck? I have a feeling I need to get home."

"You got it."

When I entered the shop, Tiffany had everything cleaned and put away for the next day.

"Thanks, Tiffany. I'm sorry you weren't there, but I appreciate your keeping the store open. It was a kickoff for a reading program at school. Woody announced their *Reading is a Treat* challenge. Anything happen while I was gone?"

"Nope, Miss Lady. You're the catastrophe magnet, so everything was fine. We sold out of donuts. I'm glad I was here."

When Colonel and I headed home, we diverted to go past the soup kitchen. Melinda stood on the sidewalk. "I was on my way to my car when I spotted you and Colonel. The two of you are becoming an institution. Okay if we walk and talk? I need to do both."

Colonel and I slowed our usual pace to match Melinda's steps as we strolled to the end of the block and back. She kept her head down, and we walked in silence. When we returned to her car, she stopped and leaned against the passenger's door. "Need to catch my breath. The medical examiner called this morning. Edward didn't have a heart attack. The M.E. said they still needed to do more tests, but he suspects poison, maybe rat poison."

I stared. "What? Did he say what led him to that conclusion?"

"He said something about bruises and unusual bleeding." Melinda shuddered. "I was so shocked, I had trouble comprehending what he was saying."

"What can I do for you?"

"You've done it. Thank you. My sister will be here on Sunday. She'll help me organize—I'm not sure what—a funeral or something. She's got rough edges but a good heart. Why don't you come to my house for dinner? Six o'clock work for you?"

"Are you sure you're feeling up to it? What shall I bring?"

"Your best appetite. I'm an excellent cook, but I haven't had much of an opportunity lately. My sister and I love to cook together. If I wear out, she'll take over. Oh wait. Do you have any food allergies? Dislikes? Preferences?"

I chuckled. "I'm a foodie. I'll eat anything, but I do prefer home cooking. I'll see you on Sunday at six."

* * *

The next morning, Tiffany fried and drizzled donuts, and I baked scones. "I enjoy our quiet mornings before the rush hits, don't you? Gives us a little time to talk," Tiffany said.

"What's up?" I asked.

"Roger wants me to apply at Georgia Southern University."

"What would you study?" I peeked at the scones in the oven.

Tiffany slammed down her spatula. "Engineering." She scowled and crossed her arms. "Go ahead. Laugh."

"If I laughed, it would only be because I'm so tickled. You are brilliant. What field? Mechanical?"

"How did you know?" she asked.

"Just fits you. Where's Georgia Southern University?" I removed the scones from the oven.

Tiffany bit her lip. "Northeast of Savannah."

"That explains why Roger wants you to apply. Do you want to apply there?'

"See. The thing is. Roger doesn't know. I applied there two months ago," she snickered.

I laughed. "You're not telling him for a while either, are you?"

"Nope. Not until I hear something from them. I applied for a scholarship too. Aunt Gee insisted. She says I've got a good chance." She rinsed her bowls and utensils and put them into the dishwasher.

I glanced at the front window and flinched in surprise when I saw Melinda Wallace at the window. She waved, and I unlocked the door. Her hair was unbrushed, and she wasn't wearing any makeup. Her beige T-shirt was crumpled, and her gray sweatpants had coffee stains. She scanned the room. "Just you and Tiffany here? Nobody else?"

"Are you okay?" I cleared my throat. "Come sit at the counter. Or would you rather sit in my office? It's the storeroom, but it's private."

"I'll just sit at the counter. Can I have coffee and two donuts?" Her smile was weak.

"How do you like your coffee?" I asked while I poured her a cup.

"Just black." After she sat, she glanced at the window. "On second thought, can I sit in your office?"

"Of course. Here's your coffee. What kind of donuts? We have classic glazed and chocolate glazed."

She wrapped her hands around her cup and hurried to the storeroom. "Whatever's convenient."

Tiffany plated one of each and handed me the plate. I joined Melinda in the storeroom. "What's going on?"

"Somebody's been stalking me. He doesn't get close enough for me to say whether he's male or female. Just a feeling I had. Sounds unreal when I say it out loud."

I shuddered. "Just a sec. I need to sit." I positioned a folding chair where I could watch the front door.

Melinda ate half of her chocolate donut. "I'm not sure I can eat the rest. Late last night I got a phone call. The voice was low. Growly. Could have been male or female. It said, 'I've been watching you. I know you're guilty.' I started to say something; I can't even remember what, but they hung up. I've been up all night. I was afraid to go to sleep."

"We need to talk to the sheriff. I trust him."

"I'm afraid if I do that, this person will fabricate something to prove I'm guilty of—what? Chasing off Edward? Murder? I don't even know."

"If you don't want to talk to the sheriff right away, how about a lawyer?"

She pushed back her plate. "I needed a little something in my stomach. Thank you. Lawyer sounds like a good idea."

"You can go out the back if you like. Where did you park?"

"I didn't drive. I left my house for a long walk to clear my head, but I wore out after a block and ended up here."

"Stay here. Use the phone." The bell jingled. "Be back in a few." I closed the storeroom door. The shadows swirled around the door, and then I saw my new customer—the tall volunteer from the soup kitchen who had dumped my donuts into the dumpster when I first took over the shop.

"Good morning." I used my best customer service voice. "What would you like? Our specials today are classic glazed and chocolate glazed."

"Classic, I guess." She glanced over her shoulder. "I expected Melinda to be at the soup kitchen, but nobody's there, and I don't have a key, and then I saw your light. Coffee too? Just three sugars and cream."

"Sure. You want that to go?"

"Oh no. I want to stay here where it's light."

Too bad.

I poured a cup, plated a donut, and served them at the counter. I slid the sugar and cream closer to her. The shadows flickered at the window.

"Are you okay?" *I'm going to regret this.*

"I'm fine." She gulped her coffee without any sugar or cream. "Not really. I got a strange call last night, and I'm feeling jumpy."

"Oh?"

She bit into her donut. "This is good. Do you make your own glaze? It was a man's voice. He said, 'I've been watching you. Why did you do it?' And then he hung up. I have caller ID, so I called right back because I thought we'd been disconnected. I was sure he was going to say more, but no answer and no voice mail."

"I'm calling the sheriff. Sounds like somebody's making nuisance calls."

"Nuisance calls?"

"That's what I think, but I'm not an expert." I picked up my phone.

"No!" She bellowed and ran out of the shop.

I was so startled that I dropped the phone. "I hope it's not broken," I grumbled as I picked it up.

"You okay, Miss Lady?" Tiffany strode to the front door and looked out.

"I'm fine. I didn't expect such a strong reaction."

"Overreaction." Tiffany frowned.

Tiffany crossed her arms and stayed near the front door while I walked to the storeroom. "Did you hear? What on earth is going on?"

Melinda frowned. "Clarissa got a call too? Now I wonder how many others were called." She drummed the desk with her fingertips. "Let's call the sheriff."

The bell jingled, and I glanced at the door. "Good morning, Sheriff. Melinda needs to talk to you in the storeroom. I'll bring you coffee and your donuts."

The bell jingled, and Shirley bustled in. Tiffany took the sheriff's coffee and donuts to the storeroom.

"I need an extra scone to go with my donuts. I got the most bizarre call last night. This person said, 'Why did you do it?' and hung up before I could answer. What do you suppose he was talking about? Doesn't it sound like a crank call to you? I ate a couple of grapes at the grocery store yesterday, but they weren't as sweet as last week, so I didn't buy any. Should I have bought some anyway and told them to charge me for four—okay, five—more? I'll go to the grocery store after this morning's appointment and give the manager some money. I'll check and see how much a pound is. That ought to cover it. Thanks, Karen. You always have the best advice."

She picked up her sack and coffee and hurried to the door. "Oh wait. I need to pay." She placed money on the counter with care and dashed out.

"Bye, Shirley," I said, but the bell had already announced her departure. I knuckle-rapped on the storeroom door.

The sheriff opened the door. "We heard."

"For the record, nobody called me."

He frowned. "You sure?"

"Would I lie to you?" I raised my eyebrows.

The sheriff snorted. "We're going to my office. Let me know if anyone else tells you about an anonymous call. You're obviously a crank-call magnet today."

After the sheriff and Melinda left, Jack came into the shop and strolled to the counter. He squinted at the board. "Classic glazed and chocolate glazed? You going retro?"

Tiffany snorted. "We need to do retro donuts sometime. Good idea, Mr. Jack."

I rolled my eyes and put two donuts and a scone on a plate in front of Jack while Tiffany poured his coffee.

"A local band is playing this evening at the town square. It's four of Alfred's boys. I promised to be there to support them. I'm working on getting the word out. Can we put a flyer in your window?"

"Of course. I'm happy to advertise local talent."

"What band?" Tiffany asked.

"*The Mudflaps.* Heard of them?"

"They're good. I'm going to text Roger."

"I'll be right back," Jack said. He returned with a large flyer.

Tiffany finished her text and read the flyer. "Food trucks too. Sounds great." She placed the flyer in the front window. "I'm sure this will help. Where else are you putting flyers?"

"Already stopped by the hardware store, grocery store, Gus's, and Ida's. I've got two left. Thought I'd swing by the drug store and the gas station."

"I need to make sure Aunt Gee and Isaiah know too." Tiffany picked up her phone and sat at the counter.

"What do you think, Karen? Want to support the local boys? I could be at your house at five thirty, and we could walk to the square."

"I'll think about it," I said.

Jack nodded and sipped his coffee. Tiffany headed to the coffee pot and jabbed me in the side with her elbow. I glared, and she raised her eyebrows. She refilled Jack's coffee.

"What's the weather going to be like? Any rain?" she asked.

"Weather's supposed to be dry and a little cool. Be a nice evening for a sweater."

"I love it when the weather turns cools. Fewer bugs at dusk," Tiffany said.

"Full moon tonight too. Perfect for an outside concert," Jack said.

These two are not going to give up.

"Five thirty is fine," I said.

"Good. See you then," Jack finished his coffee and left whistling.

"You weren't going to quit, were you?" I crossed my arms.

"Nope. You'd do the same for me, right?" Tiffany asked.

"Never." I stomped to my office.

"Pants on fire," Tiffany said in a sing-song voice.

I slammed the door.

I stared at my blank computer screen. A tap at the door broke my fury-filled concentration.

"Miss Lady?"

"Come in, Woody."

"I need to do the inventory. Is now okay?" He had his clipboard and spreadsheet.

"Now's fine, Woody. Donut first or after your inventory?"

"After." He tapped his pen on his clipboard and marched to the shelves.

I smiled at his all-business demeanor.

* * *

I checked the weather at two, three, and four o'clock. No change in the forecast. At four, I called Tammy. "You going to the concert tonight? Who with? Thought so. I have a favor to ask."

After I hung up, I dressed in jeans, a long-sleeved shirt, and a sweatshirt. The dressiest shoes I had were my cowgirl boots, and they were also my most comfortable. *No contest.*

I fed Colonel and Mia, and then Colonel and I went out back for his after-meal sniff and stroll. When a white truck slow-rolled through the alley, I waved and shook my head. Colonel and I went into the house, and I opened the front door.

A white truck pulled into my driveway, and Jack ambled to the porch. "Busted," he said.

"Again." I closed and locked the door behind me.

"What are our food options tonight?" I asked as we walked to the square.

"The tamale truck. I can't remember what else," he said.

"I haven't had tamales in forever. That sounds good. I'll bet they have a long line."

When we reached the square, Gee and Shirley had commandeered two tables next to each other. Gee, Isaiah, and Tammy sat at one table, and Shirley and Woody sat at the other.

Tiffany and Roger approached the tables from the other side of the park.

Tammy ran to meet us, grabbed my hands, and pulled me to Gee's table. "I was so excited when Isaiah said you might be here tonight. Are you going to sit at the table next to us, Ms. Donut Lady? This is thrilling. I can't believe you're actually here."

I looped my arm through Tammy's and whispered. "You're doing great. Gee's about to explode."

"Oh thank you! Thank you!" Tammy squealed. "Isaiah, Ms. Donut Lady might sit with me a few minutes later."

"That's nice, Babe," Isaiah said. He coughed into the crook of his arm.

Gee frowned and crossed her arms.

Jack took my arm and walked me to Shirley's table. "You're wicked. You know that, right?" He whispered.

I nodded. Tiffany pulled Roger on the arm and whispered. Roger's hand covered his mouth, but his twinkling eyes revealed his mirth.

I sat next to Woody on the bench. He leaned over and whispered, "We're pranking Aunt Gee, aren't we?"

"You're always right, Woody," I said.

"What?" Shirley asked. "What is Woody right about? Which is kind of a silly question because he's always right. Is it the inventory? Or did he come up with a new idea for a Friday donut? He's very smart. And talented. He's taking art lessons now. I didn't know how it would work out for the online lessons, but it's been very smooth. He says he's learned a lot. I'm really happy about that. Learning is good. Right, Karen?"

"You're right, Shirley."

Shirley beamed. Jack tilted his head and stared.

I patted the seat next to me. "Would you like to sit, Jack?"

Jack leaned close to my ear. "I'd be afraid not to."

I snorted.

"What kind of tamales do you like, Donut Lady? How about if I go stand in line for our dinner?" Jack asked.

"I'll love whatever you get. Thanks for the offer. I've had a long day."

Jack, Isaiah, Tammy, and Roger lined up at the tamale truck. Gee, Shirley, and Woody headed to the Greek food.

Tiffany stayed behind at Gee's table. "Miss Lady, you're awesome. Just wanted you to know I'm enjoying the show. Aunt Gee's about to bust a gut. Tammy's really good, isn't she? I like her."

"It would be better if I were pranking you, you know that, right?"

"You'll get me another time, I'm sure. How's Tammy going to keep Aunt Gee from hating her forever?"

"Covered. Tammy will tell Gee I bewitched her."

"Oh lord. Aunt Gee will know exactly where that came from. Brilliant. And Tammy's gone up another two notches in my eyes. Aunt Gee deserves a daughter-in-law who isn't afraid of her."

"That serious?" I asked.

"Could be. I don't have any inside information, but I got eyes, old woman."

We laughed.

"What's funny?" Jack asked as he sat next to me.

"Tiffany called me an old woman," I said.

He narrowed his eyes. "Here's your food. Let me know if you like it. I'm missing something, right? Will I hear later?"

"Maybe."

The band, *The Mudflaps*, jumped up on the stage at the square to whistles and applause. Their songs were Mudflaps originals—a cross of new rock, old rock, and classic country western with a hip-hop twist.

"Toe-tapping." Jack cleared his throat, and I laughed.

I was enthralled by the younger set hopping and jumping to the tunes. Shirley beamed while Woody flailed his arms and danced with Isaiah and Tammy.

The band closed with a tribute to Alfred. It was an original song called "Old Man's Got Your Back." I couldn't hold back the tears that flowed down my face. I glanced at the rest of the crowd. *I'm not the only one.*

I made my way to Tammy and shook her hand. She squealed and winked. I hugged her and said, "You're awesome."

Jack took my elbow, and we headed to the street. He glanced behind us. "Tammy is standing where we left her. She's applauding."

I chuckled. "Isn't she the greatest? What's Gee doing?"

"Standing with her mouth open. Folks have joined in with Tammy. She's gathered a crowd of about twenty people who are applauding you as you walk away. Am I supposed to walk behind you and applaud?"

"Don't. You. Dare." I said with clenched teeth.

Jack threw his head back in laughter. The applause and whistles behind us intensified.

When we got to my house, I said, "I suppose you're waiting while I let Colonel out."

After Colonel did his business and came back inside, I said, "Thanks, Jack. I can't remember when I had so much fun."

"It was fun, wasn't it?" He held my shoulders and kissed my forehead. I stepped back, and he left. I locked the door, threw the deadbolt, and flopped down on the sofa.

"I don't know how I feel about Jack, Colonel. I like my life as it is. I really am not interested in any complications." Colonel put his head on my knee, and I rubbed his face. "Let's go to bed."

CHAPTER FIVE

The shadows, Colonel, and Mia let me sleep in on Sunday morning. I relaxed on the back porch with my coffee while Colonel checked for any encroachment of his territory. A few clouds drifted by, and a mockingbird did its best to wake the neighborhood. Off in the distance, a dog barked. A light breeze rustled the leaves in the surrounding trees. I sipped my coffee and smiled. *It doesn't get any better than this.*

Later in the day, Colonel flopped on the floor, and Mia jumped up on my bed while I flipped through my closet. *What do I wear?*

"I always wear jeans or capris. It's too cold for capris, so it's jeans." I tossed a pair of clean jeans on the bed and frowned. "My generation either wears jeans and no makeup or fancy clothes and impeccable makeup." I strode back to my closet and flipped through the hangers. "I don't see any fancy clothes for a dinner party in here."

When I sat on the bed, Mia hopped onto my lap. "Thanks, Mia. Stressing over what to wear to dinner is silly." While I stroked her back, shadows grew in the corner. My pulse quickened, and my breathing became shallow. Mia hissed, and the shadows deflated.

"What about a gray and pink long-sleeved T-shirt? Good enough, right?" Mia meowed.

* * *

After I parked in Melinda's driveway, I wiped my palms on my jeans. Before I reached the first step, Melinda opened the door, and Pepper bounded out to greet me. I scratched Pepper's perky ears, and she licked my hand.

"Come on in. Meet my sister, Debra. Debra, this is the Donut Lady, Karen."

When I stepped inside, the aroma of chicken and herbs greeted me, but I faltered when I saw Debra. She was at least six inches taller than me and in her thirties. She wore jeans and a green T-shirt with a gray and green plaid overshirt that covered her beltline. She was lean and muscular, and her blond hair was cut short. *Prison Cop. Armed.*

"I'm a correctional officer at the Arrendale Women's Prison near Alto. You could tell, right? But I'm not at work, Ms. Karen. I'm Melinda's sister." She raised her eyebrows and stuck out her hand.

I shook her hand. "Nice to meet you, Debra, Melinda's sister."

"I'll pull the chicken pot pie out of the oven. I have an eat-in kitchen. It's one of the things about this house that I love." Melinda waved at the kitchen.

After we were seated at Melinda's rustic wooden dining table, Debra buttered her dinner roll. "Melinda told me about your first meeting after your donuts were tossed into the soup kitchen dumpster. Our family seems to have a knack of getting off on the wrong foot. I should have told Melinda to warn you."

I narrowed my eyes. "Are you sure you didn't plan to test my law enforcement radar?"

Debra froze with the roll halfway to her open mouth. "What?"

I put my hand up to my mouth too late to hide my smirk.

"Dang it, woman. You got me." Debra chuckled.

"You two are crazy," Melinda said. "If y'all don't behave, I'm not going to tell you what we're having for dessert, even though my lemon cheesecake won a blue ribbon at the county fair last year."

After Melinda served dessert, she said, "Ms. Karen, I told Debra about the calls and what the medical examiner said about Wally. Do you have any theories about the calls?"

"The calls don't make any sense to me when I look at them as a group." I took a bite of cheesecake. "Mmm. Good. I'm not sure I've ever had lemon cheesecake."

"Interesting observation, Donut Lady." Debra slipped a bite of cheesecake onto her fork. "What's another way to think about the calls?"

"I think the call to Melinda was the only significant one. I suspect she'll get a follow-up. I'm not a Clarissa fan, so my thoughts are tainted in her case. She seemed overly dramatic, and I have this feeling she's somehow involved. The call to Shirley was an obvious distraction. Everybody knows Shirley has no filters and tells everyone her business."

"I wish I'd had your common sense when I got the call," Melinda said. "I wouldn't have lost a night's sleep. Except now I wait for the next call?"

"If you don't get another call, I'd say somebody's trying to rattle you," Debra said. "Or if you do get another call—"

"Somebody's trying to rattle me, right?" Melinda rolled her eyes.

Debra and I cleared the table, and Melinda loaded her dishwasher.

"Another thing, Karen. It didn't seem appropriate to talk about while we were eating, but the medical examiner will release Wally's body on Monday," Melinda said. "He'll be cremated, but I'm not interested in a funeral. I wondered if I should contact the mother of his children. Seems wrong for him to just vanish out of their lives into thin air. What do you think?"

I frowned. "Do you think it would make more sense for the sheriff in Conway to inform her about his death first? Maybe ask the M.E. if he would notify the sheriff?"

"Good place to start," Debra said.

"What about Edward and the poison? What do you think, Debra?" I asked.

"The wife did it," Debra said. Melinda spun around and threw a towel at Debra who caught it midair.

"Did not," Melinda said.

"Fine. If you refuse to confess, my next theory is a jealous lover. Another option could be drug trade involvement." Debra folded the towel and set it on the counter. "Poison seems a better match for the jealousy angle, but that's going with the obvious. What do you think, Donut Lady?"

"I think Clarissa should confess."

Debra rolled her eyes.

"Seriously, I think it's drugs, but I can't say why," I said. "It's just a feeling. The poison thing, though. That seems personal. Maybe the poison is to implicate Melinda. To buy time? A distraction for something else?"

Debra stared at Melinda. "If you weren't my sister, I'd think you were hiding something."

Melinda sat at the table and rubbed her forehead. "Just for the sake of argument, what would I be hiding?"

"Either something damaging to your reputation or illegal." Debra joined her at the table.

"That puts us at illegal. My reputation couldn't be any more damaged with the rumors flying that I killed my husband," Melinda said.

"If Edward got a payoff for something, what would it be?" I asked while I paced.

"Whatever would make him the most money. Isn't that drugs?" Melinda asked.

"The only reason I can think that your reputation needs to be damaged is to destroy your credibility." I gazed through the window at the backyard. "Or maybe Edward hid something. Maybe the point of implicating you is to slow you down from finding something. Just be careful."

Deb rose, carried her empty glass to the sink, and filled her glass with water. "I agree. Your office was ransacked, Sis, and then you were attacked. We don't know where Edward was when your office was tossed, but then he shows up dead on your doorstep. Reminds me of a cat with a mouse. Leaves it on the doorstep." Deb shuddered. "I just grossed myself out."

"Glad you waited until we finished dessert." Melinda grumbled. She rose, and Pepper danced around her feet.

"I'll feed you, Pepper." Debra picked up the dog bowl, and Pepper trotted over.

* * *

"Been a busy weekend, Colonel. Can you believe tomorrow's Monday, already?" I fed him and Mia. After Colonel had his break outside, I relaxed on the sofa with my dog at my feet and my cat on top of my book.

"Move, Mia," I said. "I want to finish this chapter, and maybe the next." One chapter turned into another and another.

Colonel whined, and I woke. My neck and back were stiff. I rolled my shoulders. Colonel whined again. He pawed and scratched at the closed pantry door. His hackles were raised.

"What's wrong, boy? Mia trap herself in the pantry?" I asked.

When I opened the door, Mia's back was arched. She had a rat trapped in the back corner. I wretched at the putrid odor of rotting flesh emanating from the rat. I grabbed for a broom. "Move, Mia."

The rat's eyes narrowed and glowed with fire. Mia hissed and spit, and the rat lunged. He grabbed her by the neck and shook her. Mia's blood sprayed the room and me. I dropped the broom and reached for Mia. The rat flipped her into the air and sunk his sharp teeth into her belly before I could catch her. Mia shrieked and fought to get free. Colonel pushed past me with a fierce growl and his teeth bared. Colonel attacked the rodent, and three rats the same size as Colonel dropped onto him from the ceiling. Four more rats the size of leopards leaped and knocked me down. Their razor-edged teeth ripped at my neck and face. I screamed and fought to push them away. Mia went limp, and the rat tossed her to the floor. The rats severed my carotid artery, and I felt my life draining away. Colonel crawled to me and laid his head on my neck to stop the spurting blood. Shadows gathered and churned on the pantry ceiling. They plunged to the floor and blanketed Colonel, Mia, and me. The rats roared and screeched, and the room filled with the stench of burned flesh. The overwhelming stink dissipated, and silence filled the room. Mia's rough tongue licked my hand. Colonel nudged my shoulder.

My heart pounded, and I gasped for breath. Colonel nudged me again. I opened my eyes. I was on the floor next to the sofa. Colonel licked my face, and Mia cleaned my hand. The shadows danced on the back of the sofa. Mia had no wounds. I felt my neck. *No holes.* I examined my hands and arms. *No blood.*

I pushed myself to a sitting position. "I hate rats." I left the lights on in the kitchen and living room and went to bed.

* * *

On Monday morning Tiffany sang under her breath and mixed the strawberry drizzle while the last batch of donuts cooled.

I checked the calendar. "We've got the men's group from the Methodist church today. I'll get the scones started."

The bell jingled, and the sheriff strode in. "What's on the agenda today?" He read the board. "Classic and maple? What's the catch?"

I poured his coffee. "We aren't saying."

The sheriff pinched a small bite of the classic donut and examined it. He scowled and put it in his mouth and chewed slowly. "Okay to swallow?" he asked with the tiny bite still in his mouth.

"Tiffany, I need some help in the storeroom."

After we walked into the storeroom, Tiffany asked, "Are you going to tell him?"

"Nope, but if you're feeling kind-hearted, you can."

Tiffany rolled her eyes. "I can't take the pressure." She sat at my desk. "I'll come out when he leaves."

I walked out and held my index finger to my lips. I tiptoed to the door and opened and closed the door. After the second jingle, Tiffany danced out of the storeroom and whirled in the middle of the room.

She froze at the sight of the sheriff. "You're a sneak, Miss Lady," she huffed and covered her face.

"Your shoulders are shaking," the sheriff laughed.

She dropped her hands and revealed her big grin. "She did get me. Not so fair and square though. Tell her I'm not speaking to her the rest of the day."

"I've got to get to work." The sheriff dashed out, and Tiffany and I snickered.

I stacked the plates, napkins, spoons, and cups on the utility cart and rolled it into the meeting room. After I set everything on the buffet, I started the coffee maker.

"Here comes Ms. Shirley," Tiffany said. "Want to fix her coffee while I sack up her donut and scone?"

When Tiffany handed Shirley her sack, Shirley said, "A bunch of people got the anonymous caller the other night. Is that the new phone scam? I don't exactly understand how it would work. If it was blackmail or something, wouldn't they need to leave a callback number or drop off instructions or something? Aren't blackmailers supposed to write notes with cut-out words? Maybe he'll call back. Do you think I should start collecting small bills?"

The Methodist men sauntered into the shop and read the board before going to the pink meeting room.

Silas, our retired dentist, halted at the door. "Did you get one of those calls, Karen? Sounds like people are a little shook."

"No, I didn't. I think the calls were a prank," I said.

Silas nodded and hurried inside the meeting room before the door closed.

"Tiffany, we need an occasional Monday surprise when the Methodist men are here."

"I have every confidence in you, Miss Lady, and your ability to get us into trouble. I did four batches of donuts. Do I need to do more?"

"Four sounds good to me," I said.

The bell jingled, and Jack sauntered in.

"I'll check the meeting room, Miss Lady," Tiffany said.

"No, that's—if you want to, that's fine," I sighed.

Jack sat at the counter and grinned.

"Coffee, I assume. Donut or scone?" I poured his coffee and waited.

"Do you ever take a day off?" he asked.

"Of course. Sunday's my day off." I plated a classic and a scone and set the plate on the counter in front of him.

"I mean during the week." He sipped his coffee.

"Why would I want to?" I asked.

"Baseball. Best reason in the world." He wiggled his eyebrows and munched on his scone.

I filled a carafe and took it to the meeting room. "Here ya go, Tiffany. Need anything else?"

Her brow furrowed as she looked over my shoulder. "More coffee?"

"Already? On it," I said.

Tiffany frowned. "No, I meant Jack."

Whoa. I've never made a customer wait for coffee before. I need to straighten up.

As I refilled Jack's empty cup, I said, "I've been a baseball fan since I was a kid. Isn't there a farm club that plays around here?"

"I was thinking the Atlanta Braves. Wednesday. How does that sound?"

"Who are they playing? And it doesn't matter. It's not the Cincinnati Reds, is it?"

"I thought you said it didn't matter. And yes, the Reds. We'd need to leave Wednesday before noon. If we drove back after the game, we'd be on the road by midnight Wednesday, which would make for a long day. If we stayed overnight, we could drive safely back Thursday morning. Eli told me he surprised Ginny with tickets. Got me to thinking maybe we could all go together. We could share the driving back that night or stay overnight in Atlanta. What do you think?"

"I do love baseball, but I don't want to leave Colonel and Mia that long. The Braves and the Reds? Will they televise the game?"

"I don't know, but maybe I should look into a farm club. Something a little closer, and we could go more often. It would be nice to have a baseball buddy."

I nodded. *Baseball buddy. Has a comforting ring to it.*

* * *

The next morning, the sheriff stared at his coffee and donuts. His face was grim.

"Something wrong, Sheriff? Everything okay at home?" I asked.

"I wanted you to hear from me before the gossip starts flying. Melinda Wallace is being held in jail for questioning. That's all for now. Didn't want you getting mad at me."

Tiffany's eyes widened, and I sat on the stool next to him.

"Thanks for telling me. I understand you have to do your job." I met the sheriff's gaze. "Brings back bad memories, though."

"I know, Ms. Karen. Wish I could help," he said.

Tiffany poured a cup and set it in front of me.

"It helps that you're my friend. Thank you, Grady. You too, Tiffany." I sipped my coffee.

Not long after the sheriff left, Shirley scurried into the shop. "Did you hear? Melinda's been arrested. She murdered her husband. I would never have thought Melinda would do that. I was sure it was Clarissa. She was devastated when Wallace dumped her last year. Nobody knew she was seeing him until then. She would go on and on about her *Eddie* and how Melinda didn't deserve him. I just avoided her so I wouldn't have to hear it. Some people need to listen to themselves. Oversharing is not attractive at all." She sniffed, grabbed her coffee and sack, and left.

I rubbed my forehead. *Does Shirley even hear herself?*

My phone rang. "Donut Lady? This is Debra, Melinda's sister. Did you hear Melinda's been arrested? Can we meet for lunch?"

"I did hear. How about Ida's Diner at noon?"

After I hung up, I slumped against the counter. *Too many memories. I thought I was past it.*

"You okay, Miss Lady?" Tiffany asked.

I straightened up. "I'm fine. I'm meeting Melinda's sister Debra at Ida's Diner at noon."

"Can I go along? Are we going to solve this murder?"

I scowled. "Tiffany, we're bakers, not detectives. I've learned my lesson. I am not getting involved."

"I'll take that as a *yes*." She whirled around and returned to cleaning the equipment.

* * *

Tiffany and I took Colonel and Mia home before we went to Ida's Diner. We arrived fifteen minutes early and sat at a booth near the back. Mary Rose delivered our glasses of sweet tea.

When Debra arrived, Tiffany moved to my side of the booth, and I scooted closer to the window to make room. Debra sat across from us and pursed her lips when Tiffany stiffened.

"We do have our radar," I said. "Debra, this is Tiffany, my friend and baker. Tiffany, Debra is Melinda's sister and a corrections officer." They shook hands.

Mary Rose hurried to our booth.

"Sweet tea for me," Debra said. "I'm ready to order if y'all are."

"I'd like a turkey and swiss sandwich on rye. No chips," I said.

Debra nodded. "Sounds good. I'll have the same."

"And your usual, Tiffany." Mary Rose scurried away.

After Debra's tea arrived, she said, "Melinda was taken in for questioning. What did you hear?"

"That she'd been arrested for murder, and Clarissa was upset when Edward dumped her last year."

Debra raised her eyebrows. "Your news is much more interesting than mine. It doesn't take long, does it? I have to leave town this afternoon because I work tomorrow, but I'm not worried because Melinda has a good lawyer."

Debra sipped her tea and wiped the table where the condensation had dripped. "I'm taking Pepper with me. My place is a second home to her, so she'll be fine."

Mary Rose brought our sandwiches and refilled our tea glasses.

Before my second bite, I asked, "What do you want us to do?"

"I don't know. Keep your eyes and ears open."

"I can pick up Melinda's mail."

"Didn't think of that. Thanks. You've got my phone number, right? I got yours from Melinda."

After we finished our sandwiches, Debra said, "I'm buying lunch. Don't argue."

I chuckled. "Wouldn't dream of it. Thanks. I've got the tip."

"Melinda told me to watch out. You've got spells and magic," Debra snort-laughed. "And you always get the last word."

* * *

When Colonel and I got to the shop the next morning, Tiffany asked, "Are you doing okay? I had nightmares last night. It's been a while since I've had nightmares."

"I'm really sorry," I said.

"Thanks. It takes a while, doesn't it?" Tiffany shuddered. After she plopped a batch of dough into a bowl to rise, she said, "I checked the calendar. You ready for the Rowdy Rangers? Who are they?"

I laughed. "It's a group of retired forest rangers. They're an informal service organization. I think they work with Alfred and his boys too. What's our culinary plan for today?"

"I was thinking strawberry glaze and frosted coffee and maybe strawberry scones."

"I'll get busy on the scones."

After Tiffany finished her second batch, the bell jingled, and the sheriff came inside. He gazed at the board while I filled his cup, and Tiffany served his donuts. "Y'all haven't come up with a donut yet that I haven't liked."

"Sounds like the gauntlet's been thrown, Miss Lady," Tiffany said.

"I think you're right. How do you feel about broccoli donuts, Sheriff?" I asked.

He gulped. "I'd love them."

Roger came into the shop. "Love what? If we're talking donuts, I'd love them too."

When we all laughed, Roger said, "Am I fired or pranked?"

Tiffany poured his coffee. "Not fired."

"Nope, not fired," the sheriff said.

"Good. I'm used to being pranked at the Donut Hole. It's like being at home. I need donuts and a scone and my coffee to go. I'm a hard-working, dedicated deputy on duty."

"You're not on duty; you're on a break," the sheriff said.

Tiffany pointed at the counter. "Here's your donuts and scone."

"You're getting to be as magical as Miss Lady, Tiffany."

"I'll take that as a compliment." Tiffany loaded up the utility cart and went into the meeting room.

Roger picked up his coffee and pastries and followed her.

"I hear Jack's been hanging around quite a bit. You okay with that?" Sheriff asked.

I poured my coffee and sat next to him. "I don't know. I'm not sure how I feel about Jack. I love my solitude. I'd say my quiet life, but you're drinking coffee, and I don't want you to choke."

"Thank you for that," he chuckled.

After the sheriff and Roger left, the bell jingled, and Debra sauntered in. "Got coffee? Black. I got off at midnight. I dropped Pepper off at Melinda's house. I'm going to stay there a couple of days."

I poured her a cup. "Want a donut? Scone?"

She dropped onto a stool at the counter. "One of each of whatever you've got. I've heard your donuts are great."

While she munched on her scone, I asked, "Have you seen Melinda?"

"Briefly. They found rat poison in her shed. She had no idea how it got there. She would never have anything like that around where Pepper or a neighborhood kid could get into it. No lock on her shed. Her lawyer says anybody could have put it there. Can you give me a coffee to go? I need to get back to Pepper. I'll catch up with you later."

The mayor marched into the shop at eight thirty and headed to the storeroom. "I've got the morning free. Any meetings this morning?"

"Rowdy Rangers at nine," Tiffany said. "I have the room mostly set up, but you may need to rearrange it."

The Rowdy Rangers filed in, and our official greeter shook hands and beamed.

When the meeting room door closed, Tiffany said, "I've never seen a man as proud of an apron as the mayor is of his. I think he's awesome."

Shirley stomped in with a scowl, and I poured her coffee while Tiffany sacked up her donut and scone.

"When were you going to tell me?" she asked. "I thought friends told friends things. I'm you're oldest—I mean, longest—friend. When were you going to tell me? Don't distract me with coffee. Okay, I might take just a tiny sip." She gulped her coffee. "Well? You and Jack were seen coming out of the marriage license office in Conway. Did you already get married? Are you pregnant?" Her hand flew to her chest, and her eyes widened.

Tiffany snorted and dashed to the storeroom.

"I can hear you giggling in there." I patted a stool. "Shirley. Sit down and take a breath."

"You can't get out of this one, Donut Lady." Shirley frowned.

I stepped over to the utility cart, took a big breath, and turned to Shirley. "Jack and I were doing research for one of his friends. He checked the property records while I searched the marriage licenses. It's nothing exciting."

"Oh. Of course. You're good at research. I knew the whole time it was nothing. That's what I meant to tell them at the gas station when I heard about it. You wouldn't get married without a maid of honor. That would be me. And maybe Gee. Two maids of honor. Tiffany is the bridesmaid, right? Who would give you away? The sheriff or Woody? I'm glad I'm not you. That would be a hard decision. I don't understand why Clarissa was so mad, though. She's not going to be a bridesmaid, is she? Of course not. Maybe Emma and Amber."

"You done?" I growled.

"Oh. I just meant hypothetically. Because. You aren't getting married, right?" Shirley jumped off the stool and grabbed her sack. "Now I'm going to be late for my meeting. I have to run. Nice chat."

When Tiffany came out of the storeroom, she said, "I need to call Aunt Gee right away before you get another irate maid of honor yelling at you."

"You're right, Tiffany." I leaned against the counter. "Telegraph, Telephone, Tell a gas station."

"What?" she asked.

"An old saying, except I kind of embellished it to fit."

After the rangers left, the mayor straightened and cleaned the meeting room. "Anything else before I leave?" he asked.

"That's it. It's a huge help having you here, Mr. Mayor. And if you hear the current gas station gossip that I'm getting married, I'm not." I said.

His eyes widened. "Thanks for the heads up. I might just skip the gas station today. I'll let Amber know for you. See you next time."

When Tiffany and I finished our day's cleanup, I asked, "Heard anything from Georgia Southern University?"

"I haven't, and it's starting to drive me crazy. Waiting is the hardest, isn't it?"

"Did Roger apply for the job in Savannah?"

"He did. He told me he knew it was all going to work out for the best. I almost told him about Georgia Southern, but I decided to wait until he hears about Savannah. What do you think?"

"I think whatever you do is fine, but I'm wondering if it might be more fun for the two of you to share the crazy waiting together."

"I hadn't thought about that. It might be more fun. Then I could talk about it all the time and drive him crazy. What a great idea, Miss Lady."

* * *

After lunch, I settled on the sofa to read. Later, I rose from the sofa and stretched. *Finished my book.* I placed it in the bookcase next to the other books with pink covers.

After I put on the kettle to make tea, my phone rang. *Debra.*

"How are you doing?" I asked.

"Not bad. No, that's not true. A little rough. Have you had dinner? Let's meet at Ida's Diner. Thirty minutes?"

Debra beat me to Ida's and was sipping on coffee when I stepped inside the door. A man sat at the table with her. She glanced at me and inclined her head toward the counter. I claimed the last stool.

"What would you like, Ms. Karen?" Mary Rose asked.

I studied the menu. "Sweet tea and a cheeseburger. "

"You want fries?"

"Just a small order."

"I'll drop your order and get your tea."

When she returned, I said, "I can't remember who that man is over there. Talking with Ms. Melinda's sister. Drives me crazy when I forget a name."

"I know. Me too. That's Mr. Dixon. And now, I can't remember his first name." She rolled her eyes and giggled.

When Mary Rose brought my cheeseburger and fries, she set a stack of napkins next to my plate.

"Trust me. You'll need these."

I cut my cheeseburger in half and bit into the crunchy bun. The burger meat and cheese were hot, and the greasy juices ran into my hands. The dill pickle chips were garlicky, and the tomato tasted like it had been in a garden ten minutes earlier. I took a second bite before I put my burger on the plate. I grabbed a handful of napkins and wiped my mouth, chin, and hands. I picked up a fry and breathed in the earthy aroma of fried potato, salt, and hot oil.

I feasted on my hot, drippy cheeseburger and fries. Mary Rose came to refill my tea, and I pushed my plate away. I'd only eaten half my burger and a quarter of my fries.

"This was heavenly," I said. "And I'm stuffed."

"Would you like a box?" Mary Rose placed my check on the counter.

"I don't think it would reheat very well."

"You're probably right." She leaned close. "I always make my sister come with me, and we share."

Debra slipped onto the stool next to me and set her coffee cup on the counter. "Sorry I dumped you, and you had to eat alone."

"I had the delightful company of a delicious cheeseburger. So, catch me up."

"My company wasn't delightful. I'm jealous. For starters, Ronald Dixon's a jerk. He mostly talked about how his wife, Harriet, didn't appreciate all he did. Dixon's angry because after Harriet left, the county check stopped. He said Harriet probably took the boy just for spite. Do you know who he's talking about?"

"More coffee, Ms. Debra?" Mary Rose breezed by and poured without missing a step.

"Thanks, yes." Debra sipped the fresh coffee. "The most interesting part is how adamant he was that Melinda killed Edward. I reminded him that she's my sister, but it didn't slow him down. I got the impression he and Edward had a business going. He complained that all his income has been taken away from him. He'd been drinking, and I'm sure he was lying half the time. I'm just not sure which parts might have been true. I'm going to ask Melinda about him."

"The county paid the Dixons to foster a boy, but the boy was terribly neglected. He has a wonderful foster mother now. I didn't know the Dixons. Let me know what Melinda says."

CHAPTER SIX

"You going with us today, Mia?" I put her carrier by the door. Mia circled the carrier and pounced onto the top. Colonel barked, and she dashed inside.

"Thursday book club day," I said when we entered the shop. I unzipped the carrier, and Mia marched to the storeroom.

Tiffany mixed her second batch of dough while the first one rose. "I told Roger about applying for Georgia Southern last night, Miss Lady. He's never yelled at me before." She stopped the mixer and smiled. "He was mad that I hadn't told him earlier. He made me promise I'd never keep anything from him again. That is the easiest promise I've ever made."

I blinked away tears. "That's the sweetest thing I've ever heard."

Tiffany's eyes were wet too. "I know, right? And so I told him I loved him." She pursed her lips and stared at the floor.

"What did he say?"

"He said he loved me too. So, I yelled at him for not telling me earlier." She threw back her head and laughed, and I joined her.

"Way to go," I said. "You two are a great match. Roger is a wonderful man."

"I know."

The bell jingled, and Roger sauntered in. "I go on duty in thirty minutes."

"Got work in the storeroom," I mumbled. Colonel followed me, and I closed the door. I checked the calendar. "Book club. Nobody else."

The bell jingled, and I opened the storeroom door.

"You taking inventory, Donut Lady?" Sheriff asked.

"Checking our sales." I poured myself a cup of coffee and sat next to him.

Tiffany and Roger loaded the utility cart, and Roger rolled it into the meeting room.

"Getting ready for the book club," Tiffany said as she followed Roger into the meeting room.

"I hope Savannah treats my sappy deputy right," the sheriff said. "I have it on good authority that they're looking at Roger very seriously." He shoved half a donut into his mouth.

"They'll get a good man, but he'll be missed." I rose and returned with the coffee pot.

As I refilled his cup, the sheriff said, "Something's bothering Emma, but she won't tell me what it is. She's been down for a while. Have you noticed? She say anything to you? I'm getting worried about her."

"I haven't seen her in a while." I sat next to him. "Want me to stop by the hospital on her volunteer day?"

"I don't know. I don't want her to feel like I'm checking up on her."

"I can be discreet if you order me to." I smiled.

The sheriff snorted. "I should do that. Might be interesting to see if you could carry it off. But dang, I couldn't be there to watch."

Amber hurried in. "I know I'm early, but I can't stay for the meeting today. I've got court this morning. I need coffee, my maple donut, and one for the road. And a scone. Have you ever thought about a maple covered scone?"

"No. What a good idea. We'll aim for next Thursday and call it the Amber Scone."

"Oh no. You can't do that. I'll be busted."

"You're right. Forgot," I said.

"I'm going to work," the sheriff said. He rose and sauntered to the meeting room. "Going to work," he announced in a loud voice.

Roger threw open the door. "Right with you, Sheriff," he said.

"I'm leaving too," Amber said. She waved her sack as she went out the door. "Thanks for my donuts."

She bumped into Silas, our retired dentist, on her way out. "Sorry, Silas."

"Amber's in a hurry. What's she got going on?" He sat at the counter and stared at the board.

"Just court. Running late, most likely," I said. "How do you like your coffee?"

"Milk and two sugars. And a maple donut. I've got a sweet tooth." His smile didn't reach his eyes.

Never noticed that before about Silas.

"Terrible tragedy about Melinda. Never thought she'd be the type, but you just never know." He sipped his coffee, and I set his plate in front of him.

The book club streamed in. Tiffany made coffee for the carafes and carried a platter of donut holes and scones into the meeting room. As I rinsed the mixing bowl and beaters, I realized Silas had said something.

I dried my hands. "Sorry, what's that?"

"Just wondered if the sheriff's figured out why Melinda murdered Edward."

"I didn't know Melinda murdered Edward. That's interesting." I cleaned the glass on the display case.

"Yep. But I guess you didn't know they were partners. She must have gotten greedy."

I put my cleaning materials away.

"Clarissa said she knew all along that Melinda was into something crooked," he continued.

Ah ha. Now I understand. "More coffee?"

"No. I've had plenty." He checked the board and left money on the counter. I scooped up the bills and opened the cash register. I counted the money twice. *Old stinker shorted us.*

Tiffany brought an empty platter out of the meeting room. "Doc Howe already gone? He doesn't come by very often."

"Tiffany, Amber suggested a maple scone. I thought we could do that next Thursday. Maybe a cinnamon scone with a maple drizzle. What do you think?"

"Sounds good to me. I'll check Mr. Otto's secret recipes. Might be something there."

Shirley parked in front of the shop, and I poured her coffee. Tiffany sacked up her donuts and a scone.

"I love Thursdays," Shirley said. "Pink sprinkles and a maple donut. What's the scone?" She squinted at the specials board. "Cranberry-orange. My favorite. I may need to get my eyes checked. I'm having a hard time reading sometimes. The print is getting smaller. I guess they can get more words in with the smaller font. Do you need glasses, Karen? I could make an appointment for you too. You'd look good in glasses. Don't most teachers wear glasses? I know you're a retired teacher, but that counts, right? I'm going to school today. Woody is on the A honor roll. Isn't that wonderful? Although, I'm really not surprised. He's the smartest boy I know. I have to run."

* * *

That evening, Colonel, Mia, and I sat on the back porch after supper until the bugs chased us inside. The shadows hovered in the kitchen until Mia chased them to the hallway.

A loud knock at the front door startled me.

"Ms. Karen?" The sheriff called out. "Can I come in?" he asked. "I need to talk to you before anyone else does."

I sat on the edge of the sofa. He sat in the chair facing me.

"Ms. Karen, Melinda Wallace's sister Debra was found beaten and unconscious on the side of the road a mile from the Dixons' house when a neighbor came home from work this evening. Her car was on the side of the road, but he happened to catch sight of her in his headlights. She's in the hospital, but we don't know the full extent of her injuries yet."

I swallowed hard and bit my lip. "That's horrible."

The sheriff strode to the window and closed the curtains. "You know, it's a good idea to keep your windows covered at night, especially since you live here alone."

My voice cracked. "I've got Colonel, but thanks. I'll be careful."

The sheriff paced. "What did you and Debra talk about the other night at Ida's? She say anything that could help us find her assailant?"

"When I arrived at the diner, she was talking to Ronald Dixon. My impression was he approached her because she's Melinda's sister, which I thought was bizarre. Debra said he insisted Melinda murdered Edward. I'm not sure what his connection to Edward was."

When the sheriff headed to the door, I said, "Wait. What about Pepper?"

He stopped with his hand on the knob. "What do you mean?"

"Debra was taking care of her. Pepper's at Melinda's house. Somebody needs to take care of her." My heart pounded in my chest.

"I can send a deputy for her in the morning to take her to the shelter."

"No! She can't go to the shelter. She can come here. Can we go get her?"

"You can't take in every stray—"

"Pepper's not a stray. She needs her dog bed, food, and blanket. Can we go now?"

The sheriff frowned. "You're not going to give up on this, are you? I'll have a deputy meet us there with the house key."

I grabbed my purse and hurried to the door.

"What about Mia?" he asked as he opened the door.

"Mia hates all dogs except Colonel. She stays scarce or stalks Pepper."

Sheriff snorted. "I can see that."

When the deputy unlocked the front door, Pepper met me as I walked in. "Hello, Pepper." I held my hand down for a sniff, and Pepper licked my fingers. After I took her out back for a quick break, I put food in her dish while I pulled her things together.

"Ready to go?" I picked her up, and the deputy carried her things to my car.

After I parked at my house, I attached Pepper's leash to her collar. When we walked inside, I unsnapped her leash and carried her things to the kitchen. Colonel watched her from the sofa while she sniffed the living room floor and furniture. I set her bag of food inside the container with Colonel's.

Colonel eased off the sofa to greet Pepper. Mia strutted out of the pantry and jumped on the back of the sofa. She licked her paws without looking at Pepper. Pepper wagged her tail and whined at Mia.

I slipped out to my car for Pepper's dog bed and blanket. When I stepped inside, Colonel was stretched out on the sofa, and Pepper was curled at his feet. Mia scooted into the pantry.

"I guess the show's over. Glad it had a happy ending." I chuckled.

I placed Pepper's bed and blanket in a corner of the kitchen. She trotted over, stirred and fluffed her blanket, and flopped onto her bed.

"I'm going to the hospital to see Debra," I said. Colonel trotted to the door and nudged his leash.

"Will you be okay here with Mia, Pepper?" Pepper trotted to her bed and faced the pantry. *Smart girl.*

* * *

I approached the information desk. "Debra Miller?"

The desk clerk scrolled through her computer screen. "Are you family?"

I nodded. *I'm the elderly aunt at least until Melinda gets out of jail.*

"Here she is. But she can't have any visitors quite yet." She grabbed an index card and wrote. "Here's the number to call to check on her, and they will tell you when she can have visitors. That will save you from coming here and not being able to see her. You need a ride home? Your service dog is sweet. I hope it's okay. I gave him a treat. I know there are rules, but he was very polite."

I smiled. "I know he appreciated it. Thank you for everything." *Nice people are everywhere.* When I turned, I bumped into the sheriff who stood close behind me.

"Family, huh?" The sheriff asked as he walked me to my car.

"Surrogate family. Thanks for not busting me."

"And have you work some magic on me like you did on that kind-hearted clerk? No, ma'am. I like my rough edges."

After Colonel and I arrived at home, the dogs and I took a short walk, as much for me as for them. When we returned, the three of us sat on the sofa together.

Pepper climbed into my lap, and I stroked her back.

"I'm tired too. Let's all go to bed." I bolted the doors and turned out the lights.

I snuggled under my covers, and my muscles relaxed. I listened to Colonel's clicks on the hallway floor as he traveled to the kitchen and then returned to my bedroom. *Everybody's settled in. Good.*

* * *

The next morning, I woke to rhythmic yipping. Colonel loped out of my bedroom, and I threw off my covers and followed him to the kitchen. Mia was curled on top of the refrigerator. Her tail flicked in time to Pepper's yips. "Pepper, are you barking at Mia's tail?"

Mia slowed her tail, and Pepper's yips matched Mia's new rhythm.

"I'm glad y'all are friends." I opened the back door, and Pepper dashed out. Colonel ambled outside.

When I was ready to leave for the shop, Mia ran to her carrier near the door. Pepper approached her carrier, and Mia hissed. Pepper retreated and hid behind Colonel.

"Okay, then. We'll all go." I closed Mia's carrier and picked up Pepper's leash.

* * *

"We've got Pepper, Tiffany," I said when we went inside the shop. "She'll be staying with us until Melinda comes home."

"Hello, Pepper." Tiffany stooped down and rubbed Pepper's ear. Pepper leaned her head against Tiffany's hand. "You're a pretty girl."

"What's on the calendar? What are our specials today?"

"Calendar's clear. We haven't done eyeballs in quite a while. And Roger has been asking for toasted termites. Don't you think our regular customers are ready for termites?"

"Love it. What's our other type of donut and our scone?"

"Strawberry glaze. Then I'll have strawberry to make the eyeballs that stayed up too late, according to the sheriff. And for scones? What?"

"Scones with imaginary sprinkles. We haven't had imaginary sprinkles in a while either."

Tiffany lifted her hands and whooped. Pepper danced and barked. Colonel howled, and Mia hid.

I covered my ears. "Now I understand Andrew. Let's get busy on our ambitious plan."

When the bell jingled, the sheriff sauntered in. Pepper yipped, trotted to the display case, and held up one paw.

The sheriff chuckled. "I've never seen a donut hunting dog. Hello, Pepper." The sheriff crossed his arms and squinted at the board. "Hot dang. It's going to be a great day. I'm calling Roger and Josh at the gas station. I hope you made extra donuts and scones today."

"We did," Tiffany said. "We know our regulars."

I plated his termites, eyeballs, and a scone with imaginary sprinkles, poured our coffee, and sat at the counter with him. Mia prowled the shop and darted behind the counter. Tiffany put a small bowl with extra imaginary sprinkles next to the sheriff's plate.

Roger came in and hurried to Tiffany. "Termites? You did termites for me? Thank you, sweetheart." He hugged her. She blushed and pointed to the sheriff.

His big smile turned to a sheepish grin. "I love termites. I was on a break."

Tiffany laughed and poured his coffee.

"Melinda's being released today. I thought you'd want to know." Sheriff sipped his coffee and ate his termites and eyeballs.

"Thanks." I cleared our dishes. The bell jingled, and Pepper barked.

Shirley stood at the door and frowned. "Pepper's here again? More animals, Karen? Are you sure you aren't turning the donut shop into a pet retreat?"

Pepper ran a tight circle around Shirley and dashed to the display case. Pepper sat and grinned at Shirley.

"Did that little dog just tell me to pick a donut?" Shirley asked.

Tiffany snickered and hurried to the storeroom.

"Shoo, doggie. Shoo. I need my coffee." Shirley waved her hands. Pepper trotted to her and dropped into a perfect doggie-sit.

Shirley stared at Pepper. "What do I do now? She's not dangerous, is she?"

I handed Shirley her coffee. "Let her smell your hand. She wants to remember you."

Shirley closed her eyes and stooped with her hand out. Pepper licked Shirley's fingertips, and Shirley jumped back. "She tried to bite me."

"No, she likes you. She gave you a kiss."

"Can I have my donut and scone now?"

"Here you go," I said. "You did a great job of making friends with Pepper, you know. She doesn't like just anybody."

"I did? Of course, I did. Thank you." Shirley left with her head high.

"Well done, Pepper," Tiffany said. Pepper pranced to her position near the counter where she could watch the door.

Colonel wagged. "You taught her your trick of making friends? Well done, Colonel," I said.

* * *

Tiffany and I finished cleaning, and Tiffany put away the last baking pan. I picked up Pepper's leash, and Mia dashed to her carrier. Before I pulled away from the curb, I called the hospital to check on Debra.

The woman who answered my call spoke in rapid, clipped words. "Debra Miller? Her employer had her air-lifted to the trauma hospital in Macon early this morning."

* * *

When we got home, I hurried to the back door, and Colonel and Pepper ran outside. The afternoon warmth lifted my sagging spirits. I smiled while Colonel and Pepper raced around the fence. I stared at the gate. *Somebody opened my gate.* I hurried to close it, but I was too slow. Pepper bolted down the alley and vanished when she turned the corner.

"Here, Pepper. Pepper," I called. I slumped against the gate and rubbed my forehead. *How do I find her?*

Colonel barked twice and ambled to the porch, and Pepper dashed back at full speed. I slammed the gate closed, and Pepper pranced to the porch and flopped next to Colonel.

"I couldn't have handled a missing dog. Not today. Thank you, Colonel."

I glanced at the back of the house and frowned at the shadows as they drifted out of the bathroom window. *The bathroom window's open.*

I hurried inside to the bathroom accompanied by the two dogs. *Nothing looks out of place.* I closed and locked the bathroom window. I searched my bedroom, closet, and under my bed. *Windows are locked.*

After I checked the living room and the pantry, I opened the cupboard for a glass.

"I don't know what I would have done if I'd found—" I froze and stared at the bottle of red wine on my countertop. Half of it was gone, and the cork stuck out of the top.

I called the dispatch office. "Hi, Tess. Do you think a deputy could come by my house this afternoon? I think someone broke in. I've checked the entire house, and nothing's missing. But it's strange. There's a bottle of wine on my counter."

I sat at the dining table while Tess dispatched a deputy and scolded me for searching the house.

"No, I didn't smell or drink the wine. Should I have?" Tess's voice rose in pitch. *I need to remember young people have no sense of humor.*

The screech of tires in front of my house allowed me to interrupt.

"I think a deputy's here. Talk to you later."

The sheriff burst in the front door. "Don't leave your front door unlocked," he growled. He strode to the bathroom, and Mia dashed in front of him. I settled in at the dining table, and Colonel flopped next to me. Pepper ran after Mia and then yelped. Pepper returned with a scratch on her nose and curled on top of my feet.

"I closed and locked the window. I wasn't thinking," I called out.

After he inspected the bathroom and bedroom, he approached the wine bottle. "I suppose you drank only half the wine."

My eyes widened. "What?"

The sheriff chortled. "Donut you know it's hard to get the best of you?"

I snorted. "That's awful. And yes, you got me, but I'll deny it."

He joined me at the dining table. "What happened?"

"It all started with Pepper taking off down the alley. When I returned, the bathroom window was open, and then I found the wine. I poured you some iced tea." I pointed at the glass in front of him on the table.

"What do you think, Donut Lady? What's your theory?"

"Gossip has it that Melinda's husband was poisoned by rat poison. If that wine smells faintly of peanut butter, I think either someone's trying to frame me, or I called you here so I could confess."

"So how do you know rat poison smells like peanut butter? And what was your motive?"

"Teachers know things, but I can't figure out how I fit into Wallace's murder. Crime of passion?"

The sheriff spewed his tea.

* * *

After the sheriff left, my phone rang. *Melinda.* "I'm home. You have Pepper, right?"

"Yes, Pepper's with me. We'll be there in a few minutes."

After I hung up, I set Pepper's dish, food, and pad inside a laundry basket. When I picked up her leash, Pepper danced to the front door, and Colonel lumbered along.

"Not surprised, boy. Let's go."

When I turned onto Melinda's street, Pepper yipped and whined. Melinda stood at the curb. When I parked, Melinda opened the car door, and Pepper leaped out into her arms.

Melinda's eyes welled up as she snuggled Pepper. "Thank you. I was relieved when I heard Pepper was with you. Can you come in?"

Melinda led the way to her kitchen, and I sat at the table. When she opened her back door, Pepper dashed outside. Colonel trotted out and flopped down in a shady spot.

"Shall I make coffee? Would you rather have tea?"

"Water's fine for me."

Melinda handed me a glass of water. I took a long drink and set my glass on the table. "When I called about Debra, the hospital told me she'd been transferred to a trauma hospital. I didn't realize her injuries were that serious."

"I don't have the details, but I think she was moved for security reasons. I don't know where."

Melinda sipped her water and sighed. "I need some advice. The M.E. told me the Conway sheriff told Ms. Clinton about Wally's death. I need to talk to her about his ashes, but I don't think I could face her. Should I call her? That doesn't seem right."

"It does seem impersonal."

"Would you talk to her for me? Never mind. I just realized what a huge favor I'm asking."

Pepper scratched at the door, and Melinda rose to let her in. Melinda gave Pepper and Colonel a dog treat. "I've got something to show you. I found something in a box on the top shelf of Wally's closet. See what you think."

When she returned from the bedroom, she placed a shoebox on the table. She reached inside and removed bundles of paper wrapped with rubber bands. The slips were about six inches long and two and a half inches wide. "What do you think?" she asked.

The back of my neck tingled. "I'm not sure. Maybe you if you show this to the sheriff, he might know." I picked up one of the packets and took it apart to examine the paper. I set the small stack back in the box. *Feels like the paper used for money except it's blank.*

"That's a good idea. I couldn't make any sense of it."

"Do you have a computer?"

"No, I never bothered getting one because I use the computer and printer at my soup kitchen office. I'm there more than I'm at home."

"Wonder if the attacker was looking for—I don't know what— something in your office and thought you knew where it was?"

Melinda frowned and dropped the box in the basket next to the table. "I'll call the sheriff about the box in the morning and tell him Wally used the office computer. But if there was something on the computer, why did the attacker search the office? Why not just take the computer? We're pretty good with the questions, aren't we?"

"Answers seem to be a little skimpy. Will you be okay? You and Pepper are welcome to come to my house tonight. Have you eaten? Why don't you have dinner with me and stay the night? Colonel and I work tomorrow and will sneak out early. You can sleep in as long as you like."

"Maybe we'll have dinner. Sounds nice. I'll bring a few things in case I change my mind. There's a lot of memories in this house."

"Pack a small suitcase. You can return home when you're up to it."

She laughed. "Might as well. If I pack a few things and my makeup, I'll need a suitcase anyway." Melinda tossed her jacket on top of Pepper's basket, and I carried it to my car. After Melinda packed, she hauled her oversized luggage to her car, and I toted her makeup case.

Melinda and Pepper followed Colonel and me to my house.

At my insistence, Melinda put her feet up in the living room while I made salads. I turned to ask Melinda if she liked tomato, but she had closed her eyes and leaned back in the ugly chair. I didn't disturb her soft, rhythmic snore.

Colonel, Pepper, and I went to the backyard. I sat on the porch while Pepper ran, and Colonel relaxed.

I glanced to my right to the end of the alley and snickered at the white pickup truck that cruised down the street. I monitored the left until I saw the pickup go by. I ambled to the road on the right and waited. The truck stopped in the street halfway to the alley. The vehicle crept the rest of the way, and the passenger's window slid down.

"Hi, Jack," I said in my chirpiest tone.

"I hate getting busted. Every single time." Jack shook his head.

"Why don't you park and sit with me on the porch? Melinda's napping inside. I brought the dogs out for some exercise."

Jack parked near my back gate. He opened the truck door, and Roxie jumped out. I opened the gate for her, and she dashed around the yard with Pepper.

"Want to join us for supper after Melinda wakes up? I made a big salad. I'm sure there's enough for three."

"Could I redeem myself if I run to the store and grab some steaks? Steaks and salad. What do you think?"

"You don't need to do that," I said.

"Yes, I do. Then maybe I can pretend I'm contributing." He raised his eyebrows and gazed at me.

"Sounds nice. Roxie can stay and play if you like."

"She'd love it." He jumped up. "Be right back."

"You can park in the driveway when you return," I called after him.

He hopped into the truck. The sudden acceleration kicked up dust, and he was gone. Colonel raised his head. Roxie and Pepper trotted to the porch for water. Pepper ran more laps around the yard, and Roxie put her head on my lap.

The back door opened. "I wondered where y'all had gone. Sorry, I fell asleep on you."

"Have a seat. You needed the rest. I made us salads, but Jack's gone to the store to get steaks. He hovers sometimes."

"Jack's a nice guy. Rare."

I listened to the tree frogs and crickets. "Sounds like we might get a little rain tonight. It will be welcome."

Melinda smacked a mosquito.

"Let's go inside. Jack will be back soon," I said.

I called the dogs, and we all went into the house. Jack knocked at the front door and tried the knob.

"Ha! It's locked." I let him in.

"About time you caught on. Hello, Melinda. Nice to see you," Jack said.

I took the grocery sack and pulled out my largest cast iron skillet.

"What are you doing?" Jack asked. "Aren't you going to grill the steaks?" His eyes were wide, and his face was red.

"You may not have noticed I don't have a grill. Trust me. You'll enjoy your steak."

"Will not." Jack flopped onto the sofa and crossed his arms.

"What do you want me to do?" Melinda asked.

"You could serve up salad into three bowls and set the table. Plates here; silverware there." I pointed. I heated up the skillet and rubbed both sides of the steaks with olive oil, salt, and pepper.

I seared the steaks on both sides and threw them under the broiler. "You want to open the wine, Jack? Or is it for later?"

Melinda handed Jack the wine and corkscrew and set out three wine glasses. Jack poured the wine.

I pulled the steaks out of the oven and plated them to rest.

After we all sat at the table, Jack squinted at the steak on his plate.

"You going to eat it or glare at it all night?" I asked.

He cut a bite, stabbed it with his fork, and stared at it. He wrinkled his nose, put it in his mouth, and chewed. "Not bad."

"Told you," I mumbled.

"My steak's good," Melinda said.

"Mine too," Jack said.

"Don't sound so—" I was interrupted by a siren. Colonel and Roxie howled, and Pepper yipped. Mia yowled from the pantry.

More sirens joined the first. The low blast of airhorns punctuated the wail of a Federal Q siren that pierced the night.

"Sounds like a big fire," Jack said.

"Doesn't sound too far away either," Melinda said. "Can we step out on the front porch? Maybe we can see where they're going."

Smoke filled the air. "Smells like a house fire," Jack said.

"See that glow in the sky?" Melinda asked. "In the area of my neighborhood? Look at that smoke."

A rising white cloud sliced through the billowing black smoke. I gaped at the dancing embers and the flames licking the sky.

"They hit it with water," Jack said. "Big fire."

"Awesome, in a terrible way," Melinda said.

The sheriff pulled up and parked in front of my house. "Hoped you'd be here, Melinda. Your car wasn't at your house. Okay if we go inside, Karen?"

The four of us trooped inside. Melinda sat on the sofa, and I sat on the ugly chair. Jack stood at my elbow, and the sheriff stooped near Melinda.

"Melinda, your house caught fire. The neighbors called it in after they smelled smoke. By the time the fire department got there, the house was fully involved with flames coming out of the roof. The fire marshal is on the scene and will talk to you later. I can't tell you how relieved we were that your car was gone. I came here first."

Melinda stared at the sheriff. Jack strode to the kitchen and poured a glass of water. He picked up a box of tissues and sat next to Melinda. She took a long drink and handed the glass back to Jack.

"This is almost too much," she sobbed and pulled a tissue. She leaned against Jack, and he put his arm around her shoulder.

My cheeks were on fire. I frowned and turned my head away. I glanced at the sheriff, and he raised his eyebrows.

What's wrong with me? What do I care if Jack comforts Melinda?

The shadows gathered in the hallway and billowed to the ceiling. I shook my head and bit my lip to keep from smiling. *Moral support for a jealous old woman?*

"I want to go to the house," Melinda said.

"I'd advise against it. You'd have to park two blocks away, and you don't want to get in the way. The fire marshal will come by in the morning. Talk to him before you go."

"I want to go," she said.

"We'll go with you," Jack said. "Right, Karen?"

"Maybe I should stay here and take care of the animals."

"That might be best," Melinda said.

The sheriff shook his head, and Jack frowned and stared at the floor.

"Or I could go along," I said.

The sheriff nodded, Jack beamed, and the shadows danced. Melinda frowned. I coughed to keep from laughing. *No doubt on where everyone stands.*

"If you have to go, stay out of the way." The sheriff checked the back door and then left.

"We can go in my truck. We'll park on a side street and walk over," Jack rose and offered me his hand. I opened my mouth to snap at him but pursed my lips. *He's being nice.*

I took his hand and stood. He didn't release my hand. *This is getting weird.*

I removed my hand and reached for my sweater. "No need to drive only a few blocks. We can walk. I'll take this. Do you need anything for your arms, Melinda?"

"I've got a sweater in my suitcase. You know, I wouldn't have anything to wear if you hadn't told me to pack for a few days."

"Is that right, Karen?" Jack asked.

"I had a feeling."

* * *

"The sheriff was right," Melinda shouted over the roar of the diesel engines and the blasting radio traffic from the loudspeakers on the fire department equipment. "Can't really see anything from back here except fire trucks and hoses."

Jack leaned close to me. "She had to see it for herself."

I nodded. When the neighbors mobbed Melinda and bombarded her with questions, I took her arm. "We need to leave."

Melinda and I walked away, arm in arm, with Jack on the other side of Melinda. When we turned the corner, Jack shifted and walked next to me. We walked in silence to my house. When we were inside, Melinda headed to my guest bedroom, and Jack and I took Colonel, Pepper, and Roxie out back.

"You were right about Melinda's house. She did need to see it for herself."

Jack grinned. "Would you mind writing that down for me? *One time, Jack was right* is good enough. Oh, and sign it."

I laughed and swatted his arm. "No. I won't. First thing you'd do is show it to Gee."

"You're right. The temptation would be too great not to. I guess Roxie and I need to go so you can get your rest. Thanks for chasing me down and inviting me to dinner. My steak was delicious, but we need to pick out a grill for you sometime. When's your birthday?" He raised his eyebrows.

"You'd better be kidding. I'm famous for my pan-fried steak."

I called Colonel, and all three dogs scrambled to the door. When we were inside, the dogs sat for their treats.

I followed Jack to the front door but kept my distance.

"Good night, Karen." He lingered at the door.

"Good night, Jack. Thanks for everything."

He sighed and closed the door behind him. I locked the door and threw the deadbolt, and he and Roxie left.

The shadows danced in the hallway, and I headed to bed.

CHAPTER SEVEN

When my phone rang on my bedside table at three thirty in the morning, I was startled awake. My heart pounded as I snatched up my phone. *Gee.*

The words tumbled out. "What's wrong?" I propped myself up on my elbow. I was short of breath.

"Tiffany's running a high fever. She can't come to work. Isaiah will take her to the doctor later this morning. We didn't want to leave you in the lurch. Can I meet you at the shop and be your assistant?"

I slumped back on the bed in relief. "That would be great, Gee, but what about the thrift shop? How about if you help me get the donuts ready for the day, and then maybe the mayor can help with customers so you can open your shop on time?"

"I've always liked how you think, Donut Lady," Gee said. "See you in a bit."

I fed the dogs and Mia, checked the back gate, and let Colonel and Pepper out. After I dressed, Mia dashed to her carrier, and I loaded my passengers into my car. Gee was parked in front of the shop when we arrived. While I unlocked, she moved her car to the parking area behind the shop.

"What's our plan for the day, Donut Lady?"

"Let's go with classic glazed and maple donuts and cranberry orange scones. I'll start on donuts, and you can make the scones. The recipe is in Mr. Otto's secret recipe book."

I brought out the recipe book and an apron.

"I've got an apron." Gee waved her apron, threw her hands in the air, and danced. Pepper yipped and pranced with her. Gee squinted at the recipe. "Good. This is exactly how I make scones; except I don't make quite so many at a time. On it."

After I mixed my first batch of dough, I checked the calendar. "We've got the ham radio club at nine. If I text Shirley, maybe Woody can come in a little earlier and help. He's here on Saturdays to take inventory."

Shirley returned my text. "Be there at 7."

I showed it to Gee, and she laughed. "I think Woody sent the text for her. No way is that Shirley."

"I'll text the mayor too."

A half hour later, the mayor answered. "c u @ 8."

"What do you think, Gee? Read this."

Gee peered over my shoulder at my phone. "The mayor. He's always been tech-savvy."

I dropped a donut hole into the fryer to check the temperature and then fried my first batch of donuts. "How are Sandy and Mandy doing?" I asked.

Gee put a batch of scones in the oven. "Mandy is a sweetheart. She loves everybody. Sandy is a pistol. When a customer comes in that he doesn't like, Sandy hisses and spits and stalks the customer. The thing is, I agree with his judgment. He dashes off when I tell him to go find Isaiah, even if Isaiah isn't around. The customer leaves in a snit, and Sandy returns for his treat. Just a little thing Sandy and I do." She chuckled.

"I'd tell you that's awful, Gee, but I think it's hilarious."

While I mixed my next batch of dough, Gee sang a song with a haunting melody, and I hummed along. My concentration was broken when I received another text.

Tiffany: "Tammy bringing friends at ten to see Big Celebrity. Expect gushing."

Me: "Get well."

Tiffany: "Tammy's BFF will video or live stream."

I snickered and stuck my phone in my back pocket. *Don't want that just laying around.*

The bell jingled, and Pepper greeted Woody. "Ms. Shirley dropped me off to help out. Do I get to drizzle?"

"Absolutely. Would you drizzle classics and dip the maple for me? Nobody finishes the donuts better than you."

"Aw, thanks, Miss Lady. That's my favorite thing to do, next to inventory. And reading. And writing. Soccer. No, playing with Chase is my favorite." He beamed and washed his hands.

The sheriff strode in, and Pepper dashed to him. The sheriff scratched Pepper's ears and then perched on his usual stool at the counter. "Ms. Karen—" He stared at Gee and Woody. "Did you fire Tiffany? You could have warned me. Roger's going to be unbearable. What are you doing here, Gee? Who's going to run the thrift store? Hey there, Woody. So, it takes two highly trained helpers to replace Tiffany?"

"Tiffany's running a fever, sheriff. She'll be well soon." I set his coffee and donuts in front of him.

"Can I call Roger and tell him Tiffany's been fired?" Sheriff asked.

Gee and I broke into laughter. When I got my breath, I said, "No."

"Wait, Donut Lady," Gee said, "let's think about this before we make any rash decisions."

"You're right, Gee. Thought about it. No."

As I spoke, the bell jingled, and Roger hurried in.

"What's Ms. Gee right about? Tiffany asked me to pick up donuts and a scone for her. She said donuts are magic. Better than medicine."

I sacked up donuts and scones. "Here's the magic. Don't get too close to her."

"Tiffany told me I have to leave the sack on the porch and then step back to the curb."

"Smart girl," the sheriff said.

After the sheriff left and the mayor arrived, His Honor filled the carafes for the meeting room. "Sure am glad you called me into work this morning, Donut Lady. I've got a big surprise for the ham club. Even the curmudgeons will be happy."

"You talking about ole Charlie?" Gee asked. "No way. I've got to see that."

"I'll let you know when I'm making the announcement, and you can step in." The mayor waggled his eyebrows.

"That would totally make my day." Gee put the final batch of scones in the oven.

I followed the mayor into the meeting room. "Suppose you could do that at the first part of the meeting?" I asked. "Gee's going to open her shop after the meeting starts."

"Sure can." He stared at me. "But there's something else, isn't there?"

"Might be." I lowered my head.

"And you'll come get me for it, right?"

I met his gaze. "Yes, sir."

"I love this job." The mayor rubbed his hands together.

The ham radio club members filed in. The mayor spoke to the leader outside the meeting room and signaled to Gee. After Gee joined them, the leader closed the door. Shouts and applause came from the room.

Gee stepped out and shook her head. "Charlie grinned. I thought his face was going to break when the mayor announced the town had been awarded a grant for a new repeater. Charlie led the applause. Best day ever."

She chuckled and grabbed a hot pad. She bent over the oven and inhaled. "The mingled aroma of the cranberry and orange reminds me of when my grandma baked cranberry-orange muffins in her old cookstove oven. It was my job to stoke the fire and keep it hot but not too hot. Grandma said nobody understood her cookstove expect me. I think I was only seven or eight. Grandma said I was important." She took the scones out of the oven and swiped at a tear with her apron. "Don't you tell anybody I got all sentimental over the scones, ya hear?"

I saw Tammy at the front window and tapped on the meeting room door. The mayor stepped out, and Tammy and five young women tumbled into the shop.

Tammy pointed and spoke in a hushed, almost reverent voice. "There she is. Donut Lady." She clasped her hands to her chest, and the young women squealed and mobbed me. Pepper ran circles around the women and yipped. Tammy picked up Pepper, and Pepper kissed her.

One young woman hung back with her cell phone in front of her. "Let's get a group picture. Okay with you, Ms. Donut Lady, ma'am?"

"Why, certainly." I used my best regal voice. "Mr. Mayor, would you mind being the photographer?"

The mayor grinned. "Y'all might want to stand closer to the display case." After he took the photo with his phone, Tammy asked, "My phone, now, Mr. Mayor? And I want to stand next to Ms. Donut Lady. Let's shift around."

"Okay, but it's my turn to hold the puppy," the young woman on my right said.

After the commotion of the dramatic shift settled down, the mayor took a second picture.

"My phone now," one of the women cried.

"I'll post my picture. Let's do one more shift," Tammy said. "No crushing Ms. Donut Lady, though."

The second move was rowdier. Despite all the shoving, I didn't get trampled.

"How we doing?" the young woman next to me whispered.

I glanced at Gee's red face and narrowed eyes. "Better than any of us could have hoped."

"Just a second," the mayor said. "Let's try a little different placement. Those of you in the back, why don't you kneel in front?"

After the next shuffle was finished, he snapped another picture.

"I brought my favorite T-shirt," one of the girls said. "Would you autograph it for me?"

The young woman flopped a folded pink T-shirt on the counter and handed me a box of fabric markers. I chuckled, and she placed her hands on her hips. "*I* came prepared."

When one girl took off a sock, the rest copied her. I signed the T-shirt and socks. The mayor held up his hand, and Woody smacked a high-five.

The mayor pointed at the counter where Woody had set six sacks. "Thank you all for coming," he said. "In honor of your visit, our Donut Lady would like for you to accept these donuts and scones as a gift from her."

I cringed at the screams and squeals but refrained from covering my ears. The ham radio operators, who had left their meeting at the first squeal, applauded. *I understand Andrew even more than ever.*

As the girls filed out, each one hugged and thanked me. When Tammy embraced me, she giggled. "Tiffany watched the live stream. We'll post the video."

The mayor sat at the counter, and I poured us coffee.

"Wasn't that unbelievable, Gee?" I asked.

Gee nodded. "Yes. Unbelievable. It was a setup, wasn't it?"

My phone buzzed. A text from Tiffany: "Awesome."

The mayor said, "Best setup I've seen in ages. A classic for all times."

I showed Gee my phone, and she rolled her eyes. "Should have known Tiffany was in on this. I wish I could say I saw it coming, but you got me good." Gee shook her head. "Tammy did a wonderful job, didn't she? I'm right proud of that young woman."

"She sure did," the mayor said. "I almost took off my sock for an autograph too."

Woody grinned and waved his shoe. "I was ready." He and the mayor fist-bumped.

"I have to run open my store. I can't wait to tell Mandy and Sandy. Suppose I should ground Tiffany and Tammy? And Isaiah, for no reason at all?" Gee laughed as she left.

Shirley flounced into the shop. "Did y'all know you were on TV? I watched at the gas station. Josh connected his phone to the TV, and a big group of us crowded inside. Why did Gee look so cranky? Was it the lighting? I didn't know you were famous, Karen. Did you forget to tell me? We thought it was creative for you to sign all those socks. Tammy's a pretty girl, isn't she? Woody, you are handsome on TV. You too, Mr. Mayor. Karen, your hair needs to be highlighted again; it was washed out on the screen. I made you an appointment for next Tuesday afternoon. Did you know Melinda's house burned down last night? She wasn't home when it started, thank goodness. Did you hear about any more crank calls? Clarissa told me Melinda refused to divorce her Eddie. That's what she called him. *Her Eddie.* Did I tell you I heard her say to somebody, can't remember who, in the grocery store that Melinda poisoned her Eddie? Do you suppose Clarissa made those calls? No, that doesn't make sense. She got one too, didn't she? That's what I heard. I don't know what to think."

"Here's your coffee and sack with your donut and scone, Shirley."

"Thanks, gotta run. Woody and I will be back later so he can do his inventory."

After Shirley and Woody left, the mayor brought the coffee pot to the counter and refilled our cups. "Shirley can go on, can't she? Everybody thinks Edward was dealing drugs, but I think he was doing something with money. Laundering, maybe. I don't have any evidence, but a few months ago, he showed up at the bank with twenties, asked for fives and ones, and said something about poker night. I happened to be at the next window. Sounded suspicious to me, but Alfred and I weren't on speaking terms then, so I let it slide. Okay if I plan on being here Monday? I saw the county tree association on the calendar. I'd like to attend their meeting." The mayor rose and chuckled. "I just did my Shirley impression, didn't I? I'll get the pink room cleaned up."

My phone rang. *Melinda.* "I just woke up. I must have needed the sleep, but I feel like a slug for sleeping so late. I'll be there in a few minutes to pick up Pepper."

I scrubbed the equipment and organized the utensils in the dishwasher. I was cleaning the coffee maker when Melinda came in. Pepper yipped and raced to her.

"How about coffee and a donut? Or a scone?" I asked.

I caught a glimpse of a reflection of the two of us in the shop window. Melinda's makeup and hair were impeccable. I cringed at the contrast of my gray hair, out-of-date haircut, minimal makeup, and general oldness. The shadows moped around the window. *And short. If you're going to feel sorry for yourself, don't leave that out, Old Woman.* I snorted. The shadows danced.

"Coffee and a scone sound good. Thanks." Melinda sat at the counter, and Pepper flopped at her feet. The mayor rolled out the utility cart and poured Melinda's coffee while I served her a scone.

"I heard about your house. You doing okay?" the mayor asked.

"I'll be fine. I'll talk to Shirley today about a place to rent. I have a meeting in a half hour with the fire marshal at my house, but he warned me not to get my expectations up because the fire, smoke, and water damage is extensive."

"You're welcome to stay with me until you find a place, you know," I said.

"Thank you, Karen. I appreciate it, but I don't want to wear out your hospitality. I've already booked a room at the motel for Pepper and me. I called Jack. If there's anything at the house I can salvage, he'll take it to a storage unit for me."

The mayor polished the utility cart and stared. I glared, and he shrugged his shoulders and buffed the gleaming utility cart handles.

"That's really nice of him," I said.

She tugged at a lock of hair. "I offered to buy Jack dinner tonight in exchange for his truck and time, but he said he already had plans. 'Maybe a raincheck,' I said."

After Melinda and Pepper left, the mayor said, "She's got her eye on Jack, doesn't she?"

"I don't know. Not really my business."

"Karen." He frowned. "Never mind. Not really my business either."

"Sorry, Mayor. I'm feeling peevish. No excuse, except I didn't get a full night's sleep. And I've never seen the utility cart gleam like that." I snickered.

"I was awfully busy while I eavesdropped, wasn't I?"

"I've got a streak of crankiness or something. Not sure why. Not like I have any claims on Jack or anything."

"I'll just polish this here cart, Ms. Donut Lady." He flourished his cleaning cloth.

"You're terrible and my favorite mayor."

The bell jingled, and Shirley and Woody came into the shop.

"Must be inventory time, Ms. Donut Lady," the mayor said. "Woody's already gone straight to the storeroom. You want coffee, Shirley? I pour a mean cup."

"Thank you, Mayor. I wouldn't mind at all. Although, it won't take Woody long to fill out his inventory sheet. I typed it up for him. That was my contribution. He's very organized." Shirley glanced around the shop. "The little dog's gone. Are you going to get another one? I got a call from Melinda. She thinks she'll need to rent a house or apartment. I heard she'll need to rent a bulldozer. There's nothing left of her house. That's really a shame, isn't it? I'm not sure I'll be able to find her a furnished rental that will take pets, but she can find good furniture at Gee's. One of her neighbors said he thought he saw a man running away from Melinda's house right before the fire broke out, and another neighbor said she saw three kids smoking cigarettes behind her house before the fire. You finished already, Woody?"

"Yes, ma'am. Here's the list."

"I'll just take this and run do your shopping, Karen. You don't mind that I opened an account for you at the grocery store, do you? I'll be back as quick as I can. You staying for your donut with your Miss Lady, Woody?"

"Yes, ma'am." Woody sat at the counter, and Shirley left.

I placed three donuts on the counter. "Join us, Mr. Mayor?"

"Don't mind if I do."

The mayor poured coffee, and I poured milk for Woody. The three of us sat at the counter in companionable silence while we munched on our donuts.

"I never ate a donut until Woody and I had donuts together when I first met him. Just never took the time," I said.

"Sometimes it takes a friend to remind us to slow down and enjoy what we've got, doesn't it?" The major raised his eyebrows and smiled.

"Me and Miss Lady always have a donut together every Saturday. So she doesn't forget how yummy they are," Woody said.

My phone dinged a text from Tiffany: "Doc says sinus infection. Got drugs. Be at work Monday."

"Tiffany's cleared for work on Monday."

"Good news." The mayor cleared his dishes. "I'll be here in time to have the meeting room ready."

Not long after the mayor left, Shirley returned from the grocery store. Woody ran to help carry in supplies and put them on the proper shelves. When he finished, I said, "Thanks for all your help, and thanks for our Saturday donut."

After Shirley and Woody left, I leaned against the counter and soaked in the silence. Colonel woke from his nap near the reading area and stretched. The bell announced our next customer, and Carol entered with a toddler on her hip. She was dressed in black yoga pants and a red-and-white striped T-shirt.

"Didn't recognize you at first, Carol. I think I've only seen you in uniform on the ambulance."

"Guess we're even," she said. "I don't think I've ever seen you in your official pink cap and apron before."

"Coffee? Donut or scone? How about a donut hole for your young man?"

She laughed. "This is Dylan. Donut hole for Dylan sounds great. Coffee, black, and a scone for me."

She sat at the reading table and spread out a small tarp for Dylan on the floor next to her chair. She handed him a shoe box, and he squealed, dumped out cars and trucks onto the tarp, and pounded on the box. Mia dashed out of the storeroom and swished her tail in time to the beat of Dylan's drum.

After I served Carol her coffee and the pastries, I refilled my coffee and joined her at the table.

"Dylan and I stopped to fill up the mommy van, and I got an earful from Clarissa. You know her, right? She's one of the volunteers at the soup kitchen that Melinda Wallace manages. She said Ronald Dixon's going to be arrested for Edward Wallace's murder. According to Clarissa, it was all over drugs. I'm not sure about her, though. She seems to be malicious sometimes. She also said Emma's leaving the sheriff, and that can't be so. I've always considered the gas station to be a reliable source of news, but Clarissa's kind of tainted it lately."

"I'm not a Clarissa fan. I'd be hard-pressed to believe anything she says. What's tricky about her is sometimes she includes a snippet of truth."

Dylan giggled. Mia head-butted his tummy, and he giggled again.

"Mia is an amazing cat. Does she babysit?" Carol asked.

"Looks like she wouldn't mind, doesn't it? More coffee?"

"Thanks, but I want to pick up some paint at the hardware store, and Dylan has a short fuse the closer he gets to naptime. We'll scoot. Thanks for being my island of adult sanity." She smiled and gathered up her child and his toys.

After Carol and Dylan left, I flipped the sign to CLOSED and locked the front door. I wiped down the display case and counter. On my way to the storeroom, a tap at the door interrupted my thoughts about Emma and the sheriff.

I unlocked the door. "Hello, Jack. What brings you here?"

"Not much. Okay, there's a baseball game in Valdosta tomorrow afternoon. It's college ball. Whatcha think?" He stepped inside the shop and gazed at me with his brow furrowed.

"College ball? That's the best."

"Yes? And where are we going tonight for our pregame dinner? Your turn to pick, remember?"

I tilted my head. "What are you talking about? Pregame dinner? Besides, I heard you had previous plans for tonight."

"Sure 'nuf," he said. "I had plans to find a baseball game for us to go to. And we gotta have a pregame dinner."

I put my hands on my hips. "Did you stop to think I might already have plans tonight?"

"Baseball." He grinned.

I stared. "Fine. I'll call the prince and cancel my ballgown. So, engineers don't plan ahead?"

He met my gaze. "I've spent all week getting my nerve up. I was afraid you'd say no."

I frowned. "Well, no, then."

He laughed and held up his hand for a high-five. I smacked it. "Pick you up at six?" He asked. "Where are we going?"

"Six o'clock is great. It's a surprise."

After Jack left, I called Gee. "I've got a dinner emergency. I need to know a place for dinner tonight that has delicious food. Conway would be fine, but not any farther away."

"Jack?" she asked. "Never mind. Rhetorical question. I'll ask Isaiah and get back to you."

When I stepped onto my front porch, Gee called.

"I've got four or five choices. Isaiah said you might want to check them out on the internet and pick what sounds good to you. I'll send you a text." She hung up.

"Gee's efficient when she's on a quest, isn't she?"

Mia meowed. The three of us went inside. I researched the five restaurants suggested by Isaiah and stressed over types of food, cost, distance from my house, and perceived dress codes.

Cuban or Thai? Do I have Jack's phone number?

The shadows whirled in the hall.

"I could ask Melinda." I grumbled and stomped to the back door. Colonel trotted out with me, and I slammed the door when we went outside.

Chipping sparrows landed on our grass and pecked at bugs in the long grass. "Might need to mow pretty soon, Colonel."

The cardinals flitted in and out of the underbrush and flowers, and the butterflies landed on one flower after another. A neighbor's rooster crowed and was challenged by another rooster. The blue sky was dotted with high clouds. Colonel stepped to the edge of the porch and lifted his head while he sniffed the air. I breathed in. "Somebody's smoking brisket. But you're way ahead of me, aren't you? I love being in a small town. I need to remember that when I'm irritable; there's no cure like being outside."

Colonel made his rounds of the backyard. The crows clamored from an oak tree. A hawk flew overhead, and its shadow slid across the grass.

"Have I missed something, Colonel?"

After we went inside, my phone rang. *Melinda.*

"I'm hoping you have Pepper's pad, food dish, and food."

"We do. Why don't Colonel and I bring it to you? Where are you staying?"

"You'd do that? Pepper and I just got settled in. I hate to drag her right back out. We're at the new motel near town. You know where it is? If you call me when you get here, I can dash out and get it from you."

I picked through my stash of plastic sacks and found one that held all of Pepper's things. "You going with me, Colonel? Just a short ride."

I rolled down our windows for the trip. "We are what you call fresh-air freaks, Colonel." He doggie-grinned in the wind.

When we reached the motel, I parked in front and called Melinda. When she hurried outside, I handed her the sack.

"Thanks for coming all the way out here, Karen. I better get back to Pepper."

As I turned toward home, I said, "I'm glad we were available to get Pepper her bed and food, Colonel."

Jack cruised past my house at five forty-five. I fed Colonel and Mia. At ten minutes until six, Jack still circled the block.

"Should I alleviate his suffering?" Mia dashed to the pantry, and Colonel raised his head. I sauntered to the front porch. Jack slowed to a crawl. I sat on the step until he drifted into my driveway.

"Didn't want to be too early," he mumbled as he got out of his truck.

"What did you say?" I asked.

He glowered, and I laughed. "Come on in. I'll gather my things and get Colonel and Mia settled."

After the two of us were in the truck, he said, "Conway, right?"

"Yep. So, what do you think? Cuban or Thai?"

"Is this a test? Is there a wrong answer?" He smiled.

"No. I'm giving you an option. Thai or Cuban?" I leaned back and gazed at the passing countryside.

"I like both, but I haven't had Thai in a long time. Which was your first preference? We're coming up to the goat farm. See if they have any new kids when we go by."

"Thai. Unless you said Cuban. Ooo, baby goats." I smiled at the sight of bounding kids.

"Now, that's cheating."

"I thought I'd practice being social, but it felt silly." I returned my gaze to the upcoming road.

"I understand that. Sometimes you have the makings of a great socially-inept engineer." Jack slowed the truck as we entered the Conway city limits.

"Thank you. I think."

When Jack opened the restaurant door, the mixed aromas of jasmine, ginger, and sweetgrass swirled around my head. I soaked in the décor. The deep, dark red walls, shiny black-brown tables, brilliant orange and bright golden wall hangings, crystal chandeliers, and pink and white paper umbrellas hanging from the ceiling transported me to Thailand. Jack laid his hand on my shoulder and whispered. "I feel like we should have brought passports. Good pick."

The hostess led us to a table near the back. The arrangement of the tables and the muted lighting gave an aura of intimacy to the restaurant.

As she handed us our menus, she asked, "Drinks?"

"Hot green tea," I said.

"The same," Jack said.

The waitress brought our teacups and a large pot of green tea. "Ready to order?"

"Pad thai tofu, please," I said.

"Pad thai pork for me," Jack said. "Appetizer?" He raised his eyebrows, and I nodded.

"And spring rolls," he added.

I poured our tea and picked up my cup.

"Thanks for—" Jack stared at the door. "That's interesting. Todd Rockford and a young woman I've never seen before just came in."

"I'm aching to look. Tell me when I won't embarrass myself by gawking."

Jack chuckled. "Okay, now. They're being seated on the other side of the restaurant to your left."

I brushed my hair off my face and glanced to the left. My eyes widened. I turned my attention back to Jack and picked up my tea for a sip.

"You recognized her," he said.

"I saw her a while ago with Edward Wallace. Just a little startling to see her again."

He stared at me. "And there's more."

I narrowed my eyes. "What makes you think that?"

"I know my regulars." He held his cup in front of his mouth, but his eyes crinkled.

Our waitress brought our spring rolls and refilled our cups. She whisked away our empty teapot.

I took a bite. "Mmm. Good."

"Waiting." Jack took a bite of a spring roll.

"My years in prison gave me cop-radar."

"Oh. I never thought about that." He finished off his spring roll and reached for his second one.

I stared at my second spring roll. "I need to save room for Pad Thai. Would you care for it?"

"You sure? It would be a nice addition to your lunch tomorrow."

"I don't think it'd be as good warmed up. And I want to save room for dessert. I have brownies in the freezer at home, if you're interested."

"I'd heard you were a tough negotiator. So, if I eat this third spring roll, I get dessert at your house? I'm sure there's a catch somewhere, but I'll go for it." Jack wiggled his eyebrows, and I giggled.

The waitress brought our pad Thai and a full pot of tea.

"This is excellent. I've never had tofu. How is it?" Jack asked after his first bite.

"Perfect. I love fried tofu. I never cook it myself, so this is a real treat. Not sure I'll finish this generous portion at one sitting, but it'll warm up just fine, so don't worry that I'm going to make you eat tofu."

Jack chuckled. "Now that I'm off the hook, I can claim I'd eat tofu for one of your brownies."

When the waitress brought our check, she handed it to me. After she left, Jack asked, "How did you do that?"

I placed my cash into the leather folder and rose. "It was my turn, so I planned ahead. Gee or Tiffany would tell you I have magical skills, but I have years of experience in slipping notes without being detected."

As we left, I noticed Todd Rockford and his companion were involved in an intense conversation. Jack opened the truck door for me. "Just want you to know you are one complicated woman."

"Why, thank you, sir." I climbed in. "So, what was the purpose of our pregame dinner again?"

"The purpose of a pregame dinner is to make sure. Umm." Jack frowned.

I laughed. "You're busted again."

"We can plan our schedule. That's it." He beamed. "The game starts at four. Takes a little over an hour to get to Valdosta, but we'll want to be there early."

"So, if we leave at two, would that work? Should I check the weather?" I scanned the weather forecast for Valdosta on my phone. "Twenty percent chance of rain in the morning. Zero for the afternoon and evening. A little windy and cooler than today."

"Two sounds good. I've never been to a game in Valdosta, so I'm not sure if they have a concession stand. But we can find a place to eat after the game. I'll pack water for us."

"I'll bring some brownies to stave off starvation." I glanced to the west and frowned. The clouds to the west had darkened. "Looks like rain later tonight. Storms didn't use to bother me."

"Makes sense to me after the trauma you went through. Might ease up over time but you'll probably always be weather-aware. Not all bad."

"Glad you understand." My shoulders relaxed. *Didn't realize how tense I was.*

Jack cleared his throat. "Ava and I were coming home from a Christmas party years ago, and a drunk driver slammed into my truck. T-boned us on the passenger's side. Our physical injuries were not serious, but we were broken. For a long time, I'd break into a sweat at intersections and jump at sudden, loud noises. Ava was so traumatized, so terrified, that she refused to go anywhere for two years." Jack sighed. "Sometimes things are more complicated than they look."

I nodded, and we rode the rest of the way in silence.

"You still interested in a brownie?" I asked when we reached my house.

"Sure am. Guess I got lost in thought."

"So did I. It was nice not to feel obligated to talk. Thank you."

We let Colonel out for a break and ate our brownies on my back porch.

"Thank you, Donut Lady. It was a nice evening." Jack put his arm around my shoulder and walked with me to the front door.

"It was, wasn't it, Handyman?" I stepped away from his arm and met his gaze. Jack smiled and shrugged.

I double-locked the door, and then his truck drove away.

When I collapsed in my bed, the shadows filled my doorway. I rolled over and pulled up my covers.

CHAPTER EIGHT

The sound of a car woke me. Car headlights shined through my bedroom window and lit up the room. The roar of the engine intensified, and the headlights filled the window. Brakes squealed, and a car horn blared. I sat up and screamed. Shadows filled the window. The lights disappeared, and the noise silenced.

Colonel trotted to my bedside and whimpered. I trembled and stroked his back. Mia jumped up and curled next to my feet. I slowed my breathing and lay back down.

I woke at dawn and padded barefoot to the kitchen. I started a pot of coffee and let Colonel out.

I poured a cup and stepped outside with Colonel. "I need to get dressed, boy. It's cold out here. You ready to go inside?"

Colonel sauntered to the fence and sat where he could watch the birds in the neighbor's trees. I went inside, dressed, and fed Mia. I dished up Colonel's food and called him in.

"I need a good reason to stop by the hospital this afternoon. Any ideas?" Mia strolled into the pantry. Colonel finished his breakfast and ambled into the living room and flopped down in front of the ugly sofa.

"Fine. I'll go to breakfast at Ida's Diner." Colonel jumped up and nosed his leash that hung by the door.

I dropped my keys and phone into my purse and picked up Colonel's leash. When I stepped outside, I examined the grass around my bedroom window. "No tire marks. Didn't expect to see any but had to check."

The noise of a lawnmower filled the neighborhood, and Colonel trotted next to me. "That mower sounds angry to me. Somebody else didn't sleep well last night."

We walked a few blocks, and I slowed my steps. "That was a weird dream, Colonel. Not one of my usuals. Not that I have nightmares I could label as usual."

A mockingbird trilled through its repertoire of songs, and I picked up my pace. "Let's stop off at the hospital. I've got a feeling."

When we walked into the hospital waiting room, Emma sat at the information desk. "Ms. Karen, what a surprise to see you. What are you doing here? I came in to cover the night shift. Darlene Rothenberger will be here soon to cover my day shift."

"Colonel and I are on the way to Ida's Diner for breakfast and just thought we'd stop."

"You had one of your feelings? Grady's working until three today. Okay if I go to breakfast with you?"

"That would be great."

Darlene cruised into the waiting room with no limp and her back straight as she pushed a rolling walker.

"Why, Ms. Darlene, you're downright spry this morning. Is that a new walker?" Emma asked.

"My physical therapist said the way I used my cane shifted all my weight to one side and put too much pressure on my hip. She recommended a walker and suggested this rollator, as she called it. I feel great, and I've got a place to haul my plants when I garden. It's my portable potting bench." She pointed at the seat and beamed.

When Emma and I walked out of the hospital, she asked, "Did you and Colonel walk? My car's over there, but I'm okay with walking too."

Colonel dashed to the edge of the parking lot and waited. "Guess we're walking," Emma said.

When we reached Ida's Diner, Colonel barked once, and Mary Rose opened the diner door. "I saw ya, Colonel. Your order's in. Come on in, Ms. Donut Lady. Nice to see you, Ms. Emma."

After Mary Rose took our order, Emma leaned across the table. "What did Mary Rose mean when she told Colonel she put his order in?"

"Just wait."

Mary Rose poured coffee into our cups.

"Order up. Maître d' special," a man's voice called from the kitchen.

Mary Rose hurried to the window and carried a plate outside. "Maître d' special."

"Was that a steak?" Emma's eyes widened.

"Surprised me the first time too." I chuckled. "Sully and Colonel go back a long way, I was told."

"Colonel makes sure our diners have the best possible experience," Mary Rose called out as she scooted to pick up the next order. "And he doubles as our bouncer, but he prefers being called the *maître d'*." Mary Rose refilled our cups.

"Order up," Sully called.

"Here ya go. Donut Lady special and Pretty Lady special," Mary Rose said.

Emma giggled. "Thanks, Sully. I needed that."

"Knew that," Sully called. "Still true."

A tear slipped down Emma's face. "I might need to talk, Ms. Donut Lady."

"Whenever you like," I said.

"Eat up while your food's hot," Mary Rose whispered. "Sully's sensitive."

"Heard that. Am not." Sully growled.

After we ate, we strolled back to the hospital and sat on a bench near the parking lot. Emma stared at her feet. "I'm in a deep hole, and when I look up, there's no light. Only black." She squinted at me. "You know what I'm talking about, don't you?"

I nodded.

"What did you do?"

I met her gaze. "I ran over my husband."

Emma snort-laughed. "Oh lordy, Ms. Karen. I believe you.". She closed her eyes. "You're right. I'm not alone. It's hard to remember when the darkness seeps in."

A squirrel scurried across the parking lot, and Colonel raced to catch it. The squirrel zipped up a tree, perched on a branch, and scolded Colonel. The squirrel jumped to another tree, but Colonel remained frozen under the squirrel's first branch.

Emma stared at Colonel. "And I've been focused on a problem that isn't there. That's why I'm stuck." Her voice shook.

Colonel trotted to Emma and rested his head on her knee. She wiped tears off her face with her hand. "I've been obsessing about fostering or adopting siblings. It's all I can think about, but Grady's mind has been on something, and I don't know what." Emma said. "He hasn't said, and I haven't asked him."

Emma rose and stretched her back. "Of course, I haven't told him what I've been worried about either. Neither one of us is talking. I guess that's what's really bothering me. Did you know you are a talented listener? Gee says you have magic. Must have been what I needed. You and Colonel want a ride?"

"Thanks, but I need the walk, and Colonel has squirrels to find," I said. Colonel trotted to the edge of the parking lot and cocked his head. When I headed his way, he dashed to the first corner.

By the time we reached the house, Colonel was panting, and my hairline was damp. "Good walk, Colonel. I needed that."

* * *

Colonel and I relaxed in the shade of the back porch while Jack's white truck circled our block. After his second time around, Jack pulled into the alley, stopped at my back gate, and grinned. "Too early?"

"We were just relaxing. Waiting for you."

On the way to Valdosta, Jack said, "When I was a kid, we'd listen to the World Series on the radio at school and keep box scores. Our teacher said it would help us learn to focus."

"We did that too. Anybody who talked during the broadcast would be shushed by the rest of us."

Jack pointed at the smoke ahead. "Good day for a controlled burn. I never realized how important fire was for forest management until we moved to Asbury."

"Ohio, at least where I lived, didn't have the tree farming like we do here. I loved the smell of smoky pines when I was a kid. Didn't realize how much I missed it until now."

A man leaned on a rake and stood near the road. When we passed him, the man nodded and waved a two-fingered salute, and Jack returned his wave.

"You know him?" I asked.

"Nope. He waved at the pickup. Anybody driving a white pickup truck must be from around here." Jack chuckled.

After we parked at the ballpark, Jack asked as we neared the stands, "Where do you want to sit?"

"Third base side. What about you?" I inhaled. "Smell that fresh-cut grass? I've missed ballgames."

"I usually sit near first base. Why third base?"

"It's on the west side. We'll have the sun at our back."

"You're always thinking. Lead on."

When we reached the bleachers, I stepped up to the third row. "How about here? High enough to see, but I don't have to climb any more stairs."

The teams warmed up on the field. Jack elbowed me and pointed at a tall ball player with short red hair. "Keep an eye on him. Outfielder, don't you think? He hasn't missed fielding one ball."

A wild throw sent a ball sailing high over the outfielder's head. He sprinted and twisted to face the ball with an impressive high-jump as he snagged the ball with his glove.

"Did you see that?" Jack hugged me just as I leaned to the side. "Astounding!"

"Oh my goodness." His shirt muffled my voice.

Jack released me. "I'm so sorry. Are you okay? Did you say something?"

"I saw the sheriff and Tess. Over there." I waved at first base. I peered around Jack's arm.

"Well, let's go say hi." He rose, grabbed my hand, and pulled me up.

"Wait. What if—"

"What if what?" Jack cocked his head.

"Nothing." *Sometimes things are simpler than they look.* "You're right. Let's go say hi."

Jack took my elbow. I shuddered.

"What? Oh." He dropped his hand.

I led the way and glanced back at Jack. He scuffed along with his head down.

I need to talk to him.

Before we reached the sheriff and Tess, she spotted us and waved. She was a few inches taller than me, thirty years younger, and fifteen pounds lighter. Her long red hair was pulled back into a ponytail. She wore skinny jeans and a red baseball-style T-shirt with the Valdosta State Blazers logo across her ample chest. We returned her wave. My eyes widened as Emma hurried in from the entrance and waved. "Did I say you were right?"

Jack beamed.

Sheriff jumped up. "What a surprise seeing you. We came to watch Tess's nephew play. She didn't want to come alone, and we love baseball."

"Come join us," Jack said. "Karen picked out the best seats in the park."

"Are you sure?" Emma peered at my face.

"Of course, what a great idea," I said, and Emma narrowed her eyes.

"Which one's your nephew, Tess?" I asked.

"That one." She pointed at the outfielder. "That's my sister's son, Nate."

"We've been watching him," Jack said. "He's talented."

"Thanks." Tess blushed.

The sheriff picked up their seat pads and his backpack. "Who's leading the way?"

"Let's go," Jack said. Grady and Tess fell into step behind him, and Emma slowed to bring up the rear with me.

"You okay?" I asked.

"Working on it," she said.

Tess caught up to Jack and grabbed his arm. He smiled and enveloped his hand around hers. Her animated conversation was punctuated by waves of her right hand. I narrowed my eyes and tripped over a step. Emma grabbed my arm before I fell on the concrete.

"Thanks, Emma. I wasn't paying attention."

"Oh yes, you were." Emma raised her eyebrows.

When the game ended with Nate's team winning—three to one, Tess was hoarse.

"Are you going to be able to work tomorrow?" I asked.

"I have the day off," she answered in her raspy voice.

"Great game," Jack said. "Would y'all care to join us for dinner?"

The sheriff shook his head. "We've got to get back. I've got paperwork."

"And Tess needs to gargle," Emma said.

"Be right back." Tess hurried to the field where Nate waited for her with a big grin. She returned with Nate in tow and introduced us.

"Great game, Nate," Jack said. "Tess, why don't you and Nate join us for dinner. You can ride home with us."

"Really? That would be great. What do you think, Nate?" she asked.

"Sure. I'm always starving after a game."

Tess laughed. "You're always starving before a game too. Permanent condition. We'll wait for you at the exit while you change."

Nate jogged away, and Grady and Emma left. As we made our way to the exit, Tess strolled on the other side of Jack. "Thank you so much for the dinner invitation. I don't get many opportunities to watch Nate play, much less spend a little time with him."

"We weren't thinking anything fancy. Burgers or tacos okay with you?" Jack asked.

"That's perfect. I know a good taco joint if you're interested."

"Sounds great," Jack said.

I might hate tacos. Anybody care to ask me? I frowned. *Shake it off, Buttercup.*

I positioned myself between Tess and Jack near the exit while we waited for Nate. Tess prattled on, and I stared up. The field lights clicked off, and I looked for Orion's Belt in the fading sky. "The hunter," I whispered to the shadows that swirled in front of me, "but I can't quite see him yet." Across the parking lot, a car engine revved up. The back of my neck tingled, and the shadows scattered. When the engine roared, I grabbed onto Jack's shirt and yanked as I threw myself away from the fence and toward the exit. I shoved Tess, and she slammed against the turnstile.

"What are you—" Tess said.

The car smashed into the chain link fence where we had waited and spewed gravel as its tires spun when it was jammed into reverse. I was sprawled on my belly with Jack's legs on top of mine. *Not very ladylike. Darlene Rothenberger would not approve.* I raised up on an elbow and craned my neck toward the car. The driver met my gaze before he sped away. I shuddered at the depth of evil in the intensity of his scowl. *Ronald Dixon.*

Jack rolled to the side and bent down next to me. He helped me to a sitting position, and I leaned against him.

"You have awesome reflexes," he said. "I didn't even hear the car coming."

"Everybody okay? Do we need an ambulance?" Tess asked as she dialed her cell phone. "I'm calling the sheriff, and then I'll call the locals."

Nate and three other young men raced out. "Are you okay, Aunt Tess?" Nate helped Tess to her feet.

"My arm might be sore tomorrow where I hit the turnstile." She rubbed her arm. "Thanks, Karen. You're strong for your size, did you know that?"

I shook my head. "I think adrenaline took over."

Jack helped me to my feet. "You had a feeling?"

"Something like that." I broke away and stepped to Tess. "Are you sure you're okay? It'd be nice if I were polite and apologized for my sloppy tackle."

Tess laughed. "Remind me to choose you first for my warrior squad."

I didn't turn around at the screech of tires behind me. "Sheriff, right?"

Nate's eyes widened. "You've got eyes in the back of your head too? So does my mama."

Jack strode to the sheriff's car, and I closed my eyes and waited for my tongue lashing. Emma beat the sheriff to my side. "He has orders not to yell at you."

"Karen," the sheriff roared.

Emma cleared her throat. I faced the sheriff and bit my lower lip to keep from smirking.

"Karen," the sheriff sighed, "now what?"

"It was Ronald Dixon," I said. "He headed south, maybe toward the highway. I didn't get the tag number of the car, though."

"You're slipping," the sheriff growled, and Jack snorted.

Deputy cars rolled into the parking lot. Emma said, "When y'all are released, come to our house, and I'll throw something together."

Nate's shoulders slumped. "They don't need us," Jack said. "Shall we run grab you some tacos? Would that be okay, Sheriff?"

"The taco stand is only two blocks away," Tess said.

"Sure. Wait a couple minutes, and I'll clear it with Bob. We don't want anyone to think you're our escaping attacker," the sheriff said.

The arriving deputies approached Sheriff Grady who waited for them near the parking lot. The younger ones peered at us past Grady as he spoke. The local sheriff barked orders, and the deputies scattered to the fence and to their cars. Sheriff Grady, Sheriff Bob, and two deputies sauntered to our small group. Sheriff Grady introduced us.

"Ms. Donut Lady, your reputation precedes you. It's a pleasure to meet you," Sheriff Bob said. Emma elbowed me and snickered, and I glared at her. "Deputy Snider will take your statement. Would you be more comfortable sitting in a car with the air-conditioner?"

"Not really, but could we sit on a bench?"

"Certainly, ma'am," Deputy Snider said. We sauntered to the bench under the covered entrance.

"I'll take notes," he said. "I might ask you to go back over a few things for my notes. Just letting you know."

After I told him what happened, he flipped through his notes. "I think I've got it. You're very observant. You know that, right? You retired law enforcement?"

I bit my lip. *Don't say it. Ah, what the heck.* "No. Convicted felon. Twelve years in prison."

He nodded. "Knew there was something."

Deputy Snider will go far.

He closed his notebook and headed to the sheriffs. He stopped, flipped open his notebook, and then returned. "I didn't catch how you knew to get everyone out of the path of the car."

Nightmares? Shadows told me? "I had a feeling."

He stared, and I met his gaze.

"Will Sheriff Grady laugh or believe me if I write that in my report?"

"He might laugh, but he'll believe it."

"Wish me luck," he mumbled as he sauntered away.

"Ready to head out?" Emma asked. "If I can ride with you, Grady will be along later."

The four of us piled into Jack's truck. On the way home, Tess said, "This has been the most exciting day I've ever had. Wasn't this just a usual day for you, Ms. Karen?"

Before I could answer, Jack said, "Yes. You've just had a personal glimpse into the life of the Donut Lady."

I glowered, and Emma laughed.

When we arrived at Emma's, we received our assignments. "Tess, can you toss a salad? Check the fridge and pull whatever you like. Karen, set the table? Jack, would you fix drinks? We have water, beer, wine, sweet tea, and hot tea. Coffee too, if anyone wants some."

Emma grabbed a large jar of home-canned spaghetti sauce out of her cabinet. "I never get to entertain. This is exciting."

As we sat at the dining table, the sheriff came in the back door. "Ahh. Nothing beats coming home to the delicious aroma of Emma's homemade spaghetti sauce. You're awesome, Emma." He stopped by her seat and kissed the top of her head.

After we ate, Jack and I dropped off Tess. When we pulled in front of my house, I said, "Coming in?"

Jack opened the back door for Colonel. I poured two glasses of sweet tea, and we stood on the porch while Colonel patrolled his territory.

"I owe you an explanation." I stared at the dark sky. *No stars. It's Emma's darkness.*

"No, you—"

"Yes. I do. I want you to know." I sat on the steps, and Jack joined me. "I have old wounds—scars—that haven't finished healing. It's difficult for me when—" I cleared my throat. "Touch is painful for me." I felt his stare and closed my eyes. "I needed to tell you because I don't want you to think it's personal."

"I kind of thought there might have been something. I'm sorry you've gone through bad times." Jack rose. "You know you can talk to me. Anytime you want. Not pushing."

"Thanks." I took his glass and rose to go inside.

"It's hard for me not to reach out, you know?" He stuck his hands in his pockets and stared at the door. "We're still friends, right? We'll still go to baseball games and on picnics?"

"Absolutely."

After I'd locked the back door, he headed to the front door. "Good night, Karen. Thanks for telling me."

I locked and bolted the door behind him. I leaned against the door and sobbed.

CHAPTER NINE

When Colonel, Mia, and I arrived at the shop, the lights were on. *Such a comfort to see the lights.*

"Hey, Miss Lady," Tiffany said. "How was your weekend? Anything exciting happen?"

"According to Jack, nothing out of the ordinary for me."

"Oh my goodness," Tiffany dropped her wooden spoon. "That bad?"

"I'll tell you later. What's the plan for today?"

"What do you think about classic glazed bacon donuts, strawberry glazed donuts, and bacon and cheddar scones?" Tiffany pressed her lips.

I snickered. "I'd say we had a genius in this kitchen. Any meetings this morning?"

"Just one at eight thirty. A new group: *Foster Dogs and More.*"

"Their leader called last week. The group needs to expand the number of foster homes for dogs and cats. Their long-time support families are at capacity, and she doesn't want anyone to burn out."

"Are we going to buy a farm and foster dogs and cats, Miss Lady?" Tiffany mixed her last batch of dough.

I frowned in simulated thoughtfulness and tapped my chin. "That would be fun, wouldn't it? But we'd miss harassing the sheriff."

Tiffany laughed. "You are so right, but I can never guess what you're going to say next."

The bell announced the sheriff. "Smartest thing I've heard all day, Tiffany. Is that bacon I smell? Did you hire Sully away from Ida's?"

I snorted and poured his coffee. "Now how could I hire the owner away from the diner?"

"Here you go, Sheriff." Tiffany set down a plate with the two different kinds of donuts and a scone.

The sheriff bit into his bacon donut. "Mmm. Delicious." After he gobbled down his first donut, he started on his second. "I'm saving that scone for last. Did you tell Tiffany about your quiet day off, Donut Lady?"

Tiffany scowled and crossed her arms. "Now."

I grabbed two cups and poured coffee for Tiffany and me. The sheriff pointed at his cup and swallowed. "Please."

I poured his refill and recounted the previous day's events.

"Wow," Tiffany said. "I can't even take a sick day. I can't wait to tell Aunt Gee."

"I can't wait to hear your version."

The bell jingled, and Roger sauntered into the shop. I fluttered my eyelashes, and Tiffany stuck her tongue out at me.

"You are so immature, Miss Lady," she hissed as she brushed past me to the coffee pot.

"Roger, Donut Lady's trying to lure Sully away from Ida's," the sheriff said.

"Stop it, Sheriff. Word will get out, and you'll get me banned from Ida's. Then you'll have to cook my breakfast on Sundays."

Tiffany poured a cup and served up a plate of donuts. When she wheeled the cart into the pink meeting room, Roger followed and closed the door with a quiet click.

The sheriff set down his cup. "Why does trouble find you even when you go out of town?"

"That's a good question. How did Dixon know I'd be there? Tess was there to see her nephew. Is that something she does regularly? Could Tess have been his target?"

The sheriff's radio crackled, and Roger dashed out of the meeting room.

"Gotta go." The sheriff gulped down his coffee.

After they left, Tiffany said, "Roger has an interview later this week. I'm nervous for him."

"He'll do great. Look at all the things we've thrown at him that he's taken in stride."

Tiffany giggled and drizzled her last batch of donuts. "I'll never forget his face that first time we had termite donuts. I've promised I'll make a termite cheesecake when we go visit his parents on Sunday. I told you about that, right? His family's getting together at his folks' house. Aunt Gee, Isaiah, and Tammy are going. Aunt Gee, Tammy's mother, and Roger's mother went to school together. It's supposed to be some kind of big family occasion, according to Roger, but I think the occasion is to inspect me."

"That's exciting. How you going to keep Gee on her best behavior?"

"I hoped you'd throw a little magic on her." She snickered.

Shirley hurried into the shop. "Did you hear that Todd Rockford gave notice at the bank? He has a new job in Atlanta, but why would anybody want to go live where there's all that traffic when they could live here? I talked to Alfred yesterday, and he said he's not sure he wants to hire anyone else. I told Alfred he needed to stop being such an old penny-pincher. He said I talk too much. Can you imagine anybody saying that? Woody and I are having dinner with him Friday night. He wants to talk about a project he has in mind for his boys, and I told him if he wanted to talk project, we'd have to have the best project manager in town with us. He said if I was bringing my project manager, he'd bring his construction supervisor. Isn't that a stitch? He's an old tightwad, but he's got a sense of humor that kind of sneaks up on you. Thanks for the coffee and donuts, Tiffany. I never had a bacon and cheddar scone. Did you give me one? You are so talented. I have to rush. I have a meeting."

Tiffany stood at the meeting room door with her mouth open. She shook her head. "Wow. Did you hear what I heard?"

I plopped onto a stool. "I don't even know where to start."

The bell jingled, and our meeting room filled up. Tiffany scooted out for more donuts. "Didn't expect so many people, Miss Lady. Can you get more coffee going?"

After the meeting broke up, Tiffany scrubbed the equipment, and I disinfected the counter and display case.

The bell jingled, and the sheriff stepped inside with a scowl.

"Sorry, Sheriff. We don't have any donuts or scones left, and we've cleaned the coffee pots. I can offer you some water."

"Here on official business, Ms. Karen." The sheriff cleared his throat. "Need you to come to the office. The state investigator wants to ask you some questions."

"I'll get my purse and give Amber a call. Can you lock up, Tiffany? And take Colonel home? Here's my house key."

Tiffany's eyes widened. "Yes, ma'am."

I called Amber, and her administrative assistant answered. "Leah, I'm going with the sheriff to his office. The state investigator has questions for me. Could Amber meet me there? Thanks."

"I'm not sure that's necessary, Ms. Karen. But I'd do the same thing," the sheriff said.

I hung up my apron and left with the sheriff.

"Front seat," the sheriff growled when we reached his patrol car. On the way to his office, the sheriff said, "The state investigator will tell you that you aren't under arrest. A friend would tell you to wait until Amber shows up before you say anything, but I'm sure you know that."

He slammed the steering wheel with the heel of his hand, and I jumped. "In fact, I need to fill up before we go to the office."

The sheriff drove to the county maintenance building. "I'll go inside to get the pump turned on and leave the engine running for the air conditioning."

He sauntered to the service department.

I texted Amber: "On our way. Txt when u get to SO."

The sheriff opened his car door. "I'll need to turn off the engine while I refuel. Open your door or step out if you get too hot."

When the pump clicked off, the sheriff started up the car and washed the windshield and the back window. After he climbed into the patrol car, my phone dinged with a text from Amber. "At SO."

"You ready?" He peered at my phone, and I held it so he could see. "Okay, then. Let's roll."

After the sheriff parked, I said, "Thanks, Grady."

"Whatever I can do." The sheriff opened my door. When we walked into the building together, he whispered, "For the record, I hate this."

Amber strode to greet me, and her high heels clicked on the tile floor. She wore her navy suit and yellow silk shirt, and her dark hair was pulled back into a tight bun. The sheriff headed to his office while we continued to the interrogation office.

"I'll answer any questions. You don't say anything unless I say okay," Amber said.

I nodded. *This is what support is. I never had that before.*

A bald man in a gray suit, cream shirt, and dark gray tie approached us. Amber and the man shook hands. "Good to see you, Bud, although I'm not thrilled about the circumstances. What have you got?"

"Sheriff Bob arrested Ronald Dixon. Let's go into the office, and I'll tell you why I'm here. Ms. O'Brien, I'm Cleveland Pitt, state investigator. Do you mind waiting in the hall for a few minutes?"

Amber nodded. "That's fine," I said.

Roger appeared in the hallway with a folding chair. "Here ya go, Miss Lady." He set up the chair for me. "I have a message for you from Tiffany. She said, 'We got your back.' That includes me, you know." He winked and swaggered back to the sheriff's office.

Very different. A tear of gratitude escaped, and I touched it with my fingertips. *I have back up.* I folded my hands in my lap and squared my shoulders.

After an hour, Amber opened the door. "Thanks again, Bud. Let me know if there's anything else." She smiled. "I'll give you a ride home, Donut Lady."

Amber led the way to her car and opened the passenger door. After she started the engine, she said, "Ronald Dixon's attorney is trying to swing a deal on the assault charges, but the state prosecutor has a solid case. Debra named Dixon as her attacker, and Melinda and another witness—Bud wouldn't say who—positively identified Dixon as Melinda's assailant."

I bit my lip. *Andrew.*

Amber continued, "Ronald Dixon claims he knows who killed Edward Wallace. First, he said it was Melinda, then he changed his story and said it was you. Dixon said he could prove Melinda had papers— which he refused to identify, by the way—that were indisputable evidence of her culpability in an unnamed crime. He said she must have given them to you. He wouldn't elaborate on how he knows all this unless the charges against him were dropped, including any future unknown charges."

I snorted.

"I know, right?" Amber said. "At first, Bud argued a few questions wouldn't hurt, but then he agreed it was ridiculous to put you through questioning unless Dixon comes up with something more concrete and less ludicrous. Bud might try to get the sheriff to ask you some questions, but I don't think Grady will be interested. If you think of anything, let me know. Don't talk about Dixon or Wallace, including Melinda, with anyone unless I'm with you."

"You're amazing. Thank you, Counselor."

"You need me; you call me. You hear?"

Tiffany and Colonel were on my porch when we drove up.

"Good. Your posse's waiting. I'm leaving you in good hands," Amber said.

"Here's your house key, Miss Lady," Tiffany said after we were inside. "Colonel and Mia have been fed. Aunt Gee invited you to dinner tonight, but I told her you'd need to rest. You want to go to the diner, or shall I cook?"

"I'd like to put my feet up for a bit first."

"You sit, and I'll make you a cup of tea. Jack's been driving around the block. You have options."

"Tea sounds good. I don't think I'm up to going anywhere."

"You tell me what you want, and I'll do it."

After Tiffany handed me my hot tea, I said, "Roger gave me your message. Thank you."

"I told him to tell you I'd help bury the body, but he said that wasn't a good idea."

I laughed. "I knew that was what you meant."

"I heard something," Tiffany tiptoed to the front window and peeked out. "Yep. Jack's parked in your driveway and headed this way. I just realized I sneaked to the window. I might need training on being your sidekick."

Before Jack could knock, Tiffany threw the door open and hissed, "Quick. Come in."

Jack hurried inside with a furrowed brow. "What?"

I laughed. "Tiffany's working on her clandestine skills."

"That's right," she said. "I'm going to help with the investigation—what is it we're investigating this time, Miss Lady?"

Jack's face brightened, and he rubbed his hands. "So, what's our next step?"

I raised my eyebrows.

"You didn't think I'd let you two leave me out of the excitement, did you?" he asked.

"Amber said I can't discuss Edward Wallace or Ronald Dixon unless she's around."

Jack dropped onto the sofa. "That squashes everything, doesn't it? We're afraid of Amber, right?"

"Right. I've got sweet tea in the refrigerator. Who's interested?"

"I am. I'll get it," Tiffany said. She grabbed two glasses, and poured tea. "So, if we think alphabetically, could we talk about Bad Guy Number One and Bad Guy Number Two?" She handed Jack his glass.

"Thanks for the tea, Tiffany." Jack took a big gulp. "That's too obvious. What about code words? Like watermelon and dumpling?"

Tiffany and I stared at him and then burst out laughing.

"What?" Jack asked. "Too subtle?"

"That's not exactly what I was thinking." I wiped my eyes. "But it'll do."

My phone rang. My eyes widened, and I mouthed, "Melinda." Tiffany crowded me to listen when I answered.

"Hello, sister outcast," she said. "I wanted to thank you again for taking care of Pepper and to tell you the state investigator came to see me. Did he talk to you too? He said Ronald Dixon claimed you and I have some type of scheme going on, and we killed Wally because he found out. I suppose you've already talked to the investigator too. I didn't say anything about Sam Clinton and her children. Should I have? Clarissa came by to see how I was doing. I was surprised. Maybe I've misjudged her. She said Dixon murdered Wally and is trying to create a smoke screen. I think she might be right. What do you think?"

"I didn't—"

"Pepper and I are moving. I might try to call Jack to see if he can go to dinner tonight, but I'm not sure there's really anything there as far as he's concerned. He's a nice guy, but a little standoffish. Have you noticed? Pepper and I are going to stay at Debra's place until she gets out of the hospital. I'll find an apartment near her. It's good to be close to family, don't you think? Well, you've got my number. Stay in touch."

Melinda hung up. Tiffany's eyes were wide.

Jack's phone buzzed. He glanced at it and put his phone face down. Tiffany snickered, and I carried my cup to the sink. *He didn't even answer. Why am I so pleased?*

"So, what did Melinda say?" Jack asked.

I scanned my surroundings with exaggerated stealth. "Melinda said dumpling claimed she and I conspired to kill watermelon."

Tiffany spewed her tea. "Dang it, Miss Lady. You're supposed to warn me."

"One more, Tiffany. Jack, she also said you're standoffish." I sat in my chair and smiled.

Tiffany snorted. "Thanks for the warning."

Jack frowned. "I prefer to think of myself as *mysterious*."

Tiffany grabbed the dishcloth and wiped the table. "I'll see you in the morning." She tossed the cloth into the sink. "Call me if you need me to hide in the back of Jack's truck while he circles your neighborhood, Miss Lady." She giggled, and Jack's face reddened.

"More tea?" I asked after she left.

"In a minute. I've been thinking about what we talked about yesterday. I want to try an experiment." He put his arms on top of the table with his palms down. "Whenever you're ready, put your hand on my arm. You can move it away any time."

I tilted my head and narrowed my eyes. He met my gaze and smiled.

"You won't grab my arm or anything?"

"You know I won't."

I peered at his face. *He's right. I trust him.*

I rested my left hand on the back of his right forearm. His arm relaxed at my touch. I reached out with my right hand and placed it on his left forearm. Colonel came to my side and nudged my elbow. My hand moved up Jack's arm and closer to his elbow.

"How you doing?" He asked.

"Fine. Not nervous at all." I didn't move my hands.

Jack maintained his gaze. "Good. I thought you might be okay if you were in control. You can reach out for me anytime you want."

I removed my hands slowly. "Very astute. Thank you."

"Did you hear that, Colonel? I'm astute. Add that to mysterious." Jack stuck out his chest.

My phone dinged. A text from Tiffany. "Warning. Guac calling."

I laughed, and Jack leaned to look at my phone. "Guac? Guacamole's calling?"

"Keep up. Gee's going to—"

My phone rang, and Jack rolled his eyes.

"Hello, Gee."

"You have to eat. Get Jack to come with you so you can have a glass of wine with me. Bring Colonel and Roxie. Mandy misses having company, and Sandy will hide. We eat in an hour, and cocktails are served when you walk in the door. Shake a leg." She hung up.

"Would you like to go to dinner with me at Gee's? That's a rhetorical question. You can choose not to, but you have to call Gee and tell her. And Roxie and Colonel are invited too."

"Sounds great. Do I have to give back my *Astute* badge for the guacamole gaff?"

"Only if Gee finds out."

"But she doesn't know she's—oh. I get it. If she finds out she's guac. Then I'm umm, in a jam?"

"Well done, sir."

Jack bowed. "Thank you, Madam. She we fetch the lovely Roxie?"

"Where are we going?" I asked when we left the outskirts of town.

"Just a few more miles. Roxie and I live out in the country."

My eyes widened when we pulled into a long dirt driveway that led to a brown clapboard farmhouse with a wraparound porch. "I didn't realize you lived in the country. Your home is beautiful."

"My old friends couldn't understand why I stayed, but I'd feel cramped on a city lot."

"I can see where they'd think you'd be rattling around, but it's so peaceful here." I climbed out of the truck and strolled to a nearby azalea bush. "I love the bright pink blossoms."

Jack opened the front door, and Roxie raced to join Colonel, who investigated the country smells. Colonel sniffed from the middle of the yard to the edge of the surrounding woods.

"Colonel looks like he's found a rabbit trail," Jack said.

I gazed at the well-kept lawn, the tall pines, and the oaks with spreading branches.

"Are the woods yours too?" I asked.

"They are. I like having a natural habitat for wildlife. Come around to the back. I'd like for you to see my raised bed garden."

I wasn't used to the uneven ground. I focused on my balance. When we reached the back, I stared. "It looks like an open-air greenhouse with the chicken wire all around it."

"I love the wildlife, but I'm not willing for them to eat my peas and sweet potatoes." Jack chuckled.

"I suppose we'll have to leave. Thank you for the quick tour. I love being outside."

Jack offered his arm, and I grabbed hold as we strolled over the uneven ground to the front of the house.

Jack whistled, and the dogs dashed to the truck.

On our way to Gee's, Jack asked, "So would you be Kale?"

"Never," I said in my iciest voice. "I am cantaloupe. Spelled with a K."

Jack smiled. "What about Tiffany? Not Tomato, right? Tartare? That's it, isn't it?"

"It's much better than Tossed Salad, which was what I was thinking."

"I'm a pretty good cook," Jack said. "I'll have to invite you to the cabin for dinner sometime."

"The cabin?"

"That's what Ava named our place the first time she saw it."

I nodded. "Very fitting. It has the look of a cabin."

"Here we are." Jack pulled in front of Gee's house.

Colonel whined.

"Colonel and I are excited to be at Gee's, but don't tell her. She'll be insufferable," I said.

Roxie crowded Colonel and matched the tone of his whine. "Roxie and I are excited too," Jack said.

The dogs scrambled to the door, and Roger let them inside. Mandy stretched and ambled to Colonel. "Gee and Tiffany are in the kitchen. No room in there for me." He grinned.

"About time you showed up, Donut Lady.' Gee called from the kitchen. "I started without you. You want white or red? Tell Roger. He's tonight's sommelier."

"What's a sommelier, Miss Lady?" Roger whispered.

"Wine steward. Person who pours the wine." I matched his tone.

"Would that be white or red, madam?" Roger tossed a small towel over his arm.

"I'll take whatever Gee's having."

"And, Mr. Jack?" Roger asked.

"I'm driving. Don't want to get in trouble with the law."

"Whole reason you got the invite," Gee said. She strolled into the living room. "Tiffany kicked me out of the kitchen. She can be awfully bossy when she's frying chicken. Never interested in a little friendly advice."

Roger handed me a glass of wine, and Gee sat next to me on the sofa. "So where are we on the investigation? Do you think Ronald Dixon attacked Melinda and her sister? Did he kill Edward Wallace too? And what about those warning phone calls everybody except you and me got?"

Roger cleared his throat. "Y'all are getting into a conversation that could get me fired. I'll take my chances in the kitchen with Tiffany."

Jack pulled a chair close to the sofa. "What do you think, Karen?"

"I have more questions than answers. As far as the phone calls, I think Clarissa made them, and Melinda was the target. Clarissa was the only one who identified the caller as 'he.' Everyone else said 'a voice' called."

Gee scowled. "What if she just happened to say he? That's a little flimsy."

"You're right, Gee. All I've got is a feeling. No motive. No evidence."

Jack nodded. "If you have a feeling, that cinches it for me, but you're right that we don't have any evidence."

"True," I said. "Debra was found near Dixon's property. That's not much except Melinda could identify her attacker."

"You're right," Gee said. "What if Melinda told Debra that Dixon attacked her? Maybe Debra was going to confront Dixon."

"Melinda told me she didn't know her attacker, but Debra would have recognized Dixon from Melinda's description."

"Dinner's on the table," Roger announced. The dogs followed us to the dining room until Gee said in a stern voice, "Stay." Mandy, Colonel, and Roxie flopped in the doorway.

I hope nobody has to leave here in a hurry," Jack said. "Those dogs have the doorway blocked. Can you believe all three of them are in that tiny space?"

While we passed the fried chicken, mashed potatoes, gravy, rolls, and green beans around the table, Roger poured and served sweet tea.

"Good job, multitasking, Roger," Jack said.

Roger served himself a generous portion of mashed potatoes. "If sommelier is what you call someone who pours wine, what do you call someone who serves tea?"

I rolled my eyes, and Tiffany nodded. Gee and Tiffany set their forks on their plates and folded their hands.

"Roger," I said.

Jack choked on his green beans. "Dang, Karen. Give a guy a warning."

Gee and Tiffany laughed and dug into their food.

"Remind me not ask any of you three a simple question," Roger mumbled.

When dinner was over, Gee shooed Tiffany and Roger away. "You did the cooking and serving. I'll take care of the dishes."

"I'll help," I said.

"I'll supervise." Jack beamed.

"You two go on," Gee said after Tiffany and Roger disappeared. "I can work faster by myself, and you have an early day tomorrow, Donut Lady."

"You win this time, Gee. Thanks again for a great evening."

Jack walked into the house with me and let Colonel out back. "Karen, if something comes up, call me. No matter what time of day or night."

I gazed at him. "You got one of my feelings?"

He met my gaze. "No, but I want you to know, I'm here for you."

Colonel trotted back into the house, and Jack locked and bolted the door.

When Jack reached for the front doorknob, I patted his arm and smiled.

"Thanks," I said.

After he left, I locked and bolted the door and raced to the window to peek. He swaggered to his truck, and I giggled.

I'm as silly as he is.

Colonel and the shadows followed me down the hallway to bed.

CHAPTER TEN

I woke at eleven when my phone buzzed a text. I fumbled in the dark and stared at the screen. *Melinda.*

"@ park. Pepper's hurt. Can u help?"

Mia jumped on my bed and meowed.

"I can't turn her down. I hate to bother Jack, but this is a little strange."

"Give me a few." I texted and then dialed 911.

"Deputy on the way," Tess said.

"Send him to the park. Melinda texted me for help and said she was at the park. Is Deputy Jeff on duty tonight?"

"Yes, ma'am. I just diverted him."

"Thanks. I'll meet him there. Hopefully, with apologies."

Text from Melinda: "Hurry."

After I threw on jeans and a sweatshirt over my pajamas, Colonel and I left the house. I locked and bolted the door. *What if somebody's trying to get me away from home?*

Before I pulled out of the driveway, I called Jack. "I'm okay. Sorry to wake you, but Melinda sent me a text and said Pepper's hurt at the park. Jeff's going to meet me there. Can you watch my house?"

Jack hung up on me. *I'll take that as a "yes."*

Text from Melinda: "Help!"

I called Melinda. No answer, so I pulled out of my driveway. When Colonel and I arrived, I parked next to Jeff's patrol car.

"Do you see Jeff anywhere, Colonel?"

I stepped out of the car. When I opened the back door for Colonel, he jumped out and stood facing away from me with his hackles raised. I called Melinda again, and the phone rolled to voice mail.

Jeff sprinted to my car. "I heard a car drive away from the other side of the park right before you pulled up. You didn't pull in near the playground first, did you?"

"No."

"I ran to see who it was, but all I saw was the taillights of a sedan. Do you know where Ms. Melinda's staying?"

"The new hotel on the outskirts." I shivered.

"You cold? Let's climb into my car." He opened the passenger's door for me and the back door for Colonel. He spoke on his radio before he slid behind the wheel. "I've asked Tess to check with the hotel. I didn't find anyone or anything at the park with a quick search. I need to ask, could someone be pulling a stunt?"

I handed him my phone, and he scrolled through my texts.

"Jack's on his way to my house in case this was a ruse, but Colonel's hackles raised when we first got out."

"Do you think Colonel will help me search the park again?"

"I don't know. He might. We can try."

"No, ma'am. You stay in my car. If you see anything, call Tess."

Jeff opened the back door for Colonel. Colonel's hackles rose. "What is it, Colonel?" Jeff headed to the park, and Colonel blocked his path.

"It's my job, Colonel. We'll look after each other. Let's go, boy." Jeff waved his hand, and Colonel sat on Jeff's feet.

Jeff opened the back door. "Guard Ms. Karen, boy." Colonel hopped in, and the locks clicked.

My phone rang, and I jumped. *Tess.* "Sheriff's on his way. I've got him on the radio. Where are you?"

"Locked in Jeff's patrol car."

"Putting you on hold a second."

Jeff's flashlight sliced through the darkness as he continued his search.

Tess came back on the phone. "I had trouble understanding the sheriff because he was laughing so hard. He says he'll be there in a minute, and he's promoting Jeff." Tess snickered. "Sorry."

"It's okay, Tess. Just don't let him think he's funny. We'll all suffer."

"Yes, ma'am, you got that right."

When the sheriff walked up to Jeff's patrol car, I put my wrists together and held them up for him to see. His eyes widened, and he turned his back on me. After his shoulders stopped shaking, he turned back with a frown. I raised my eyebrows, and he rolled his eyes.

Jeff reappeared, and the sheriff strolled to meet him. *Too dark to read lips.*

My phone rang. *Jack.*

"Jeff locked me in his patrol car," I said. I pulled the phone away from my ear. *Why is that so funny?* "I'm not under arrest, and I hate not knowing what's going on." I hung up. *There. My turn.*

The sheriff slid in the driver's seat. "Tess called the motel. They said Melinda Wallace checked out today. When customers complained about a barking dog, they checked the room, and Pepper was there. They called Alana on the after-hours number for the animal shelter. Alana called Tammy, and Tammy picked up Pepper."

"Today? She called me earlier. What time did she check out?"

"They said she loaded up her suitcase and left around six. She called at nine and said she meant to check out when she left."

"That's after she called me." I rubbed my forehead. "Doesn't make sense."

"What did she say when she called?"

"She said she was moving to Debra's. She wouldn't have left Pepper willingly. She adores Pepper."

"Jeff found Melinda in the park. Deceased. There was a needle with a syringe still in her arm. It has all the appearances of an accidental overdose, but we're not assuming anything."

"She didn't send the texts, did she?"

"What do you think?" The sheriff narrowed his eyes.

"She didn't answer any of my calls. Somebody else sent them."

He nodded. "I can't discuss an active investigation with a civilian."

"Fair enough. Can I go home? Jack's circling my house."

"I'm assigning Jeff to patrol your house tonight."

My phone rang. *Gee.* The sheriff leaned over to listen.

"Hello, Gee."

"Isaiah was at the gas station. You know about Melinda, right? It's getting scary. Tiffany said she could stay with you. That makes the most sense to me. I'm asking nicely. Please?"

"What do you think, Sheriff?" I asked.

"I think the gas station's timing on news borders on freaky."

I scowled.

"Oh, you meant about Tiffany. If Roger says okay, then it's okay."

"Did you hear, Gee? It's up to Roger."

"Well, that squashes that. Roger's a regular bear when it comes to Tiffany."

"I have Colonel. Sheriff's assigned Jeff to patrol my house tonight. Why don't we figure it out tomorrow? Everybody's tired right now."

"You win, Donut Lady."

After we disconnected, the sheriff said, "You know Emma's going to want you to stay with us. Just throwing that out for discussion. I'll follow you home."

When I pulled into my driveway, Jack and Roxie hopped out of his truck. I climbed out of my car, and Jack opened the back door for Colonel. The sheriff waved and pulled away.

"You okay?" Jack's brow was furrowed.

"Come inside, and I'll catch you up."

I sat on the sofa, and Jack settled in with me.

"Thanks for coming. Read the texts." I handed him my phone.

Jack scrolled.

"The texts aren't from Melinda. Jeff found her body in the park."

"So, this was a way to get you to the park? Why?"

"I have no idea."

"Are you sure?" He turned to face me. "Then why did you call Tess and me? You had one of your feelings, didn't you?"

"Yes." I met his gaze. "I just realized you came to the house like I asked. Why didn't you go to the park instead?"

He shrugged. "You asked me to guard your house. I figured you had a reason."

I was too slow to cover my yawn. "Sorry," I said. "Guess I'm wearing out."

"Why don't you go on to bed? I'll just sit here on the sofa. I'll follow you to the shop in the morning."

"Jeff's going to patrol my house tonight, and I've got Colonel. You and Roxie go home. And promise me you'll go straight home, so I don't have to stay up to see if you're driving past the house."

Jack scowled. "You'll call me, right? If there's anything. Anything at all?"

"I called you tonight."

He smiled. "Yes, you did."

He rose, and he and Roxie headed to the door.

When he reached for the doorknob, I touched his arm and added a light squeeze. "Thanks, Jack."

He blushed. "You're welcome. I'll see you in the morning."

I locked the door and threw the deadbolt then sauntered to bed with Colonel at my side.

* * *

My alarm sounded at four. When I headed to the front door twenty minutes later, Mia scampered to her carrier. I zipped it closed and opened the door. Jack's white truck was parked at the curb. He waved and jumped out.

"I thought you left around four or four-thirty. Want a ride?" He opened his back door, and Colonel jumped into the truck.

"Did you run home, drop Roxie, and change your shirt so I'd think you just got here?" I narrowed my eyes.

"Dang, didn't think of that." Jack took Mia's carrier from me. "You riding with us, or are we following you?"

I rolled my eyes and climbed into the truck. "Did you ever think I might need my space?"

Jack pulled away from the curb. "Nope. Do you?"

I crossed my arms and turned my head toward the window so he wouldn't see my smirk. "I might."

"What's the specials for today?" He asked when he parked in front of the shop.

"I never know until I get here. Sometimes Tiffany's already got something in mind, and sometimes we just make it up."

"Ahh," he said. "Collaboration and magic."

When we walked into the shop, Jack opened Mia's carrier. Tiffany glanced up and raised her eyebrows. "What? Did you have overnight company after all?"

"Yep," Jack said.

"Did not," I said. "I would have checked with you and Gee first. And Shirley, Woody, Amber, the mayor, and Emma. And maybe taken a poll at the gas station."

Tiffany laughed and covered the dough to rise. "Sorry, Jack. I believe Miss Lady. She's got an entire town to answer to."

I headed to the storeroom for my apron. "What's the plan for today?"

"Only one meeting—The Historical Society at nine. They are going to induct new members today and requested their cranberry-orange scones. It might be a test or something for the new members. I thought we could have chocolate-dipped donuts. You have any ideas for our second donut?"

"How about peppermint-glazed?"

"That sounds good. Why haven't we ever thought of peppermint before? I'll add sprinkles."

"Perfect. You staying, Jack? Or you want to come back later for donuts?"

"I'll come back for donuts."

"You want a coffee to go, Mr. Jack? I put a pot on early for Miss Lady."

"Thanks. That would be great."

After Jack left, Tiffany wrote the day's menu on the board. "Cranberry, orange, chocolate, and peppermint. Seems like a strange concoction of flavors."

I cocked my head. "Then let's declare Wacky Wednesday."

Tiffany waved her wooden spoon and danced. "This is my Wacky Dance."

"I'm going to get ahead of you," I said as I hurried to make scones.

"How many batches today? Four?"

"Let's go for six."

I pulled the last batch of scones out of the oven. "I'll drizzle these when they cool. Is that your last batch?"

"Last one," Tiffany said.

The bell jingled, and the sheriff stared at the board. "Ah. Normal donuts today."

I chuckled and poured his coffee. "Yep. Just another normal Wednesday."

The sheriff sipped his coffee. "I forgot to tell you yesterday. We got the results back on the bottle of wine at your house. Just wine. No rat poison. No additives."

"So, intimidation."

"Seems like it. We still don't know why. Is this peppermint with the sprinkles? Genius. Let me guess. Donut Lady's idea."

"How'd you know?" Tiffany asked.

"He saw Jack at the gas station," I said. "I know my regulars."

The sheriff guffawed. "I see why Gee grumbles she can't get anything past you."

I sipped my coffee. "Sheriff, I've been thinking—"

"Oh lord." The sheriff rolled his eyes.

"Hush. I think we have two different criminals. One is a killer who uses chemicals. The other one is Ron Dixon, the thug who uses brute force."

The sheriff finished off his peppermint donut. "Interesting theory. Could their motives be the same, just different methods?"

"I think Dixon is taking orders. He doesn't strike me as an independent thinker."

"Do you think Dixon knows who the killer is?" Tiffany asked.

"I have a feeling he doesn't have direct contact with his boss. What do you think, Sheriff?" I rose. "More coffee?"

"Thanks. I have no idea what to think, but I've learned your feelings are always right."

"I have another question. Maybe two," Tiffany said. "Do you think there's only one killer? Or could there be a third criminal, and the two murders are unrelated? Never mind. Too convoluted and now my head hurts."

"Should I go with chocolate or orange next?" The sheriff stared at his plate.

"Chocolate," Tiffany said.

The sheriff broke his chocolate-dipped donut into fourths and popped a piece into his mouth.

I refilled our coffee. "Two different murderers using similar methods to kill a married couple two weeks apart seems unlikely."

"What about a copycat killer?" The sheriff asked.

"Wouldn't a copycat killer use poison? Seems like the killer has access to some pretty potent drugs. Maybe a drug dealer? What did the toxicology report show for Wallace? Just rat poison?"

The sheriff frowned. "Good point. I only got an oral report, not the full report. I'll get a copy."

The sheriff polished off his donut. "Can I have my scone in a sack? Y'all have given me work."

Tiffany brought him a sack for his scone, and I handed him coffee in a to-go cup.

After the sheriff left, Shirley charged into the shop. "My partner decided to change the regional agents' meeting to today. We never have the meeting on a Wednesday, but Charlotte called it an emergency meeting. Nobody misses her meetings. I have no idea what could be such a big emergency that it couldn't wait until our quarterly meeting next week. She's working on the agenda, and I need to get donuts. Did you know Melinda Wallace was murdered? It's a shock to everyone at the gas station. Clarissa said she heard Ronald Dixon arranged it. Why would that be an emergency for the agent community? It's terrible that Melinda Wallace's house burned down, and now she's dead. Where's her dog? Is Pepper okay? Can I get a dozen donuts, donut holes, and a dozen scones? There's going to be close to forty agents there. The office is going to be crowded. Maybe my math is off. How many donuts do agents eat? Should I get more? Woody is really good at math. I guess I can't go to the school and get his opinion. He knows a lot about donuts too. I'll just run by school real quick. I'll be right back."

Tiffany beat her to the door and handed Shirley a to-go cup. "Take a breath, Ms. Shirley. We'll help you. Sit at the counter and drink your coffee while we pull together your order."

Shirley carried her cup to the counter. Tiffany and I boxed up donuts, donut holes, and scones for Shirley.

"Shirley, you have three dozen donuts, a dozen donut holes, and two dozen scones. You should be fine," I said.

"Thanks. And you were right, Tiffany. I needed coffee."

The bell jingled, and Jack sauntered in. "Can I help you carry out your order, Shirley?"

Jack followed Shirley to her car with the pastries.

Tiffany dropped the last of the donut holes into the fryer. "I've learned to listen to Ms. Shirley. She's a wealth of information, isn't she? Where is Pepper, Miss Lady?"

"She's with Tammy." I pushed the cart into the meeting room.

"I knew you'd know. I'll take over the meeting room in a second, but I suspect we'll see the mayor today. He checks the calendar at least once a week. I think he arranges his schedule around our meetings."

The mayor bustled in wearing his pink *Got Sprinkles* ball cap and hurried to the storeroom. "Historical Society today, right?"

"Yes, sir," Tiffany said.

Jack came into the shop. "When does Shirley breathe? Do you know how many times she told me she was in a hurry?"

"My theory is that she's part alien. Maybe from Saturn." I poured coffee for Jack and set his cup on the counter.

"I'll take a Wacky Wednesday," Jack said.

Tiffany's eyes widened. "Oh, I get it. Saturn because she can talk rings around anyone? Am I right?"

"That's it." I smacked her hand in a high-five and set the plate with two donuts and a scone next to Jack's cup.

The mayor stood at the display case. "Cranberry-orange is the Historical Society's theme scone, right? Chocolate dipped. Chocolate is good for the heart and long life. They'll love that. And what's that third one?"

"Peppermint. We'll let you come up with its story," I said.

The mayor chuckled. "You know peppermint was an old remedy for indigestion, headaches, and sinus problems. Let's see what they come up with."

The Historical Society flowed into the shop. After the leader closed the door, Tiffany and I grinned at the sounds of laughter.

"I always thought the Historical Society would be stuffy, but they remind me of the historical fiction books I used to read. They are a rocking, rowdy crowd," Tiffany said.

The bell jingled, and Roger came in. His eyes narrowed, and he crossed his arms. "I'm here on official business."

I fluttered my eyelashes at Tiffany, and she mirrored Roger's stance and glared.

I rolled my eyes and crossed my arms too.

The mayor stepped out of the meeting room with an empty platter and stared at us. He shrugged and crossed his arms. "Are we playing Simon Says?"

Roger guffawed. "I tried to get a rise out of Tiffany, but all I get here is two sassy women who give me grief."

The mayor strode across the room and pumped Roger's hand. "Congratulations, son. You've reached full adult manhood." The mayor laughed. "Tiffany, can we have a refill for the platter?"

Tiffany glanced at me, and we broke our poses simultaneously.

The mayor's eyes widened as he handed the platter to Tiffany. "Awesome synchronization."

"So what's your official business, deputy?" I asked.

Roger shuffled his feet. "Sheriff says I'm assigned to keep you out of trouble, Miss Lady, but I need to talk to Tiffany first. Will you be okay if we leave for a bit?"

"Of course, I've got the mayor here, and we can hold down the fort. Take as much time as you need."

Amber came into the shop. She wore gray heels and her dark gray suit with a red silky blouse. "My dad here?"

I poured her coffee. "He's in the meeting room with the Historical Society."

She sipped her coffee. "Good. I'm supposed to get a picture of him at the meeting." She stared at the display case. "Oh dear. No maple?"

"Try a peppermint. I'd like to know what you think."

Amber took a tiny pinch and put it in her mouth. "Mm. I like this. Maple will always be my first love, but this is wonderful. Can I have one to go after I snap Dad's picture?"

When Amber opened the meeting room door, she said, "I'd like to take a couple of snapshots of my dad." The Historical Society members burst into applause and shouts of conflicting requests for pictures with the mayor.

After Amber came out of the room and closed the door, she said, "I thought I was going to just get a picture of Dad, but everyone wanted to be included in the photo. The leader tried to split up the members into six groups, but then friends had to be next to each other, and the shorter people who were behind taller members tried to climb up on chairs. Now I know how police officers feel trying to talk someone off a ledge. And naughty? I never saw so many bunny ears. I could never be a photographer."

"Sit for a break, Amber. This is why I appreciate your dad so much. The folks just love him. I'd have put them in time out for their outlandish behavior."

I refilled her coffee, and Amber stirred in extra sugar. "When I told you not to discuss Wallace or Dixon with anyone, I neglected to admonish you about staying away from killers. My mistake. The gas station is buzzing. One version says your magic saved Deputy Jeff from an attack. Are you okay?"

"There must be something I know or have that keeps me in the crosshairs of the killer, but I don't know what it is."

"I'm stumped too." Amber picked up her donut. "See you later. I'm sugar-charging for court."

Tiffany and Roger came into the shop with their arms around each other, and their faces were radiant.

"Oh my goodness," I said. "I'll sit. You tell."

"We went for a stroll to the park. Roger's accepted the position in Savannah—"

"And Tiffany said she'd marry me." Roger grinned.

I clapped. "I cannot tell you how happy I am for both of you. Does Gee know?"

"Can we go tell her right now? We won't be long." Tiffany danced on her toes.

"Of course. I'll be fine. Take the rest of the day, if you like, Tiffany. The mayor will help me."

"We won't be long. Roger has just a little time off."

After Tiffany and Roger left, I squealed. "Wedding, Colonel!"

The mayor raced out of the meeting room. "You okay?" He peered around the shop. "Where's Tiffany?"

"She and Roger went to talk to Gee. She'll be back soon."

His face lit up, and he mumbled as he returned to the meeting. "Oh boy. Oh boy. Oh boy."

I scrubbed the counter and the stools. I loaded the dishwasher and polished the sink. I gave Colonel and Mia a treat and swept the floor. I stood in the middle of the shop and scanned for another task. Colonel nudged my hand, and I scratched his ears. "I can't wait to hear what Gee said."

The meeting ended, and the Historical Society chattered as they left. The leader approached the display case. "Do you have two dozen donuts? I'd like to take them to the hospital. Actually, how many do you have left? I'll take all you've got."

"I may have a little over two dozen. I'll sell you two dozen, and you can take what I have."

After she left, the silence in the shop enveloped me.

The mayor pushed the cart to the sink. "I love that group, but they sure are noisy. When will the news about Tiffany and Roger be public? Do you know?"

"They should be back soon, and we'll find out. How did you guess?"

"Easy." He waved his hand. "Only one reason Tiffany and Roger would leave you to see Gee. I'll stick around until they get back." He unloaded the cart and returned to the meeting room to clean up.

I tackled the dirty dishes from the meeting room.

"That it?" I asked when the mayor carried trash to the back door.

"Yep. I need to sweep and take the trash to the dumpster."

I hand-washed the coffee pots and set them on the drainer to dry.

"I'm feeling antsy," I said after the mayor returned. "If I had some paint, I'd be painting the shop."

The mayor sat on the stool beside me. "If you had paint, I'd help you. What color?"

I raised my eyebrows. "I'm not authorized to make paint decisions without Woody."

"That boy is remarkable, isn't he? I understand he's really blossomed in school. Shirley has turned out to be a wonderful foster mother. I never would have guessed."

"Sometimes I forget how amazing she really is. Like every single morning when she comes in to get her coffee and donuts."

The mayor chuckled with me.

Roger's deputy car pulled up in front of the shop. After a few minutes, he swaggered to the passenger's side, opened the door, and took Tiffany's hand to help her out.

"My heart just melted. They look like a prince and a princess." I rested my hand on my chest and sighed.

Roger gave Tiffany a light kiss and stepped away.

"This is like a romantic movie," the mayor said. "We need violins playing in the background."

Roger drove away, and Tiffany waved from the porch.

Tiffany floated into the shop. "You're going to get a call from Aunt Gee, Miss Lady. She said she needs you to help her plan the wedding." Tiffany twirled, and the mayor and I applauded.

I held out my arms, and we hugged. "I'm so excited for you, Tiff."

"Would you be my Maid of Honor, Miss Lady?"

I stepped back and peered at her face. "Isn't there—"

"Nope." She raised her eyebrows. "Don't pull out your *old* card. You're my best friend."

"I'd be honored. It won't be a big wedding, will it?" I frowned.

The mayor laughed. "I'm leaving."

I sat at the counter. "Did you and Roger talk about a date?"

"He leaves for his new job in three weeks. We talked about deciding before he leaves. I was thinking in late August. Right before school starts."

"School?" When I realized my mouth was still open, I snapped my jaw shut.

"I was accepted by Georgia Southern University. I got the letter yesterday." Tiffany's eyes widened. "Oh no. I forgot to tell Roger."

"Let's lock up. You want a ride to Gee's?"

"I think I need the walk to clear my head," she said.

Jack pulled up in front of the shop as Tiffany left. Jack put the windows down, and Roxie jumped to the front seat and leaned out with a grin.

When Jack came into the shop, he stopped to pet Colonel. "Tiffany was bouncing down the road. Good news?"

"The best. She and Roger are getting married. No date yet, but they may decide in the next few weeks before Roger reports to his new job."

After I locked up, we joined Roxie in Jack's truck. On the way to my house, I said, "Tiffany asked me to be her maid of honor, and Gee wants me to help her plan the wedding. Busy times ahead."

"Perfect opportunity to exercise your magic, Donut Lady."

* * *

When we pulled up in front of my house, Jack said, "I've got a meeting with Alfred after lunch. We've got some plans to make for the summer. I kind of told him I already had lunch plans. Would you mind having lunch with me?"

"I ate lunch with Alfred once at the diner. He is so fastidious. And he eats so slowly." I chuckled. "Want to have lunch here? I have fixings for sandwiches and cold tea in the refrigerator, and brownies in the freezer."

"Best offer I've had all day." Jack picked up Mia's carrier, and we all went inside.

"Won't take me but a second to mix up chicken salad." I pulled out my ingredients and a bowl.

Jack refilled water bowls and let Colonel and Roxie out back. "Your grass is growing like crazy. I'll have the boys do a little yard maintenance tomorrow. You okay if we attack the yard tomorrow morning?"

"You don't need—" I glanced up from my cutting board. "That would be great. Want to come by the shop mid-morning, and I'll send you back with some donuts?"

Jack beamed. "The boys would love it."

Big step for me. This letting other people do things for me.

I cut the sandwiches in half and poured our tea. "Lunch is ready when you are."

"Looks good. Can we sit on the back porch?"

"I do love a picnic. Even if it's just on the porch."

While we ate and watched the dogs play, Jack said, "The latest at the gas station is that Melinda's sister identified Dixon as her attacker. As far as Melinda's concerned, the consensus is divided between accidental overdose and murder, with the majority leaning toward accidental overdose."

"Drug addicts know who else uses," I said. "I don't have any sources here though."

Jack frowned. "I might."

I rose, and the dogs raced to the porch. "What time's your meeting with Alfred?"

Jack glanced at the clock on the stove as we went inside. "In ten minutes. Want to go to the bank?"

"Actually, I wouldn't mind visiting with Todd Rockford before he leaves town. Dogs should be fine here."

When we entered the bank, the teller asked, "Where are Colonel and Roxie?"

"Hiding out in air conditioning." Jack headed to Alfred's office.

"They're the smart ones," I said. "Todd Rockford around?"

"Yes, ma'am. He's in his office." She turned to the drive-up window.

I tapped on Todd's open office door. He glanced up and flashed his boyish smile. "Ms. Karen, it's nice to see you. Please, come on in and have a seat."

"I heard you accepted a position in Atlanta and wanted to wish you the best." I returned his smile as I relaxed in the visitor chair.

He rose, closed his door, and pulled his chair to the side of his desk. "Which one of us is in trouble?"

I met his gaze. "It isn't you, so it must be me."

"Are you in danger?" The sincere look of concern on his face was heart-warming.

"Maybe, but I don't know why. I wanted to run some questions by you. Do you know if Melinda Wallace was an addict?"

"I don't think so, but that's just my gut reaction. Her soup kitchen clients would have known, and they never said anything. Some of my old childhood friends traveled a dark path for a while. Edward Wallace was a different story, however. He was rumored to be a dealer. It was never obvious how he made his living, but he threw around a lot of money and was vague where it came from."

"You know I saw you with a companion in Conway."

"I know. I also know you've never said anything, and I want you to know how much we appreciate it."

I raised my eyebrows. "We?"

He narrowed his eyes. "My wife was transferred to Atlanta."

"I understand. I had a feeling." I rose to leave.

"Wait," he said. "What can I do for you?"

"I think I'm supposed to know something about the murderer, but I don't know what it is. Was Edward moving from drugs to something else? Do you know anything about Sam Clinton?"

"Edward may have shifted his greed to dangerous ground. I can't say anything more than that. As far as Sam is concerned, have you talked to her? You might want to."

He scribbled on the back of a business card and handed it to me. The phone number had an Atlanta area code. I turned the card over. It was from the restaurant in Conway.

"I picked up the card as a souvenir," he said. "Text me anytime, especially if the nightmares are crushing."

His bank business cards were on his desk. I printed my phone number on the back of one and gave it to him. "My cell. Good to have backup."

I stuck out my hand, and Todd grabbed me in a bear hug. My face mashed into his chest, and the mix of sweat and soap reminded me of Jack.

"Oof." My voice was muffled.

Todd stepped back. The dismay on his face telegraphed his concern.

"I'm fine." I smiled. "I need more sincere spontaneity in my life. Thank you. It's good to have friends."

Todd smiled and put his arm around me while we walked to the bank lobby. Jack waited at the door and glowered. I stopped and shook Todd's hand. "Thank you, Todd. Don't let the biddies get you down."

He threw back his head and laughed. "Mr. R. told you that too, didn't he? He was certainly a force. Thanks for everything." He kissed me on the cheek and turned to his office.

Jack's face was red, and he took a step toward Todd. I wrapped my arm around his and led him to the door. "We'll talk in the truck."

"What was that all about?" Jack asked with a growl after he'd started the truck.

I pulled on his arm and held his hand. "Don't get huffy with me, mister. You're the one who helped me realize I can trust my friends."

He sighed. "So, what was that all about?"

"Todd told me to talk to Sam Clinton."

"Road trip. When do we go?" Jack asked.

"How about tomorrow after I close the shop? Do we take the dogs?" I checked my phone. "Rain tomorrow, maybe a thunderstorm. Friday might be better."

"Friday it is then. Where are we going to dinner to celebrate your new-found trust in friends?"

"You can go to dinner wherever you like." I raised my eyebrows. "I have laundry and housework to do before I can call it a night."

He stared at the road. "Okay. But we have lunch in Conway on Friday, right?"

I rolled my eyes. "Yes. Lunch on Friday."

* * *

After dinner, I relaxed on the ugly sofa with my latest book. Mia hopped onto my lap and Colonel curled on top of my feet. I propped my book at eye level on the back of the sofa and read. When my phone rang, I disentangled my feet and scooted Mia off me and onto the sofa so I could get up. The shadows slid from the hallway to the kitchen.

My eyes widened as I picked up the phone off the dining room table. "Debra, it's a surprise to hear from you."

"I'm out of the hospital and recuperating at home. We'll have a small, private service for Melinda next week. After we finalize the day and time, I'll get the details to you, but that's not why I called."

I sat on the dining chair. "I'm glad to hear you're out of the hospital. I am so sorry for your loss."

Debra spoke with a catch in her voice. "Thank you. Melinda considered you a good friend. The reason I'm calling is I need some help. Melinda always wore Mother's ring, but it wasn't—."

I turned on the burner under my teapot and waited for Debra to continue speaking. The shadows billowed into the pantry.

She cleared her throat. "She wasn't wearing it. I know she liked to remove it when she worked at the soup kitchen. I was hoping it might be there. Do you mind looking?"

"Not at all. Do you know who might have a key?"

"Maybe the building owner? I don't know, but Melinda always hid spare keys. Her two favorite hiding spots were on a nail about knee-high in a shed or taped to the underside of a table. Is there a shed or something at the soup kitchen?"

The shadows poured out of the pantry and huddled under the dining room table.

"No shed, but there's a picnic table at the park she liked. Would she have left the key in such a public place?"

"That's exactly what she would do. No one could tell what the key was for, and if they took it, Melinda always had another one hidden somewhere else."

"I'll check the park. What does the ring look like? I can't remember seeing it."

"It wasn't flashy. Silver band with a single green emerald. Our mother's birthday was in May. Her grandmother gave her the ring on her sixteenth birthday."

"I'll check the park after lunch tomorrow and give you a call."

After we hung up, I brewed my tea. "Colonel, do you suppose Melinda hid other things besides keys?" I sat on the sofa and propped up my feet. "What else could she have hidden?"

The shadows thinned, their color changed from black to pale gray, and then they disappeared.

CHAPTER ELEVEN

My neck hurt when I woke. I rose to stretch, and the floor rocked. I reached for the sofa to steady myself, but it wasn't there. Instead, I grabbed onto the railing of a sailing ship. I peered down, and giant waves washed over the deck and soaked my feet and my legs to my knees. I clutched the railing to keep from being swept overboard. The waves pulled away. *Tsunami?* My heart pounded. A foghorn sounded in the distance, and fog rolled in, except it was shadows, not fog.

I turned to run, but an open treasure chest lay at my feet. I bent down to pick up the small emerald ring on top of the jewels, and a hand reached up from the chest and grabbed me by the throat. The hand squeezed, and I couldn't breathe. I grabbed for the hand, but it wasn't there.

The shadows encircled my ankles and jerked me to the ground. They dragged me away from the chest, and I gasped for breath. I opened my mouth to scream, and hands clutched my mouth. I bit down, but they pried and pulled my jaw until I heard it snap. I tried to scream, "Find the ring; find the ring," but my jaw hung loose and guttural noises replaced my words. I rolled away from the railing and fell off the sofa.

"Find the ring; find the ring," I sobbed.

Colonel whined and licked my face. Mia mewed and licked my neck.

I leaned against the sofa. Tears rolled down my face. "Need to find the ring." I wrapped my arms around Colonel's neck and held on.

* * *

I woke at three thirty. I was on the floor with Colonel and Mia sleeping next to me. I struggled to my feet, stiff-walked to the kitchen, and put on a pot of coffee. While it perked, I headed to the shower where hot water ran down my back and loosened my tight muscles. I breathed in steam until the water turned tepid. When the spray turned cold, I stepped out and shivered as I wrapped myself in a rough, oversized towel. I coughed at the overwhelming odor of scorched coffee and left puddles behind me as I made my way to the kitchen to turn off the burner.

I opened the back door, and Colonel trotted outside. Mia meowed her complaints until I fed her. After Colonel came in, I fed him and dressed.

"Let's go, Colonel. You going, Mia?" Mia scampered into the pantry, and the shadows followed her. Mia hissed, and the shadows scattered.

* * *

The bell jingled when Colonel and I walked into the shop. Tiffany glanced up from her mixer. "You look awful. Nightmares?"

I headed to the storeroom for my apron. "This one was different though. I need to sort it out. What do you think about bacon scones with maple drizzle?"

"Pig in a poke?" She grinned.

"Do we have enough bacon?" I opened the refrigerator. "Nope. Let's plan it for tomorrow."

"How about nightmare scones? Strawberry scones with dark chocolate drizzle?"

"Sounds like therapy to me. I'll be happy to see my nightmares being gobbled up."

After Tiffany sprinkled her second batch of pink-drizzled donuts, the sheriff sauntered into the shop, and Roger swaggered in behind him. The sheriff sat on his usual stool, and I served him coffee, his two donuts and a scone. He frowned at the menu board. "I expected the pink-sprinkled and maple donuts. After all, it's Thursday. But nightmare scones?"

"Sweet and dark. Sweet, so you'll help us get rid of them, even though they are dark," I said.

"I love that," Tiffany said.

"Sweet inside and dark outside. Just like you, Sweetie," Roger said.

"What?" Tiffany dropped her wooden spoon, and it clattered on the floor.

"No. Wait. That came out wrong. You're not a nightmare." Roger's eyes were wide. "Could you change the name, Miss Lady?"

"Nope," the sheriff said. "Once it's on the board, that's it."

Tiffany and I laughed, and Roger peered at her. "So, I'm not in trouble?"

"I wouldn't go that far, Roger," I said.

The sheriff snorted and headed to the door. "Back to work. See y'all later." He waved his scone on the way out.

Roger gave Tiffany a quick peck on the cheek and hurried out behind the sheriff.

"We're terrible, aren't we?" Tiffany picked up the wooden spoon and dropped it into the sink.

The bell jingled, and Andrew opened the door with hesitation. He stared at the floor and asked in a soft voice, "May I buy a donut?"

"You most certainly may," I said. "Do you want a maple or a pink-sprinkled donut?"

"I like sprinkles." He trudged to the counter. His face was somber.

I placed a pink-sprinkled donut and two donut holes on his plate. Tiffany poured him a glass of milk.

"I don't think I have enough money for milk too." He frowned at the counter.

"Milk comes with a donut, free. Most people just skip the milk and have coffee. Might be why you didn't know that." I perched on the stool near the cash register.

"Ms. Melinda was your friend, wasn't she?" I asked.

He took a swig of milk. "Ms. Melinda was my best friend. But she died."

He crammed both donut holes into his mouth. Colonel lumbered to him, and Andrew reached down to rub his ears. He swallowed and gulped more milk.

"Milk is good with donuts," he said. "Ms. Clarissa called my mama at our hardware store. I can't work at the soup kitchen anymore."

"I'm sorry to hear that. I know you liked working there."

"Mama said it's okay. Ms. Clarissa is grouchy."

"Amen." Tiffany mumbled.

He folded his hands in his lap and stared at the floor. "Ms. Tiffany is going away to school. She's smart. She could teach me to make donuts."

Tiffany and I stared at each other. Tiffany shrugged.

"She is smart. What do you think, Ms. Tiffany?" I asked.

"I think Andrew can be my helper and learn how to make donuts." She stood in front of Andrew. "Do you want to start on Monday?"

Andrew jumped up from his seat. "Yes. I'm a hard worker. What time do you want me to be here? I can tell time."

I held my hand up and wiggled my fingers.

"Five o'clock," Tiffany said.

Andrew reached into his pocket and placed folded bills on the counter. "I'm leaving a tip for Ms. Tiffany to go to school. Mama said that's the right thing to do."

"Thank you, Andrew," Tiffany's voice cracked.

I coughed to clear my throat. "See you Monday morning, Andrew."

He nodded. "Five o'clock."

After he left, Tiffany leaned against the counter. "Don't that beat all?"

"You sounded just like Gee. We need to get moving before the book club shows up."

The bell jingled, and Jack strode into the shop. "Here to pick up donuts."

"We already packed them up for you and the boys." I set the boxes on the counter. "I wasn't sure how many, so here's three dozen donuts and two dozen donut holes. Give me a second, and I'll have a coffee and a donut for you."

"Lot of donuts here," Jack picked up the boxes. "But you know they won't go to waste. And coffee sounds great. Thanks." He frowned at the boxes and his coffee on the counter. "I'll have to make two trips. Be right back."

"I'll carry your coffee and travel donut for you," I said.

After I returned from helping Jack to the truck, Tiffany asked, "What boys?"

"Jack said my yard was out of control. He and some of Alfred's boys are trying to make me look respectable."

Amber hurried in, and I handed her two maple donuts. "How did you know?" She asked as she bit into the first one.

"You're dressed for court on book club day. Must be an important case."

"Bingo." Her voice was muffled by her last big bite of donut. "Gotta run."

* * *

At the end of our day, Tiffany asked, "Do you think Andrew will be able to pick up making donuts?"

I chuckled. "Did you know that's exactly why Woody and Shirley were here your first day?"

"No." Her eyes widened. "They thought I couldn't make donuts?"

"Woody thought you could. He said you were smart. Shirley was Shirley."

Tiffany shook her head and laughed. "So, will you be able to catch a nap this afternoon? I think Gee's got housecleaning plans for me."

"The afternoon forecast includes thunderstorms. Not my personal favorite. I may catch up on my housecleaning chores after I run a few errands."

* * *

After lunch, I rechecked the weather forecast. "No rain for two hours. Forecast still shows heavy storms later, though. Why don't you stay home, Colonel, and guard Mia?"

Colonel trotted to the front door and nudged the handle with his nose.

"Or we can both go." I grabbed my lightweight blue jacket in case the rain blew in early. "We do like to go to the park. You'll be good cover for me."

When we reached the park, Colonel whined. When I opened his car door, he chased a squirrel to a tree and peered up into the boughs while the squirrel chattered. I sauntered to Melinda's picnic table and sat on the bench seat.

Hard to believe Melinda won't appear. I miss her flair.

I peered at the ground under the table and bent to pick up a leaf. I craned my neck to examine the underside of the table.

Wow. A key.

I pulled on the tape and straightened up with an oak leaf in one hand and a key hidden in the other. I set the oak leaf on the table and examined it. Colonel trotted to my side.

"This leaf comes from a white oak tree. See the rounded edges? And that's the grand total of my knowledge about oak trees." I dropped the key into my purse as I picked it up, brushed the leaf to the ground, and ambled to the park's water faucet. I rinsed the dog bowl and filled it for Colonel. While he drank, I studied the tops of the trees. When I glanced around the park, I caught the flash of a figure as it stepped behind a tree. When Colonel finished drinking, I hung the bowl back on its hook and headed to the dog play yard. Colonel dashed to the gate and waited for me. I threw the ball for him, and he chased it. After the third time, he returned the ball to the box and stood at the gate.

"Ready?" I glanced at the sky. "Let's go home. Clouds are getting darker."

When we got home, I called Debra. Her phone rolled over to voice mail. "It's Karen. Hope you're feeling better. Catch you later."

I shuddered at the rumble of distant thunder and turned on the burner under the tea kettle. Mia head-bumped my leg, and the shadows swayed in the hallway.

"Let me make my tea, and then we can snuggle on the sofa. Y'all going to let me read?" Mia dashed to the sofa and claimed the corner next to my lamp. The shadows slid into the pantry.

After my tea brewed, I moved Mia and turned on the light. Mia curled around my feet, and Colonel flopped next to the sofa. I sipped my tea and opened my book.

A sharp crash of thunder woke me. The house was dark. I reached for my flashlight in the table drawer. When I turned it on, the shadows slipped away. I held my book in one hand and the flashlight in the other.

"I need a headlamp so I can read. It's too hard to hold the book and turn pages with one hand." Colonel jumped on the sofa and laid his head on my book.

"I know you'd help if you could. Thanks, Colonel."

My phone rang, and I disengaged myself from my guards. *Jack.* "You doing okay, Karen? I know storms aren't your favorite these days."

"No electricity, but we're fine."

"I'll be right there."

"No. I'd worry about you on the road. We're fine. Really. I have my flashlight, a cup of tea, Mia, and Colonel."

"Let me know if anything changes. I'll be there after the storm passes by."

I rolled my eyes after he hung up. "I'd say he's a worrywart, Colonel. But it's kind of nice to have a friend who cares."

My phone rang. *Gee.* "You okay? We don't have any power."

"I don't either, but we're fine. Colonel and Mia are good company."

"Mandy is the poster child of relaxed. Sandy, however, is taking the storm personally. He's at the window hissing." She chuckled. "Call if you need us. I told Tiffany witches love storms, except when a house falls on them, or a tree falls on their house."

I laughed. "You're terrible, Gee. I'm proud of you."

"It's what I do," she said as she hung up.

As I set my phone on the table, it rang. *Shirley.* "Hello, Miss Lady. Ms. Shirley said I could call you," Woody said.

"Thanks for calling, Woody. We're fine."

"We don't have any lights, but Ms. Shirley gave me a flashlight. Chase doesn't like storms. She's sitting on my lap."

"Mia and Colonel are sitting with me too. Thanks for calling." *I have friends. Real friends.*

* * *

After the storm subsided, Jack called. "I'll be there soon. I want to check your yard after the storm."

"I have some errands to run. I won't be here."

"What about dinner? You have any plans?"

"I actually do. I plan to have a grilled cheese and go to bed early." I crossed my fingers. *Hope he takes this the right way.*

Jack cleared his throat. "But we're still going to Conway tomorrow, right?"

"Of course. I'm just tired, not angry."

"Good. Not good that you're tired, but you know."

"I know. I meant to tell you the yard looked nice when I got home. I'm sure it appreciated the rain. Why don't you inspect tomorrow when you pick me up to go to Conway?"

"I do have some things I could take care of around here. One of my old trees lost several branches. Didn't hit anything, but the driveway's a mess."

After we hung up, I jotted down my grocery list. Colonel joined me at the door when I was ready to leave. "I thought you'd stay here, but it might be smart to have a little backup."

I parked in the alley in back of the soup kitchen. "I'm nervous about advertising that we're here. Let's see if the key works in the back door."

The key unlocked the door. I relocked it after we went inside. The eerie silence was broken by the clicks of Colonel's nails on the tile. The snick-snick of my shoes and his taps echoed down the hall.

I had forgotten Melinda's office had been searched. It was still a mess of overturned furniture and papers on the floor. I started with the desk, and Colonel flopped on the floor near the hallway.

I inspected and then righted the wheeled office chair to sit. When I pulled on the middle drawer, it opened only part way. I found a letter opener and slid it under the drawer where it seemed stuck. When I tugged hard, the drawer came out. I flipped it over and found a manila envelope taped to the bottom of the drawer. "Well, this goes with us." I put it in a grocery sack that I found on the floor. I sorted through the drawer contents. *No ring.* My search of the remaining drawers turned up nothing. No false bottoms. No more taped items.

I turned in the chair to rise and spied an electrical outlet behind me with one of the screws loose. I used the letter opener to unscrew the plate. I hoped to find a ring, but there was nothing inside except wires. I replaced the plate. *No sense in giving away secrets.*

"Maybe I'm overthinking this, Colonel. Melinda wasn't hiding her ring. She just took it off when she was working." I smacked my forehead. "In the kitchen."

I picked up the sack, and Colonel and I clicked and snicked to the kitchen. "Most people take off rings and put them on the sink, but rings get knocked down the drain. Melinda wouldn't take the chance."

I stood in the doorway with my hands on my hips. "If I took off my ring every time I worked in the kitchen, I'd always put it in the same place. Right, Colonel?" I scanned the kitchen. "I'd first go to the handwashing sink." I opened the last drawer on my right before I reached the sink. *The ring!*

Colonel and I headed to the back door. Colonel raised his hackles and growled—soft and low. The scratching of a key at the front door made my skin crawl.

"Let's go, boy." I whispered.

We went out the back door, and I locked it behind us. When we arrived at the grocery store, Colonel took his position near the entrance to greet customers while I shopped.

Clarissa was in the produce section. *Maybe she won't notice me.* She popped grapes into her mouth and glanced around. She glared at me and flounced to the rice and beans section.

I picked out three apples and headed to the meat section for bacon. I loaded my cart with bacon and wheeled to the checkout.

Clarissa came up behind me. "I have only three items, Karen. Can I go in front of you?"

"The ten items or less lane is empty. Might be quicker if you go over there." I smiled.

She glowered and stomped to the lane next to me. Before she reached it, another customer stepped in front of her with a cart. I squinted at the magazine rack to keep from laughing.

She waited outside. "You think you're so smart, Karen. I'm going to be the next director of the soup kitchen. You should have been nice to me. Not only will your donuts not be allowed there, but I know you went to prison for murdering your husband. I'll bet you murdered Melinda and my Eddie too." She stormed to her car.

"She's one angry cuss, isn't she, Colonel?"

Colonel and I dropped the bacon off at the shop. By the time we got home, the sky was red and orange as the sun slid into the horizon.

After I fed Colonel and Mia, I grilled my cheese and green chili sandwich. While I ate, my phone rang. *Debra.* "Forget what I said about the ring. You need to stay away from the soup kitchen. I hear Wallace was in deeper than we thought. Just stay away. I'll get the ring when I'm well enough. Gotta go."

She hung up before I could say anything.

"Well, that was bizarre. So, what do I do with the ring?" I pulled the ring out of my pocket and put it on the table. *Plain sight will have to do for now.* I dropped the ring into my junk drawer along with other costume jewelry that I'd never worn but couldn't bear to part with.

I opened the manila envelope and found a stack of papers. *Invoices?* I slipped the envelope into a file folder and dropped the folder in with my old tax papers. *Maybe not my best idea, but I'm tired.*

CHAPTER TWELVE

The alarm sounded. I opened one eye. *No ocean waves or floods. Maybe I'm awake.* I kept one eye closed and hung my legs over the side of the bed. Colonel tapped into my bedroom and licked my knee. "Thank you, boy." I plodded to the kitchen and let him out.

"Happy Friday, Mia." She darted out of the pantry when I poured her food into her bowl.

Colonel ate while I dressed. When Colonel and I approached the front door, Mia scooted into her carrier.

After I opened the shop door, I moaned at the sweet aroma of hickory-smoked bacon.

"Good morning, Miss Lady. I found the bacon." Tiffany waved her spatula.

"We may want to double up on the scones. What do you think?"

I pulled my apron off its hook and checked the calendar. "D.R. Board meeting. Did I put that on the calendar?"

"Ms. Darlene called earlier this week. I can't remember what you were doing. She's the chairwoman of the soup kitchen board."

I grimaced. "What do you think she'll say about our bacon scones?"

"I can make them more ladylike with a little addition of a splash of red drizzle." Tiffany bit her lip.

"Lipstick on a pig?" I snort-laughed and laughed even harder at my snort. After I settled down, I wiped my eyes. "Yes. Let's do pig in a poke for scones and add bacon to our batter for lipstick on a pig."

"Oh lord," Tiffany said. "I may just have the shortest engagement in history. What else?"

"How about blueberry drizzle for support the blue?"

"National Law Enforcement Day. Got it. I'll post the menu. Too bad we didn't come up with this yesterday. Aunt Gee has a big ole pink piggy bank."

"Really? You mind calling her and asking if Isaiah can bring it by? I'll give Shirley a quick call."

Ten minutes later, Isaiah tapped on the door. He carried a garish pink pig the size of a five-gallon bucket in his arms. I hurried to open the door for him. He placed it on the reading table. "If this isn't where you want it, Miss Lady, tell me. You don't want to try to move it. Mama says after you collect your money, smash the pig. She doesn't want it back, and there's no other way to get the money out. There's already some money in it. When she had it on display, people dropped in coins."

I stared. "That is one ugly pig. It's a wonder she didn't con me into taking it when I got the ugly sofa and the ugly chair."

Isaiah chuckled. "When I asked her, she said she felt sorry for you with your house falling in on you and all. I'm grounded for saying she missed an opportunity."

Twenty minutes after Isaiah left, Shirley and Woody trooped into the shop. Woody carried posters.

"You got your stands, Karen? Woody designed the poster while I fixed his breakfast. I actually put a bowl, a spoon, a glass of milk, and two boxes of cereal on the table. I like to give him a choice. He ate while I printed."

"We're an awesome team." Woody beamed.

"Yes, you are," I said. "Thanks, Shirley for jumping right on it. The posters are great, Woody. I love the font you chose for National Law Enforcement Day, and your *Feed the Pig and Support Foster Care?* Cute design. Love all the children holding baby pigs."

Tiffany leaned over my shoulder. "You drew the kids and pigs, didn't you, Woody? In what? Ten minutes? You are one talented dude."

Woody hung his head. "Thanks, Tiffany. Ms. Shirley got me some awesome software and a tablet for drawing on the computer."

I handed the three posters and a pen to Woody. "Please sign them for me. An artist needs to sign his work."

Woody glanced at Shirley who nodded. He scrawled his name on each poster.

As they left, Shirley brushed away tears from her cheeks and mouthed, "Thank you, Karen."

After they left, Tiffany said, "I got a little choked up too. I'm in awe of Woody's talent and Ms. Shirley's ability to bring it out. And have you noticed how ideas explode in this shop?"

"They do, don't they?" I tilted my head and admired Woody's posters before I headed to our prep area. "Break's over. We need to finish up before the sheriff comes in."

"Yes, ma'am." Tiffany saluted and hurried back to her fryer while I mixed the third batch of scones.

The bell jingled, and the sheriff sauntered in. He stared at the board. "We need to get the water tested in here. You two are demented. So, we've got *Pig in a Poke*, *Lipstick on a Pig*, and *Support the Blue*." The sheriff narrowed his eyes. "Explain."

I stared at the ceiling.

"Okay, fine." Tiffany grumbled. "The bacon scone with maple drizzle is the pig in the poke. The bacon donut with strawberry drizzle is the lipstick on the pig, and the classic with blueberry drizzle is support the blue line. All Miss Lady's ideas. I just do as I'm told." She smirked and crossed her arms.

The sheriff guffawed, and I applauded. Tiffany curtsied using her apron and turned back to her fryer and drizzles.

I poured coffee for the sheriff and gave him one of each pastry. "In honor of National Law Enforcement Day, all donations go to the county Foster Care program."

The sheriff bit into the scone first. "This is really good. My compliments to the unhinged minds who come up with this stuff. Is it really National Law Enforcement Day?"

"Is now." Tiffany and I said in unison. We high-fived as Roger swaggered into the shop.

"Why do I feel this will not end well for me?" He stared at the board.

Tiffany poured him coffee, and the bell jingled when Darlene Rothenberger rolled in with her walker. She stopped short and read the board. The mayor bustled in behind her and almost crashed into her.

"Ah," he said. "National Law Enforcement Day. Glad you took my suggestion to celebrate today with donations to the county Foster Program." He winked when he breezed past me to the storeroom for his apron.

"What do you think, Darlene?" He asked when he returned wearing his pink *Got Sprinkles?* cap and apron.

"I think it's brilliant," she said. "Must have been Tiffany's idea." The mayor took Darlene's arm and walked her to the meeting room.

"She's always been smart, you know," Darlene continued.

"Ms. Darlene's right, you know," Roger said.

I stood behind him and batted my eyelashes.

"Miss Lady, you are so annoying sometimes." Tiffany slammed a platter of donuts onto the utility cart, marched into the storeroom, and slammed the door.

"Am I in trouble?" Roger asked.

"Dare you to go ask Tiffany," the sheriff said. "More coffee, please?" He drained his cup.

I refilled the sheriff's cup and poured a cup for myself. "Go." I waved at the storeroom.

The rest of the board strolled in and stopped to stare at the board and the pig.

"Come in, please," the mayor said. "The meeting's in here."

The board members filed into the meeting room. When the sounds of laughter and applause came from the room, I exhaled.

"You are not allowed to ever win a lottery." The sheriff sipped a coffee. "I need my daily dose of deranged. Keeps me sane."

I spewed my coffee, and he jumped up from his seat and danced a jig.

"Talk about demented," I mumbled as I cleaned the counter and dabbed at my apron.

Darlene stepped out of the meeting room, and the sheriff froze. She said, "Carry on, Sheriff. Nice to see people who are happy. Karen, may I speak to you privately for a minute?"

Darlene took my arm, and we strolled to the back door. "What do you think of Clarissa? Just between you and me. I need to know."

"Not much." I met her gaze.

"Thank you." She returned to the meeting room.

"Sheriff, what can you tell me about Debra?" I asked.

"Why?" He peered at me.

"She called me and asked me to get something for her. Then called me back and essentially told me never mind. Is she impulsive? Do you know?"

"I know her only professionally. I wouldn't think she's impulsive, but I really don't know. Was it anything I need to know about?"

"I don't think so. She said she'd take care of it when she's well."

He drank his coffee. "And you can live with that. Right?"

"Sure can. I've got plenty going on without more complications."

The bell jingled, and Jack strolled in. "Am I in the wrong place?" He asked.

"Nope." The sheriff winked at me. "Complications," he said in a soft voice.

"Tell my deputy he still works for this county if you see him." The sheriff put folded bills into the pig. Roger tore out of the storeroom and opened the front door.

"Ready to go back on duty, Deputy?" the sheriff asked.

"Yes sir." Roger held the door for the sheriff and blew a kiss to Tiffany, who stood outside the storeroom door.

The board meeting broke up. Each board member filed past the pig and deposited a check. I could have sworn Darlene was the only one that required assistance in walking when they came in, but each woman hung onto the arm of the mayor or Jack as she fed the pig.

Tiffany's eyes were wide. "What's going on?"

"Looks like the grand promenade to me," I said.

"Part of the service." The mayor scooted back to the meeting room to assist the next board member.

"I heard at the gas station about National Law Enforcement Day at the Donut Hole," each customer who came into the shop said.

"We've got a regular busted fire hydrant stream of people showing up this morning." Tiffany filled another large pot to brew coffee for the benefactors who jostled for coffee and National Law Enforcement Day donuts and scones. "Isn't it great?"

Tess raced in. "Fill up some boxes for the department. I've got a boatload of cash for the pig. Pigs feeding the pig. They said that. Not me." She giggled and handed a sack to the mayor. "Who will smash the pig, Ms. Karen? You going to take a photo? We need one for the department wall. This will be an annual, right? Tiffany, you're awesome. Roger can't stop talking about you. He's really proud of you. We all are."

"What's he saying, Tess? Is he mad at me?"

"It's all for a good cause. Just roll with it, honey." Tess laughed.

"Tess, would you send the sheriff here around eleven thirty to smash the pig?"

"Sure will." Tess carried her boxes of pastries out of the shop.

"This is going to be the shortest—"

"Oh hush, Tiffany. Just roll with it, O Deranged One," I said.

"We've got enough donuts and scones for an hour or so at this pace," Tiffany said. "You okay with that?"

"Absolutely. I can take being nice just so long."

Tiffany snorted. "I knew that."

Another group of customers trooped inside. I was heads-down taking money while Tiffany handed out donuts and scones. The mayor and Jack diverted everyone to the pig before each customer left. I smiled at my next customer and realized it was Silas.

"Looks like it's going great, Karen. Congratulations. You're a marketing genius, but you know that."

"Thanks, Doc. Everything going well with you?"

"Sure is." He glanced around and lowered his voice. "I heard Debra's under investigation for Melinda's death. Something about not reporting Melinda's drug dealing or something. Did you know about that?"

My eyes widened. "No. So, Melinda was involved with drugs?"

"Sure was. Not easy for most people to spot a drug abuser. Guess you're not that experienced. They're good at fooling people."

"My goodness. Who would have thought?" I shook my head and turned to my next customer.

Silas strode to the front door without buying anything. I snickered when the mayor collared him and accompanied him to the pig. Silas pulled out his wallet with a reluctance that rivaled a slow-motion football play on television.

The customers dwindled toward the end of the morning. The sheriff and Roger showed up at eleven thirty. Roger carried a hammer. "Tess sent us with a hammer, just in case," the sheriff said. "Who's taking pictures?"

"I will," Jack said.

"Mayor, you need to be in the picture too," I said. "Keep your cap and apron on. You're our official walking billboard for the Donut Hole."

"Billboard?" The mayor chuckled.

"Or representative. Sometimes words escape me." I rolled my eyes.

"Not believing that," Tiffany said.

The bell jingled, and Gee and Isaiah rushed into the shop with Andrew in tow. "We stopped to pick up Andrew at his parents' hardware store. We couldn't miss this," Gee said.

The sheriff stood in front of the pig with the hammer poised to strike. "Can't do it. There's something sacrilegious about a sheriff breaking a pig. It's in the oath of office or something. You do it, Donut Lady. On behalf of the foster children."

"What? Is this a setup?"

"Yes, ma'am." Tiffany giggled.

"Go ahead, Old Woman. Do it," Gee said.

"Okay, but I'm not using a hammer. What do we have, Tiffany?"

"We've got Mr. R.'s old rolling pin. I don't use it because it's so heavy."

"Hand it here. If it bounces off and knocks me unconscious, Gee, it's on you."

Gee crossed her arms. "Just do it."

The mayor stepped back. "I have every confidence in you, Donut Lady. Pieces of ceramic will fly everywhere."

I clutched the rolling pin with two hands, raised my arms up over my head, and slammed the pig square between the eyes as hard as I could. I lost my balance when the rolling pin shattered the pig's head and bounced on the table. The mayor caught me before I fell, and everyone applauded.

"Man, that was one great action shot," Isaiah said.

"You streamed it?" Tiffany asked.

"Sure enough." Isaiah flashed a thumbs-up. "And just got a text from Josh at the gas station. He said *awesome*."

The pig's head was busted open, and its face had fallen onto the floor.

"Why did you go for the head, Karen?" Jack asked.

"I'm not answering that." I flipped my hair, and Gee snickered.

Jack pulled out the money, and the mayor and Roger counted it. Andrew pulled over a trash can and swept the floor while Tiffany picked up the larger pieces.

"Okay if we have a training day tomorrow? Tiffany asked.

I nodded.

"Andrew," Tiffany said, "Would you like to be here tomorrow for your first training day?"

"Yes, ma'am. I'll be here at five o'clock."

Roger and the mayor left to deliver the funds to the county office.

"Everything's cleaned up, Miss Lady," Tiffany said. "Okay if I go with Aunt Gee?"

After everyone left, I locked up, and Colonel, Mia, and I headed home where Jack's truck was parked at the curb. He strode from the corner from the front yard to the side of the house.

When I opened the back door to let Colonel out, Jack pointed at a tree in the middle of the yard. "There's a broken limb about halfway up. The boys and I can take care of it tomorrow. You ready to leave?"

"Soon as Colonel is inside. I'll meet you out front."

As we headed to Conway, I asked, "What do you know about Silas Howe?"

"Not that much. He retired ten or so years ago and keeps to himself. I don't see much of him around town. Why?"

"Just wondering. He doesn't seem to have cared much for Melinda."

"I can't imagine what the connection might have been."

"Have you ever thought about raising goats?" I pointed at a handmade sign painted on a piece of plywood: *Goats for Sale.*

"Can't say that I have. What about you?"

"Not really, but I like to watch them."

Jack pointed at a field. "Corn looks good." He drummed his fingers on the steering wheel and turned on the radio. Country music blasted through the speakers, and I covered my ears. Jack reached for the volume and turned it down. "Sorry. Roxie and I drive with the windows down."

I chuckled. "Colonel and I do too. Sometimes we forget the windows are down when we ride through town, and one of our favorite songs comes on. I sing, and he howls."

"What kind of music do you like?" Jack asked.

"Mostly 70s. Decade of unappreciated music." A roadside sign marked the Conway city limits. "Wow. We're in Conway. Time went by fast."

"I found a café that specializes in salads and ice cream." Jack grinned.

"Are you kidding?"

He shook his head. "Ice cream is no joking matter."

"I agree."

When we entered the café, we were greeted by the sweet aroma of home-churned ice cream. The lime-sherbet colored walls were dotted with drawings of vegetables riding in hot air balloons and all imaginable colors of ice cream in cones. While we stood in line at the café, I stared at the menu overhead. "Blue Yardbird sounds great, Chicken, blue cheese, pecans, strawberries, and blueberries. Yum."

"I think I'll have Wild Boar. Barbeque pork with hot sauce and pickles sounds good, but how can that be a salad?" He squinted at the board. "Oh. Wild Boar Salad on a Bun. That's what I'm having."

I chuckled. "Salads for every taste. Smart folks."

We found a booth and sipped sweet tea. "How do you know Todd Rockford?" Jack asked.

"I know him from the bank. Shirley and I talked to him about remodeling the shop. But there's no good way to explain why I trust him without betraying a confidence." I stared at my hands. "A glib answer would be that I knew his family, but that's not true." I met Jack's gaze. "He's a good friend."

Jack nodded. "Thank you."

A young man in jeans and a green shirt brought us our plates and refilled our tea. We dug in, and after we ate, I read through the three pages of the ice cream menu. When the young man appeared, I said, "Black cherry with sprinkles."

"Yes, ma'am. Single or double? Cup, sugar cone, or waffle cone?"

"Sugar cone. Single scoop."

"Mint chocolate chip. Single scoop. Sugar cone," Jack said.

We waited at the cash register for our cones and took them outside. We strolled down the block to window-shop while we ate our ice cream.

"This is the way to eat ice cream," Jack said. "Hot, humid day. Blistering heat from the sidewalk, except I think we're supposed to be barefooted and jumping from shady spot to shady spot. Eat your ice cream as fast as you can before it melts down your hand, but not so fast you get a brain freeze."

I laughed and licked the side of my cone where ice cream dripped.

"Great lunch. Thank you," I said after we climbed into the truck.

On our way to Sam Clinton's, Jack asked, "Do you want me to wait or go inside with you?"

"Let's play it by ear."

The front yard was mowed, and the peeling paint had been scraped and touched up. A real estate *For Sale* sign was posted in the yard.

"Interesting," Jack said.

When we reached the porch, I rang the doorbell.

The young woman who answered the door was slim and just over five feet tall. She had straight, long black hair and dark skin. A toddler hung onto one leg, and an older boy peeked from behind her. Their big dark eyes stared at me.

My eyes widened, and she laughed. "Come on in, Donut Lady. Todd told me to expect you. This is Jack?" She held out her hand, and they shook hands.

"Just give me a second. I was about to give the boys a snack."

Except for a few scattered toys, the living room was clean and tidy. "We have a potential buyer coming to look at the house later today. My challenge is to stay two steps ahead of these boys."

I followed her into the kitchen, and Jack stayed in the living room. The eat-in kitchen was cheery. The boys munched on carrot sticks and crackers and slurped their milk.

"I'm Sam Clinton's sister. My name's Marty. Martha Rockford, but you probably figured that out. The boys are my nephews, and Todd and I are in the process of adopting them. My sister died earlier this year in a tragic crash—just before Charlie turned two. Her husband was Edward Wallace's nephew. Chuck died while she was pregnant. He was in law enforcement too. In fact, that's how they met. Chuck and I worked together. Can I offer you some tea?"

I sat at the dinette with the boys. "I'm fine. We just had lunch at the Salad and Ice Cream café."

"Well, you are set then. So that's the quick background. What can I tell you? Oh, one other thing. After Chuck died, Edward Wallace deeded the house to Sam and set up an annuity for her. Wallace had been estranged from the family for years. Evidently, he and Chuck had kept in touch. Making arrangements for Chuck's children is probably the only decent thing he's ever done."

"So, you were investigating Wallace?"

"I can't really discuss any of that with you, but I remember you from the diner." She winked.

"Some people are saying that Melinda murdered Wallace." I put my hand on the table, and the littlest one handed me a half-eaten carrot.

Marty laughed. "Charlie likes you. Melinda would never do anything like that. I didn't know her, but Todd liked her. Todd doesn't like just anybody. You know that."

"It appears that I have something from Melinda that the killer wants. At least that's the feeling I have. There are so many side players with private agendas, it's hard to differentiate between fact and distracting rabbit trails."

"Welcome to my world." Marty shook her head. "I can tell you I think you are wise to trust your feelings. You do have a reputation, you know. I've attended classes with Roger."

I shook my head and laughed. "I can see why you and Todd are relocating. This area might be a little crowded for you to work."

"You are so right. Todd and I have been talking about it for a while. He's looking forward to being a stay at home dad. He might take on a freelance contract once in a while after Charlie's a little older. Or not."

The six-year-old drained his milk and stood next to me. "You're like my teacher."

I raised my eyebrows at Marty. She said, "Caleb."

"Thank you, Caleb. I used to be a teacher."

"I know that. I like teachers." He stayed by my side.

"Well, it's unanimous," Marty said. "You've received the full family approval, Ms. Donut Lady."

"What can I do for you, Marty?" I asked.

She furrowed her brow and stared at me. "Surprising question. I don't know. Give me your cell phone number. It's nice to have contacts."

I pulled out my Donut Hole business card. "That's my cell phone. Text or call anytime."

She scrawled on the back of my card and gave it back to me. It said *Chuck* with a phone number. "That's my personal cell. Chuck recorded the voice message for me, so don't be put off if you call."

I gave her another Donut Hole card.

"Can I have a card too, Donut Lady?" Caleb asked.

"Card," Charlie said.

I gave each boy a card.

"Consider us your personal fan club," Marty chuckled.

"Thank you for your time, Marty." I rose to leave.

Marty helped Charlie out of his booster seat, and the boys and I marched to the living room. Marty followed us.

"Here's the parade," Jack said. "Are we ready to go, Donut Lady?"

"Yes, we are." When I reached the door, I said, "Thank you, for everything."

"Thank you, Ms. Karen. We enjoyed meeting you."

When we pulled away, Jack asked, "Good meeting?"

"Yes, I understand why Todd wanted me to meet Sam. We'll talk about it later. Right now, I've got a lot to process. Is that okay?"

"No." He peeked at me and chuckled. "Of course, it's okay. Let me know anytime you need a sounding board. Meanwhile, what do we talk about on the way back? Oh look, there are some longhorns. What do you know about raising longhorns?"

"I don't know anything. I think I'd be better off with chickens on my hypothetical farm. What about sheep? Which are easier to take care of goats or sheep?"

"Oh man. Now my brain's spinning. Sounds like a fun research project," he said.

"Does, doesn't it? Where do we start?"

"Check the county extension. See if there are any classes."

I pulled out my phone. "Poultry classes too?"

"Might as well," Jack said. "Do I need to start reading up on building chicken coops?"

"Hypothetically, yes." I mumbled while I searched for classes on the extension website. "Here's a class on growing mushrooms. That might be more my speed. Less likely to stress over a mushroom failing to thrive."

Jack slowed the truck. "And here we are. Asbury."

"Thanks for being my chauffeur, and lunch was great."

"I'm going in with you to be sure everything's okay, and then I'll see you tomorrow. The boys and I will clean up the trees in the morning."

After Jack left, I fed Colonel and Mia while the shadows frolicked.

After I climbed into bed, I remembered. *The papers from Melinda's desk. Tomorrow. Too tired.*

CHAPTER THIRTEEN

The alarm sounded. I plodded to the back door and let Colonel out. *Papers.* I pulled out the file folder and slipped it into the pocket on Mia's carrier. *I'll look over the documents at the shop when we have a lull.*

The three of us entered the shop as Tiffany covered her first batch of dough. "I have Andrew's training plan written up for today. I'll have the plan for the week on Monday."

I checked the calendar. *No meetings.* I pulled out a new apron and ball cap for Andrew and set them on the counter near the cash register. "Here's Andrew's uniform. What's the plan for donuts?"

"Classic glazed and chocolate dipped donuts."

"Excellent. I'll make cinnamon scones with vanilla glaze. I have a feeling we'll have a big crowd today. Might want to make five batches. No, make it six."

Andrew appeared at the door at ten minutes to five. When I opened the door, he said, "Mama helped me sign up for food safety classes."

"That's great, Andrew. The Donut Hole pays for training. Ms. Tiffany has your work plan for today."

Tiffany showed Andrew how to drizzle a classic. She did one, and then he drizzled two.

"Well done," she said. "Drizzle this batch, and then we'll work on chocolate dipped."

When the sheriff came in, Andrew had finished up his first two batches of drizzled and dipped donuts and was drizzling scones.

I poured two cups of coffee, one for the sheriff and a second one for me. Andrew served the sheriff his donuts and scone with Tiffany's coaching.

"Thank you, Andrew. Did you help make the donuts?"

"Yes, sir. I drizzled the classic and scone and dipped the chocolate."

"Nicely done," the sheriff bit into the classic and sipped his coffee "You'll be getting a letter of appreciation from the foster care folks, Donut Lady. Y'all are geniuses at raising money and awareness. I hear more people signed up yesterday for the foster parent training than signed up year to date."

"I didn't even think of that." My voice cracked, and my cheeks warmed.

"Emma signed us up. She told me she's been thinking about adopting siblings, but she decided the foster program is where we're needed right now."

I cleared my throat and sipped my coffee.

"You're a softie," the sheriff said in a quiet voice.

I scowled. "Don't let it get around."

Sheriff snorted and finished off his chocolate donut. "I'm taking my scone for my snack. I've got paperwork to catch up on."

Papers! "Can you and Andrew hold down the fort, Tiffany? I've got paperwork to do."

"Sure, Miss Lady."

I picked up Mia's carrier and went into the storeroom. I closed the door, pulled the papers out, and sat at my desk. I read the first page, flipped to the next to read. More of the same. *Dates, initials, amounts of— drug orders?*

I peeked out. *No Roger.* I put the envelope back in Mia's carrier and stuck her carrier under my desk. *I don't want to call in and create a big production.* I sent the sheriff a text: "Stop by shop later."

The, bell jingled, and Shirley and Woody came into the shop. Woody had his clipboard.

"Hi, Andrew. Glad you're working with Ms. Tiffany. She's nice."

"Yes. She's not grumpy," Andrew said.

"I take inventory on Saturdays." Woody headed to the storeroom.

"I know," Andrew said.

"I hear people signed up for the foster parent training program in droves yesterday," Shirley said. "I got calls asking me questions. I told them the program had a pamphlet that answers all the questions much better than I can. I'm not a foster program expert. At all. I learn something new every day. That's good, right? Did I tell you what the emergency agent meeting was all about? Some of the agents tried to change the logo colors for the association. They said the colors were outdated. They might be right, but they tried to go behind the officers' backs. Not the smartest move, right? So, two agents are on probation now. I never knew an agent could be put on probation, but Charlotte had the charter and pointed it out. It was fascinating. The vote wasn't even close. Wasn't Woody's artwork amazing? He says he works best under pressure. I don't. I get too flustered when—"

"Shirley. Coffee?" I placed her coffee on the counter. "That's my subtle way to say take a breath, you know."

Shirley pursed her lips and nodded. She sat with her coffee and a donut at the counter and relaxed her shoulders. "Love coffee," she said.

Andrew uncovered his ears and carried dishes to the sink. Tiffany rinsed a dish and placed it in the dishwasher, and then Andrew copied her.

"Shirley, weren't you and Woody scheduled to have dinner with Alfred last night?"

She nodded and smiled with her lips still pursed.

I rolled my eyes. *Of all times for her to decide to keep quiet.*

Woody came out of the storeroom. "Got my list. Time for our donut, Miss Lady?"

"Sure is."

Woody sat next to Shirley, and I poured my coffee and his milk while Tiffany served up our traditional Saturday donuts.

Woody bowed his head and held hands with Shirley. Andrew mimicked Woody and folded his hands. Tiffany glanced at Andrew and did the same.

"Thank you for donuts, family, and friends," Woody said.

"Amen," Shirley said.

"Andrew, Miss Lady and I eat a donut together every Saturday," Woody said.

"Yes," Andrew said. "What's next, Ms. Tiffany?"

"Rinse utensils and scrub bowls and pans."

Woody finished his donut and milk. "Ready to go shopping, Ms. Shirley?"

"You know I'm well now," I said. "I can do my own shopping."

"No, you can't." Shirley frowned. "Woody and I look forward to shopping together for you every Saturday."

"Then I can fill in anytime you need me to," I said.

The sheriff came in as they were leaving. "Needed a break from desk work," he said.

"I've got a paperwork question. Can you come to my office? Need coffee?"

"Maybe later," he said.

I closed the storeroom door behind us. "Do you want to sit?" I asked.

"No. What's going on?"

"I found some papers in Melinda's office."

He sat. "Of course, you did."

"Debra called me and asked me to look for her mother's ring. She thought it might be in Melinda's office at the soup kitchen. Melinda hid a key under a picnic table in the park."

He shook his head. "You'll fill me in about that later, right?"

"Anytime. Anyway, the key was to the soup kitchen. At first, I thought Melinda hid the ring in her office. I looked for it and found a manila envelope taped to the bottom of her desk drawer."

"And you'll give me more details about that too?"

"Yes. I realized she wouldn't hide the ring while she worked; she'd just put it somewhere safe. I found it in a drawer in the kitchen. And then Colonel growled, and I heard someone unlock the front door. So, we left by the back door. I parked in the alley. I forgot to tell you."

"Does this have a short version?"

"This is the short version."

He sighed. "I was afraid of that."

"So, then Debra called me and told me not to bother getting her mother's ring. I didn't tell her I already did. Or that I found an envelope."

"I'd forgotten about the envelope," the sheriff said.

"So did I." I pulled it out of the file drawer and handed it to the sheriff. "I remembered it last night. I'd put it—never mind, that's the long version. I brought it with me to work this morning. I looked through it and sent you the text."

He frowned. "That's it?"

"Yes. Short version. Oh, one more thing—"

He glowered.

"—after you look at these."

He opened the envelope and read the first page. His eyes widened, and he flipped through the remaining pages. "Who knows you have this?"

"No one. I put the drawer back before I left."

He leaned back in the chair. "You didn't see who came into the building?"

"No. Colonel and I left, and before you ask, no one could have seen my car unless they drove down the alley."

"Thanks. Stay close to your phone. I'll get back to you as soon as I find out what's best for you. What was that one more thing?"

"Before Melinda's house burned, she showed me bundles of blank paper she'd found in a closet that were two inches or so wide and six inches long. All uniform. She must have dropped a small stack of them in the basket when we packed up Pepper's things."

The sheriff's eyebrows raised.

"Anyway, I found the stack when I put the basket away. I'd forgotten about it until we talked about paper. I have them in here." I pulled an envelope out of my file cabinet and handed it to the sheriff.

"That's it? Nothing else?"

"Not that I can think of offhand."

The sheriff shook his head and left with the envelopes.

Tiffany asked, "Are you okay, Miss Lady?"

"Yep. Just needed a professional opinion on some of my paperwork."

"We got a call from Alfred. His boys are helping people clean up yards this morning from the storm. He wanted to know if we had ten dozen donuts. The men's church groups have jumped in to help. He wants to surprise all the workers. The mayor's going to pick up."

"We have that many?"

"Sure do." She unfolded donut boxes. "Andrew, I always ask Miss Lady how many donuts to make. The recipe book of secrets says make three to five batches. Sometimes Miss Lady has a feeling we need more, and we always do."

"Yes," said Andrew.

The mayor showed up in his ballcap. "Can I take an apron?"

"Certainly," I said. "The donuts are on us."

"Nope. Not acceptable. Alfred said you'd say that. He wants to pay for them. No special discount either." The mayor smiled and grabbed his apron from the storeroom. "He already wrote the check. Here ya go. And he included money for Tiffany's school fund."

"That's amazing. Thanks. And thanks to Alfred."

"Between you and me, I think Ms. Shirley has had an impact on our local banker." The mayor winked.

Tiffany and Andrew helped the mayor load up his car with donuts.

"Are Ms. Shirley and Mr. Alfred seeing each other?" Tiffany asked when she and Andrew returned. "Funny, she hasn't said anything."

"She mentioned that she and Woody were going to advise Alfred on a project, but I couldn't get any details out of her this morning."

Tiffany inspected the dishwasher. "Andrew, I like the way you organized the dishwasher. Really efficient."

"Yes," Andrew said.

"Our Monday lesson will be making donuts. Can you be here at three forty-five? That's when I mix up my first batch of dough."

"Yes."

Shirley brought in a sack of groceries. Andrew helped Woody carry in boxes and bags. Woody shelved items while Andrew swept the shop.

"How was dinner last night, Shirley?" I asked.

"Nice," she said.

"We might do a project with Mr. Alfred and Andrew," Woody added.

"Yes," said Andrew.

"We've got a full schedule today," Shirley said. She rushed to the door, and Woody hurried to catch up with her.

I glanced at Tiffany and shrugged.

After Woody and Shirley left, Jack sauntered in. "The donuts were a hit. The boys cleaned up a ton of debris all over town and loaded it onto the county trucks. The county couldn't have managed the aftermath without their help."

Jack cocked his head and watched Tiffany and Andrew clean. "You been fired, Donut Lady?"

Tiffany laughed. "You notice we can't even get her to sit down."

I sat at the counter. "I'm on a break now."

Jack took the seat next to me. "Let me know when you're ready to go home. I can't wait for you to see what the boys did to your yard."

Tiffany and Andrew put away their cleaning equipment and hung up their aprons.

"You can keep your cap or leave it here, Andrew," Tiffany said.

Andrew strode to the storeroom and returned without his cap.

"Do you want a ride, Andrew?" Jack asked.

"I walk."

"So do I," Tiffany said. "See you Monday morning."

"Three forty-five," Andrew said.

As the two of them walked away, I locked the shop. Jack carried Mia to my car. "I'll follow you."

I parked in the driveway, and Jack parked at the curb. When Jack headed to the backyard, I said, "I'll take Mia inside. Colonel and I will meet you in the back."

I stuck my key into the lock, and the door swung open. I eased the door closed and carried Mia around the house to the back. Colonel followed us.

"Jack, come with me to your truck for a second."

"Why?" Jack asked as he followed me to the street.

I stood in the street, next to the driver's door. "My front door was open. I need to call the sheriff's office."

"I'll go check." Jack headed to the house.

"Wait a second, Jack. There might be someone still inside. I always double-lock when I leave."

I pulled my phone out of my pocket and called nine-one-one. "Hi, Tess. My front door was not secure when I got home. Jack was in the back, but he's here with me now. No, I didn't go inside."

The sheriff turned the corner and approached from the north, and Roger arrived at the same time from the south. Roger leaped out of his patrol car and ran to the back. The Sheriff strode to where we stood.

He crossed his arms. "What happened?"

"When I put my key into the lock, the door opened. I closed it. Very quietly and walked to the back and asked Jack to join me right here. And then, I called Tess."

"Stay here." He spoke into his radio on his way to my house and stepped up onto the porch. He tried the door, but it didn't open. He tried again and pushed with his shoulder.

"That's strange. I didn't lock it, Jack. I just closed it. Do you suppose it was locked but not latched??"

Jack stepped closer. "Seems like it."

The sheriff's radio crackled, and then he strode over to the truck. "Who has copies of your house keys?"

"Only Shirley."

The sheriff bit his lip.

"You going to be around for a few minutes, Sheriff? I'd like to get new locks and install them," Jack said.

"Take your time. I'll be here."

As Jack climbed into his truck, Roger returned to the front. "Back's locked. Nothing seems to be out of order."

"Karen, I'd like for you to wait in my car while Roger and I check your house."

"Front or back?" I asked.

"Tempting," the sheriff chuckled. "Your choice, Donut Lady."

"Front." I growled.

The sheriff started his cruiser. When he opened the back door, Colonel jumped in, and the sheriff set Mia's carrier on the seat. I slid into the passenger's seat.

"Y'all will be more comfortable in the air conditioning. Can I have your key?"

I still clutched the key in my fist. I handed it to him.

He turned the key over in his hand a few times. "Shirley called Tess a few minutes ago and said the spare keys she kept in her office were missing. The last time she used one of them was two weeks ago, so she doesn't know when they disappeared. Jeff's on his way to her office."

After he closed the door, I pushed the lock. The click of the four doors comforted me, and I leaned back in the seat.

I was startled awake by the sheriff tapping on my window. I unlocked the door and stepped out. He opened the back door, and after Colonel jumped out, he picked up the carrier.

"No sign of anyone. Appears to be nothing out of place, but you'll know if there is."

When I stepped inside, the shadows were agitated to the point of panic. "Are you okay?" I asked.

"What?" Sheriff asked.

The shadows drifted to the floor and slid down the hallway.

"Just a little self-talk."

The sheriff frowned. "Whatever. Do you see anything that's been disturbed? Anything missing?"

I scanned the room. "The file cabinet. One of the drawers isn't quite closed." I pulled the second drawer open. "Old tax records. I filed them in chronological order. I'd have to go through them to see if anything's missing." I flipped through. "All the years are here. But this is where I had the papers I gave you. How could anyone know?"

I opened the top and then the bottom drawers. "These files are out of order too. Whoever came in must have gone through each drawer."

"Nothing obvious missing?"

The shadows raced back from the hallway and dashed to my bedroom, and Mia chased after them.

"Not at first glance, but I'll have to go through the papers. I need to check something else in the bedroom."

I opened my junk jewelry drawer, and the emerald ring sat where I'd left it. I opened my jewelry box on the top of my dresser, and my two silver quarters were missing. The folded drawings and notes from Woody when he was younger were still there.

The sheriff stood in the doorway. "The emerald ring's in the drawer where I stored it," I said. "I'm missing two silver quarters from my jewelry box, but I didn't have anything else of value in it."

As we returned to the living room, he said, "The intruder apparently searched for the two things you took from the soup kitchen."

"Are there security cameras at the soup kitchen? I didn't think of that before."

The sheriff stared at me. "There were, but we were told Melinda disconnected them because of the cost. I can't remember who said that. I'll put Roger on it. It's the only thing that makes sense." He crossed his arms. "I'm worried about your safety, Karen. Could Tiffany stay with you, or could you stay with someone? Gee? Shirley? Never mind. Not Shirley.

You're welcome to stay with Emma and me. Sparks needs somebody to stalk beside me."

"I'll think about it."

"Think about what?" Jack asked as he came into the house.

"Security system." I glared at the sheriff who raised an eyebrow.

"Security system sounds good to me. I'll research and install one for you. You want to hook into the sheriff's office?"

"I don't think so," I said.

The sheriff rolled his eyes. "I'll talk to you later, Karen. Let me know if you think of anything else."

Jack carried his tools and the sack from the hardware store to the back door.

I accompanied the sheriff to his patrol car. "Security systems were on your mind, weren't they? Not a bad idea if you insist on staying at your house alone," the sheriff said.

"Thanks for not busting me, except now I owe you, don't I?"

The sheriff chuckled. "Sure do, Donut Lady."

"There is one more thing. Do we know who owns the soup kitchen?"

The sheriff's eyes narrowed. "Roger can add that to his list of documents."

When I returned to the house, Jack had the packages for the new locks opened. "I'm keying all the locks to one key again."

"I didn't realize Shirley kept my key with her keys for rental properties. Makes sense from her point of view, but I'm not sure it's a good idea. What do you think?"

Jack filled a glass with water from the kitchen faucet. "Hope it's okay I helped myself. I'd suggest we give Shirley a key to your shed where we can put a spare house key in case Woody or Shirley needs access to your house."

"That's an excellent idea. While you're installing locks, why don't I run to Gus's shop for sandwiches? I'd offer you lunch, but I don't have much here. What would you like?"

Jack inspected the locks on the door. "Lunch sounds good. I'm not picky. One of Gus's specials is fine for me. If you're getting Gus's homemade lemonade, I wouldn't mind one too."

After I picked up my purse, Colonel trotted to the door. "It's too hot for you to wait in the car, Colonel." He nudged the door.

"Fine. I'll call in the order." I called and ordered two specials and two lemonades. When I opened the front door, Colonel bounded to the car. As I pulled into Gus's parking lot, Colonel growled.

"What's wrong with you, Colonel?"

His hackles raised, and he growled again.

Clarissa, Tess, and Alfred were headed into Gus's shop. Silas pulled up and pushed ahead of everyone else. Colonel barked, and Tess sauntered over to my car.

"Hi there, Colonel," she said. "Hey, Karen." She slid into the passenger's seat, and Colonel licked her neck. "Love you too, boy." She rubbed his face.

"I called in my order. Do you mind sitting with Colonel a minute while I run in?"

"Of course not," she said.

When I reached the counter, Gus waved his knife at a table near the front door. "Got your order over there."

I found the sack marked *Donut Lady*. After I paid, I hurried back to my car. "Thanks for sitting with Colonel, Tess."

"He's a sweet boy," Tess said. Colonel growled. "What is it, boy?" She glanced toward Gus's. "Ms. Karen, looks like Silas has two lemonades."

When Silas reached my car, Colonel's growled louder.

"Ms. Karen, Clarissa noticed you forgot your lemonades. Thought I'd save you the trouble of coming back. Colonel sounds a little nervous."

Clarissa hurried past us with her nose in the air. Colonel continued his growls.

Silas handed the lemonades to Tess and sauntered back into Gus's.

"Two lemonades?" Tess asked. "Never mind. I'm sorry. That sounded like an interrogation question."

I laughed. "Jack's installing new locks for me."

"That's great," she said. "Mr. Jack is one of the nicest men I know." She reached for the door handle but stopped. "What do you know about the new teacher, Mr. Collins?"

"He's Woody's language arts teacher, and he came from Atlanta. Woody thinks he's awesome, which makes him a star as far as I'm concerned. I've never met him, though. Is he cute?"

"He's dreamy. And he's nice too, but he's nice to everybody. Whoa. You just interrogated me." Tess's twinkling giggle escalated to a contagious laugh, and I joined her.

Tess wiped her eyes. "Thanks for that. I needed to talk to someone. No way could I have told any of the guys at the department that he was dreamy. I gotta grab my lunch and get back to work."

Tess jumped out of my car and raced into Gus's.

"So, whadda ya know, Colonel. Tess has a crush on Mr. Collins."

When we arrived at home, Jack met us at the driveway and took the drinks inside while I carried the sack.

Jack set the clear plastic cups on the dining room table, while I plated our sandwiches.

"That's funny," he said. "The lemonade is cloudy. What makes lemonade cloudy, do you suppose?"

His words made my skin crawl. "Don't drink any." I grabbed my phone.

"What? Are you okay?"

"No. Stay away from the lemonade. I'm calling the sheriff."

When the sheriff answered, I said, "Sheriff, I've got a feeling about some lemonade I brought home from Gus's."

I stared at Jack. "The sheriff hung up."

"He'll be here in seconds, not minutes. Your feelings are uncanny."

Sheriff tore through the front door. "Did either of you drink any lemonade?"

"No." Jack furrowed his brow. "I'm a little lost here."

"Tell me what happened. And summarize this time, Karen."

I glared. "I picked up our lunch at Gus's. After I got in my car, Silas ran our drinks out. When I got home, Jack said the lemonade was cloudy. It is cloudy."

"Why did you call me?"

"Rules I learned in prison. Never drink an open drink that has left your sight. And never, ever drink a cloudy drink."

The sheriff squinted at the murky liquid in the clear cups. "Good catch, Jack. Definitely cloudy. I'll get the techs here to pick it up. What about the food, Karen?"

"Probably just fine, but I'm spooked. How about eggs and toast for lunch, Jack?"

The sheriff placed our sandwiches back into the sack. When the technician picked up the drinks, the sheriff followed her out with the food.

I opened the refrigerator door. "You have a choice. Grilled cheese or eggs cooked to order with jam and toast."

"Grilled cheese sounds good. What are you having?"

"I'm having my usual yogurt." I pulled out my cast iron skillet. "How about an apple?"

"Split one?"

"That's perfect. I'll brew some tea."

After lunch, Jack finished installing the locks. "I tested the locks on the back door, and the keys worked fine. Want to check the front?"

Colonel joined us as we stepped outside. I locked and unlocked the door latch and the deadbolt. "Smooth," I said.

Jack brushed sawdust remnants off the door. "I'll have copies made of your house key and shed keys. Did you have any preferences for a security system? I recommend one with a live feed that sends data to your phone."

"I'll leave the system decision up to you."

Jack ran his hand down the doorframe. "Door still has a good fit."

My peripheral vision caught a figure step behind a parked car on my right, but when I turned, there was no one there.

Jack rose and inspected the top of the door. "I'll see if the hardware store has a solar-powered system. Won't be long."

I smiled as Jack jogged to his truck. *He certainly loves a project.*

As he turned the corner at the end of the block, Clarissa appeared from behind the car. She strode to my house and up my walkway. Colonel flopped down on the porch and closed his eyes.

Clarissa stared at the porch. "Karen, I know we aren't friends and probably never will be, but you should know I've seen a man around your house every day this week on my morning walk around the neighborhood. When I get close, he ducks behind your house."

I frowned. "Can you tell who it is? What does he look like?"

"I don't know who it is. He's medium build—reminds me of the Methodist men. But I've seen him every morning while you're at your donut shop. He gives me the creeps."

"Thank you, Clarissa. Sounds creepy. You might want to change your routine."

"But I've always—" She stared at me. "You have one of your feelings, don't you?"

"Not really sure, but it's smart to be careful."

"Thanks." She strode to the sidewalk and said over her shoulder, "We might be friends someday after all." She crossed the street and hurried away.

"That was a surprise, Colonel."

He opened his eyes.

"Ready to go inside?" I unlocked the door, and he lumbered inside.

I locked the door behind us. "That'll make the sheriff and Jack happy."

The shadows shimmered in the kitchen sunlight. "So, what do you think? I have a feeling Clarissa told the truth." The shadows darkened and whirled to the hallway. "Goes against the grain, doesn't it?"

Jack's truck parked at the curb. I opened the door just as Jack reached the porch, and Roxie bounded into the house.

"Were you going somewhere?" Jack asked.

"Your truck told me it was you."

Jack's eyes widened, and I laughed. "No, it didn't talk to me. I recognized the sound of your engine. No luck at the hardware store?" I pointed to his empty hands.

"No, they didn't have what I wanted, but they ordered it for me. I ran home to let Roxie out, but she wanted to come along. Why don't y'all come to our house for dinner? I'll grill steaks."

"What do you think about potato salad? And I can bring brownies." I opened the back door for Colonel and Roxie, and they dashed out.

Jack followed me to the kitchen. "Sounds like a party to me. Want to bring Mia?"

"That's a good idea. I'd be nervous with her by herself. I need to run to the store to pick up potatoes and a few other things. We can be there in a couple of hours."

"Why don't you make the potato salad at my house? We can all go to the grocery store in my truck. We'll wait for you while you shop, and you won't be driving home by yourself tonight."

"I hadn't thought of that. I'll pick up the ingredients for brownies and leave a batch for you in the freezer."

"This is sounding better and better." Jack grinned.

I set the carrier by the front door, and Mia dashed in. Jack let Colonel and Roxie inside, and after I locked up, we all climbed into Jack's truck. As Jack pulled away from the curb, I smiled at the sound of the engine.

"What?" Jack asked.

"My imagination is fanciful sometimes. The truck's engine is purring," I said.

Jack cocked his head. "Yep, I can hear it."

I snickered at the smugness in his voice and jotted down a list on an old envelope I found in my purse.

Jack dropped me off at the grocery store entrance.

"Won't be long," I said.

CHAPTER FOURTEEN

I grabbed a grocery cart and headed to the produce section first. I ticked off items on my list: *potatoes, celery*. Next was the baking aisle: *flour, sugar, cocoa, baking powder*. I wheeled past the plastic container section and stopped when I spotted a covered container the flour would fit in. I stood at the side of my cart to compare the different sizes and picked one to inspect the label for the capacity information.

"Finally caught up with you. You don't take hints, do you?" Silas leaned against the handle of my cart. "Where is it?"

"What? What hints? What are you looking for?"

"Don't play dumb, Donut Lady. That bumbling oaf Dixon was supposed to run you down. I left you a little wine, but you didn't pay any attention to the warning. I found out Wallace was freelancing. When I reminded him who he worked for, he was stupid enough to tell me he had records of sales with names and addresses of suppliers and buyers.

Melinda claimed she didn't know where he'd put the files. I saw you take the envelope out of Melinda's desk. Where is it?"

"I don't know what you're talking about." I narrowed my eyes.

He opened his right hand he'd held at his waist. I stared at the syringe with an uncapped needle and milky contents. "A little fentanyl and heroin. Felon and a drug addict. Not a surprise, but you had everybody fooled for a long time. They'll find the drugs hidden in your shop. Town's going to talk about you for a long time. Maybe Tiffany will get caught in it too."

I stared at his dark, soulless eyes as they shifted to pools of death. When he lunged at me with the syringe, I pushed the cart with all my strength and threw him off balance. He fell against the shelves and to the floor and landed face down.

I ran to the front of the store to customer service. When I realized he hadn't followed me, I pulled out my phone and called nine-one-one. My heart pounded. "Tess, I'm at the grocery store. Silas tried to kill me. A syringe. He said it had fentanyl and heroin. He might have fallen on it."

A scream and shouts from the aisle where I last saw Silas filled the store, and the manager dashed toward the commotion. Customers left their carts and hurried to the exit. "I think somebody found him." The wail of a siren and screech of tires announced the arrival of a cruiser.

The sheriff ran inside and growled. "Where?" I pointed to the aisle where I left Silas.

Jack dashed into the store. His face was white. He grabbed me in a tight hug. "Lord, Honey. You scared me. Are you okay?"

"I'm—"

He took my face in his hands and kissed me with a gentleness that made my knees weak. He buried his face in my hair, and I closed my eyes and wrapped my arms around him.

"I'm fierce," I mumbled.

Paramedic Carol came in behind a stretcher wheeled by firefighters. She whispered as she passed me. "Fierce and a beast, Donut Lady."

Jack released me but held onto my elbow when the sheriff strode to us.

"Karen, if you'd like to go home, I'll be there later to take your statement." The sheriff's voice conveyed a kindness that touched my heart and caused me to tear up. He frowned. "Are you okay? Do you need Carol to check you out?"

"Thanks, but I'm fine." I brushed the dampness off my face. *Toughen up, Buttercup.*

As Jack and I turned to leave, the sheriff pulled Jack aside and spoke in a low tone. Jack's eyes widened. I bit my lip. *I can't believe it either, Jack.*

We walked to the truck in silence. When Jack opened the truck door, I breathed in the familiar, comforting aroma of dogs.

I pulled out my cell phone and called Amber. When Leah answered, I said, "Is Amber available to meet me at my house? Tell her I'm okay."

"Thanks, that's the first thing she'll ask me. She's in a meeting, but I'll get a note to her."

Leah hung up.

"What did she say?" Jack asked.

Before I could answer Jack, my cell rang. "She'll be there in five minutes." Leah disconnected again.

"Five minutes."

"Are you sure you're okay?" Jack asked.

"I'm fine."

Jack snorted.

"Okay, I'm a little shook up."

"You're the most amazing woman I know, Karen. And you're the fiercest calamity magnet in the state." He chuckled.

I frowned and turned my head toward the window to hide my confusion. *You called me fierce. And amazing?*

Amber was on the porch when we pulled up to my house. She ran to the truck and jerked my door open. "You're not being brave, right? You are okay?"

"Yes. Silas attacked me with a syringe in the grocery store, and I knocked him down with a cart. I think he stabbed himself with his syringe."

Amber's eyes widened. "Let's go inside. Okay if Jack comes in, or do I send him away?"

"He can come in."

Jack carried Mia inside. When he opened her carrier, she dashed to the pantry. The shadows followed her and slammed the door. Jack let the dogs out back and opened the pantry door.

"I should check this door." Jack closed and opened the pantry door and examined it. "Or install a cat door so Mia doesn't get trapped inside the pantry if she's alone."

I snorted and sat on the sofa. Amber narrowed her eyes and joined me. The sheriff strode into the house and stared at Amber.

"Is this official?" he asked.

"Not at all," Amber said.

"Good. I'll have Roger get an official statement later. Silas died on the way to the hospital. What happened, Karen? Unofficially."

"Silas lunged at me with a syringe, and I pushed the cart between us. He lost his balance and fell. I ran to the front office. He must have injected himself."

"Good summary. Now, tell me the long version."

I raised my eyebrows. "Are you sure?"

The sheriff leaned back in the ugly chair and groaned. "Yes. Go ahead."

Jack scooted a kitchen chair around and faced the sheriff and me.

"I was trying to decide which container would be best for five pounds of flour. I pulled my cart closer to me so I wouldn't block the aisle. I stood with my hand on the front of the cart. Silas grabbed onto the cart's handle. At first, I thought it was in his way, but then—" I took a big breath and exhaled.

Jack asked, "Water?"

"Yes, thanks."

After he filled a glass with water, he handed it to me. The cool water soothed my dry throat. Amber took the glass and held it for me.

"He asked me where it was, but I didn't understand what he was talking about. He told me the papers I found in Melinda's office were Edward Wallace's records of drug sales. He said he left the bottle of wine as a warning, and Dixon was supposed to run over me. He implied he killed Edward and then Melinda because she wouldn't tell him where the envelope was."

The sheriff shook his head. "Silas owned the soup kitchen building. You were right. The security cameras still worked."

I nodded. "Makes sense. The rest is kind of a blur in my mind. He wanted to know where the envelope was, but it seemed much more personal than that. He said there were drugs in the shop. He wanted to ruin my reputation, and he intended to implicate Tiffany too. His eyes." I shuddered.

Jack's face tightened. He rose and paced.

"Easy, Jack," the sheriff said. "Get yourself a glass of water."

"I'll take one too, Jack, if you don't mind." Amber winked at me. "Being a good friend of the Donut Lady takes a certain amount of fortitude."

"No kidding." Sheriff mumbled.

Jack handed Amber a glass, and she toasted me.

The sheriff rolled his eyes. "What else?"

"I pushed the cart at him as hard as I could, and he fell. I ran to the front. Oh. He told me the syringe had fentanyl and heroin. When I got to customer service, he wasn't behind me. I called Tess."

I remembered Jack's kiss and touched my lips. Jack grinned, and I dropped my hand. My face warmed. Amber raised her eyebrows. *My lawyer's going to interrogate me later.*

"He didn't say anything about counterfeiting?" The sheriff asked.

"No. He did say Wallace was freelancing."

"Unofficially, there's a drug task force that appreciates Wallace's information. And the paper for counterfeiting is in the right hands. Also unofficially. I'll send Roger over later for an official statement. We'll need to search the shop. Is that okay with you, Counselor?"

"Certainly. Just let me know when Roger will be here. Get a warrant, and I'll open the shop."

"Will do." The sheriff rose.

Amber set her glass in the sink and left with the sheriff.

Jack put his glass on the dining table. "I need a little time to digest all this." He opened the back door and called Roxie. The two of them left. The latch clicked with a finality that ripped into my heart.

I stared at the door. Mia jumped onto the sofa, and I stroked her back.

"I guess that's that, Mia."

I took my water to the back porch. Colonel flopped down at my feet. I gazed at the sky as loneliness and sadness filled my chest and overflowed into my heart. I put my face in my hands and sobbed. Colonel nudged my arm and laid his head on my lap. I hugged his neck and soaked his coat with my tears. Shadows surrounded me, and I was comforted by the light breeze as they swayed.

The door behind me creaked.

"You're supposed to keep your front door locked, Donut Lady," Jack said.

He sat on the porch next to me. "I bought an azalea bush. You can help me decide where to plant it at my house. I have more room there so I can plant an azalea every time you scare me. I have a feeling my yard will be overrun with blossoms." He wrapped his arm around my shoulder and sighed. "Unless there's any way I could talk you out of being a calamity magnet?"

ACKNOWLEDGEMENTS

Huge thanks to my husband for his patience while I wander off into the world of my imaginary friends.

Thanks to my family and friends for their support and to my beta readers. A special thanks to Watson who doesn't miss a thing.

Thank you for reading. If you enjoyed the Donut Lady's story, tell a friend, post a review, subscribe to the Judith A. Barrett newsletter, and read

SWEET DEAL APPEALED, BOOK 4.

The past haunts the Donut Lady when her dead husband's sketchy brother, who had blocked her appeal of the wrongful murder conviction, arrives in town. How does a counterfeiter fit in his scheme?

Meanwhile, a silent stalker intends for Donut Lady to die.

Subscribe to the newsletter!

Look for the Subscribe button on www.judithabarrett.com

ABOUT THE AUTHOR

Judith A. Barrett, award-winning author, lives in rural Georgia on a farm with her husband and two dogs. She writes thrillers, post-apocalyptic science fiction, and cozy mystery novels. Stories with a twist!

When she isn't writing, Judith is working in her garden, hiking with her husband and dogs, or rocking on her front porch while she watches the sunset.

Website   https://judithabarrett.com

Newsletter   Subscribe to her eNewsletter on her website

Let's keep in touch!